CONNER'S ODYSSEY

BOOK TWO - ENLIGHTENED

To Carrie Steltz

Enjoy :)

Ian C. Bristow

ISBN-13: 978-1523350704

ISBN-10: 1523350709

DEDICATION

To Trevor Bristow, who has been an invaluable resource.

To everyone else that has been there to encourage me.

CONTENTS

CHAPTER 1

A Hero's Welcome

The soothing sounds of a flowing river caressed Minna's ears as she drew a bucket of water from its crystalline depths. Normally she would have appreciated its peaceful tones, but today the tranquil sounds were unable to ease her anguish. Thoughts and images of losing the one most precious in her life plagued her mind.

The last time she had seen her son, Medwin, he had set out on a mission to destroy Vellix for his crimes upon Rohwen and its people. That was nearly two weeks ago. She could not bear the thought of losing him mere weeks after she had lost her husband in battle.

She headed back to the village, fighting the urge to cry. Medwin was just a boy. How did he expect to defeat a man as powerful as Vellix? Why did he have to go? Why couldn't he have sent the elders with the Conner boy to do it? Medwin was chief now, after all. He had the authority to do so. Surely, Yorick could have helped lead them to a victory.

"Mother..."

'Please, not again,' Minna thought pleadingly. Medwin's voice had been calling out to her randomly, always saying the same thing — just "Mother." On the one hand, it was nice to hear his voice, but deep down, she wished the delusions would stop. It just made her want to see him that much more.

"Mother, I'm home!"

'Please let it stop,' she thought, feeling desperate as she turned instinctively to look in the direction of the voice she so longed to be real.

Medwin was entering the village, accompanied by a small, deformed hunchback.

Minna dropped her bucket of water and raced toward her son. She pulled him into an affectionate embrace. "Oh, my son!" she exclaimed, tears welling uncontrollably. "I was so worried!" Before another word could find its way out, she broke down entirely and bawled into Medwin's supportive shoulder.

"Mother — Mother, it's okay. I'm fine," Medwin said, pouring as much sympathy as possible into his words. He glanced around and noticed the scene between him and his mother was quickly becoming a spectacle. Many people in the general area had started to stare at them. "Mother, please…" He appreciated her affection, but he was chief. It was important to him as a leader to show the tribe his strength.

Minna released her son, but continued to gaze at him through glossy eyes. "I thought I would never see you again. I — I thought V — Vellix would surely kill you," she sobbed.

A large group of the tribe gathered around them.

"Mother, it's okay now. I am home. I'm safe." Medwin gazed into his mother's intense, dark eyes, and a twinkle of joy gleamed back at him. He turned to face the group. "My people," he started, raising his hands as if he could embrace all of them at once. "I have returned bearing good news. Vellix and his Mirthless are no longer of any threat to the people of Rohwen."

The trees shuddered as an enormous cheer of joy exploded into the dry, late-summer air.

Medwin raised a hand to silence his people. He looked down at Moxie, who had been standing timidly in his shadow. "This is Moxie. If it were not for his bravery and courage, I would be dead, and Vellix's reign would have continued. He will be staying with us, permanently, as my guest. He is to be treated as one of us. Honor him." Medwin gave Moxie a nudge forward. "Go on Moxie. Don't be shy," he added encouragingly.

The little hunchback stepped forward nervously. A crowd of people gathered around him to introduce themselves. Moxie was overwhelmed. He had never been the center of attention like this. In fact, before Vellix had subjected him to his experiments, he was an outcast. No one had wanted him. It was not until he met Conner, Medwin, and Zelimir that he finally found true friends.

"Give him some space," said Medwin, noticing that Moxie was becoming uncomfortable with all this attention.

A man near the back of the crowd started to make his way forward. "We must celebrate the return of our chief!" he pronounced.

Murmurs of agreement came from all around the group. They dispersed, heading in different directions to prepare for the evening's festivities. Some of the men went over to a fire-pit, while others set off toward their huts. A group of women moved in the direction of the river, eager children babbling excitedly at their heels.

"May I have a word, Medwin?" asked the man who had made his way from the back of the crowd.

"You may," Medwin answered, turning his attention to a man covered in battle scars but wearing an expression much less abrasive than his appearance. "Thane!" Medwin cried when he realized who stood before him. "It's good to see you!"

"Thank you, sir. I am sorry about your father… Nayati was a great man."

An awkward pause followed Thane's statement before Medwin finally responded. "Thank you, Thane..." As Medwin answered, he battled to keep his expression hard, hoping to conceal the emotions that had exploded within him at the sound of his dead father's name. But he might as well have written his feelings in bold print across his forehead for all the good it did it to try and hide them. His eyes sparkled as tears urged him to let go. To break down. To release the poison that had coursed through him for the last two weeks.

"Sir…" Thane shifted his feet uncomfortably, as if he felt that to pursue their conversation at this point was less than tactful. He pushed on, meeting Medwin's eyes with a thousand words of solace and understanding that have no spelling. "The elders wish to hold council with you as soon as possible. They are most anxious to learn of your journey … and to talk of your plans as chief."

"I am ready now," Medwin replied, bringing his chin up with pride. He knew his father would be ashamed of him if he lost sight of important matters in a piteous display of sorrow. "Moxie, you shall join me in council," he said with one hand rested upon the hunchback's shoulder.

Moxie looked up at Medwin, full of disbelief. "You would like *me* in your council?"

"More than anyone, Moxie," Medwin replied with a broad smile. "Thane, inform the elders that we will meet now."

Thane bowed before leaving to carry out his orders.

"Mother, will you prepare a comfortable place in our hut for Moxie?" Medwin asked, careful to use gentle tones.

"Of course, dear," Minna replied, still unable to conceal her overwhelmed emotions.

"Thank you."

"Yes, thank you!" Moxie added, throwing a backwards glance at Minna. He followed Medwin through the village until they came upon a hut larger than the rest. Long strips of bark and moss covered its sturdy oak framework, weatherproofing the interior from wind and rain.

Inside there were forty seats arranged around the hut's outer edge. At the back of the circle was a seat taller than the rest. Medwin moved to the back of the hut and sat in the higher seat; Moxie stood beside him.

The elders filed in, followed by the warrior captains. As they took their seats, Medwin noticed that a few men were missing: two captains and three elders. Yorick, the elder who should have settled directly to his right, was among them.

"Where are the others?" he asked casually, assuming they had a good reason for being late.

Some of the elders looked down. Others exchanged meaningful looks of sorrow, but none of them spoke.

"They did not survive the battle," Thane finally answered.

Medwin absorbed Thane's words for a moment before he replied. "I am ... sorry to hear that." It was a hard loss to swallow — especially Yorick, who had been his father's right-hand man for many years. Medwin knew he could have learned much from him about his father, things that had never been his right to know as a child. Now, it seemed that these questions would remain unanswered.

"I assume they had a proper burial?" he asked, a heavy stone of grief settling into the place in the pit of his stomach where he kept the one that belonged to his father.

"A few did," uttered one of the elders, "but Yorick and Slone's bodies were never recovered, sir..."

"We searched tirelessly..." another added. "...But with no success," he finished despondently.

"I see... Thank you for your efforts," Medwin replied quietly.

"Sir, not to seem indelicate, but perhaps we should move on to matters in need of discussion?"

"I agree, Inoke," Medwin responded bureaucratically.

"I think," Inoke continued with an official tone to match Medwin's, "that we would all like to know what happened on your journey." His age-lined face flexed into an expression of genuine interest as he gestured to those around him.

"Well," Medwin started, scanning the room to let everyone know he was addressing them equally, "as you all know … Conner, the wolf, and I set out shortly after the battle ended. We traveled for what felt like an endless five days and eventually reached Botanica. The Botanicans were kind enough to feed us before we continued our journey. From there, we headed north, toward the Morik Forest; that is where we met Moxie." Medwin gestured in the direction of Moxie, who had taken to lingering in a deeply shadowed recess at the back of the hut.

Moxie made a shy sign of acknowledgment at the mention of his name and then tried to become as invisible as possible once more.

"Moxie was one of Vellix's prisoners for years within the depths of Mt Cirrus," Medwin said, pity for the hunchback seeping into his tone.

There was a quiet hum of interest at this news.

Medwin allowed the muttering to die down before he continued. "As you will have already concluded, he escaped his prison. This is what led to his meeting us. His usefulness was abundant. He showed us a secret entrance into Mt. Cirrus. He then went on to save Conner and me from certain death. We were extremely foolish to enter a fight with Vellix in his comfort zone. He was far too powerful for us alone.

If it wasn't for Moxie's immense courage, Vellix would still control Rohwen."

"So it is official?" asked a highly decorated warrior captain. "Vellix has been defeated?"

"Yes, Clavis," Medwin answered. "Conner was able to defeat him after Moxie and a large group of Vellix's own creations came to our aid."

"What has become of Conner then? Where is he?"

A flash of grief struck Medwin's face like lightning. "Conner has returned to his own world..." Medwin paused briefly before he addressed one of his warrior captains to change the subject. "Akamu, I wish to inform the Idenites, Botanicans, and if we can locate them, the Edelish peoples of their freedom from Vellix's tyranny. When council has ended, send our two fastest messengers to the Idenites and the Botanicans. Then form a group of our best trackers to search for the Edelish."

Akamu bowed in acknowledgment of his orders.

"What of the Ryvelians?" asked Inoke.

"As far as they are concerned, I am in need of the wisdom of my entire council. I feel that for one man to decide the fate of so many lives would be an act of extreme ignorance."

"This is a very wise outlook, sir," said Inoke. "Might I suggest a vote?"

Medwin nodded. "Unfortunately, as we are all well aware, on the subject of the Ryvelians, there are really only two options. Either we send our warriors to eradicate them for their obvious alliance with Vellix during his reign, or we act humanely, and give them a chance to live peacefully now that their leader has been defeated. We will vote with a show of hands. Those in favor of an attack, raise your hand."

To Medwin's disgust, twenty hands went up. He thought mercy meant more to the men he had held in such high esteem since his childhood.

"This leaves us with an even vote," said Thane, who was one of the men that had not raised his hand. "What do we do?"

"The vote is not even," Medwin replied coolly. He pulled Moxie out of the shadows. "Moxie is as much a part of this council as any of us. He didn't raise his hand."

Moxie gawked at Medwin, horrified that he had just been used as the vote to tip the scales.

"That makes the vote twenty in favor of an attack, to twenty-one who are not," Medwin said, deliberately ignoring Moxie's distressed expression. Moxie would just have to learn that he ranked on the same level as everyone else in council.

"What?" snapped one of the oldest-looking elders. "You are going to allow this — thing to partake in the vote of our council? As if his opinion is worthy among us?"

"His opinion *is* worthy among us, Zuma. In fact, based on the words you just spoke, I would say his opinion is worth more than yours."

Zuma stood up, looking outraged. "I was in your father's council for the entirety of his term as chief! And I was in his father's before that! Never, in all my years, was I treated in this manner! If you wish to take the advice of this — this thing over one of your own tribe elders, then don't expect to find me among those with whom you take council!"

Medwin gazed at Zuma seriously. "Very well. It pains me to see you act as foolishly as this. I know my father held you in the highest respect. But, if you can't see past the appearance of the person that is the *sole* reason Vellix was defeated, then so be it. You may dismiss yourself."

Zuma glared at Medwin furiously before storming out of the hut.

"I didn't mean to make trouble for you, Medwin," Moxie said, sounding distressed.

"You didn't make any trouble, Moxie. Zuma is acting disgracefully."

"Sir, what are your plans for the tribe laws during your term as chief?" asked one of the elders, evidently ready to move on from the uncomfortable confrontation that just took place.

"I won't be changing anything, Beynon. I intend to govern the tribe in the same fashion as my father did. I only hope that I can gain the same respect from my people as he did."

"You will," Beynon said confidently. "You have your father's wisdom."

Medwin couldn't help but smile at Beynon for his compliment. "Are there any other topics in need of discussion?" he asked, looking around at his council searchingly.

Nobody seemed to have anything to bring up.

"If that's it, then let's celebrate." Medwin got to his feet and left the hut, Moxie close behind.

"Hey, Medwin — Medwin!" A girl was waving energetically from one of the smaller huts nearby, her dark hair flowing in the breeze like gleaming hangings of silk.

"Zyana, how have you been?" Medwin asked as he approached her. "It's great to see you!"

"You too! …So you're chief now?" she asked, fixing him with an impressed gaze.

"Yeah."

Zyana fell into a strained silence, suddenly too aware of the fact that Medwin's becoming chief surrounded an incredibly painful topic. "So, what happened to that Conner boy?" She trudged on, not realizing it was the only other subject remotely as painful as the one she had just steered away from. "I heard your mother telling mine that he was some sort of special person or something. I'd like to meet him. Where is he?" Zyana glanced around the general area, as if hoping he would suddenly show himself.

"Conner is gone…" Medwin said bitterly. "He went back to his world."

"*His* world? What do you mean, 'his world?' You're not seriously trying to tell me…"

"I know it sounds weird, but it's true. The reason he was even here in the first place is because he found some kind of gateway between our worlds…" When Zyana appeared less than convinced, Medwin decided it was only fair to give her the best explanation he had — one that he knew to be true, yet still found hard to believe. "We were on our way back from Mt. Cirrus."

Zyana's expression quickly became attentive.

"Conner said he could hear his mother calling him..." Medwin paused to see if Zyana had picked up on how strange it would be for someone to announce that at random. Her expression became more captivated than ever. He carried on.

"…At first, I thought he was hearing things, delusional. But then I heard the voice as well… I knew he had come from another world, but it was still very strange to hear a voice calling from that world... Anyway, you don't have to believe me, but it's the truth."

"I believe you," Zyana replied quietly, sounding awed.

Moxie shifted restlessly from behind Medwin.

"Who is that standing behind you?" Zyana asked, craning her neck in order to get a glimpse of the little hunchback.

"This," Medwin said with a smile, "is Moxie." He pulled Moxie out of hiding. "He's staying with us."

"Oh, it's nice to meet you, Moxie," Zyana said; when she extended a hand to shake Moxie's, she didn't show the slightest bit of disgust at his deformities. "My name is Zyana."

Moxie shook her hand and retracted his quickly.

"You don't need to be shy," Zyana told him reassuringly. "This is your home now."

"Zyana is most kind," Moxie said, twisting his fingers around one another.

Zyana opened her mouth to reply, but her words were cut short as Thane called out from over by the fire.

"Medwin, come over here! I would like my boy, Luka, to be your first initiation. He has just returned from the Cliffs of Elders."

"It was really nice to see you again, Zyana," Medwin said, giving her his best version of a, "duty calls," look. "We'll talk later?"

"Of course," Zyana replied with a passive smile, resigned to the fact that Medwin had a great many responsibilities more pressing than holding a light conversation with her.

As Medwin strode toward the fire, Thane called for his son to come forward. Luka marched over and stood in the flickering shadow of his father.

"Nice job," Medwin congratulated him, grinning. He was quite proud of Luka, knowing only too well the skill and effort it took to scale the cliffs.

Thane handed Medwin a bowl full of the white pigment they used to paint their traditional markings.

Luka currently had a single stripe painted around his upper arms and lower legs. He got them at the age of five: the day he had started his warrior training.

Medwin dipped two fingers into the bowl of pigment and swirled them around, then he reached out to Luka and painted second stripes above the first, symbolizing his manhood.

Luka turned proudly to face the observing tribe. He threw his hands to the sky and let out a fierce cry of joy; before the powerful note of his voice died away, a group of tribesmen met it with an energetic rhythm, beating their goatskin drums vigorously.

Soon, beautiful melodies were fluttering playfully around long droning notations as wooden flutes and didgeridoos joined in. The music was powerful, yet subtle — beautiful, yet rigid.

Medwin danced joyfully with his tribe, yelling at the top of his lungs. He allowed the rhythm to occupy every inch of him, and it flushed away his poisons: his father's death, Conner leaving, Zelimir's sacrifice…

* * *

Moxie looked around at all of the Satrian people, dancing in celebration. He couldn't help but feel left out. He knew that he didn't really fit in. Grappling with his own insecurities, he left the village to sit alone in the forest. He plopped down on a mossy old tree stump that had rotted dramatically. After eating a few of the grubs living within the loose bark, he hugged his knees and looked up at the stars through the treetops as they swayed entrancingly with the wind.

An owl flew overhead, setting out for its nightly hunt.

Moxie shivered impulsively as he gave the bird a second glance. He could have sworn its eyes had glowed red. The memory of being carried off to Mt. Cirrus by the Mirthless crept into the back of his mind like a black panther, waiting to prey on his entire conscious.

"Moxie... Moxie, where are you?"

"Over here, sir."

"Why aren't you celebrating with us?" Medwin asked, even though he was sure he knew the reason.

"I don't fit in here," Moxie replied pitifully. "I don't fit in anywhere." He looked down with his face in his hands.

"Come on, Moxie. You *will* fit in here. Just give it some —" Two large birds clashed together above Medwin's head, cutting his words short.

Nerve piercing screeches and cries cut through the evening air like a sharp blade as the birds started to battle with intensity. Feathers and talons blended in a blur, making it nearly impossible to decipher which bird was winning.

Then, after a powerful strike, one of the birds gained control of the fight and drove down its enemy in a spiraling dive. As they slammed into the twig strewn forest floor, it became clear what breeds the birds were: owl and hawk.

The owl tried to squirm back to its feet, but the hawk lifted its leg and thrust its talons into the owl's wing, allowing them to sink deep. The owl cried out madly in pain.

"Who sent you?" The hawk interrogated. When it got no response, it lifted its leg and dug its talons into a fresh section of the owl's wing.

The owl shrieked worse than ever and started speaking. Its voice was dry and raspy, and full of malice. "Okay!" it grumbled. "I'll talk! Just get your talons out of my *wing!*"

The hawk removed its talons but left its foot hovering over the wing, just in case.

"It was —" A blow dart struck the owl in the neck before it could speak, killing it instantly. Its glowing red eyes faded to black.

The hawk took flight immediately and started circling the area in search of the one who had fired the dart. After a few passes, in which it was unable to locate the culprit, it landed on a branch near Medwin and Moxie.

"You are Medwin?" asked the hawk.

Medwin yanked himself from a state of astonishment. "I am," he answered, feeling a little unsure of what to think about the scene he'd just witnessed and wondering how this hawk knew his name.

"I am Lolani. I was Vivek's hawk."

Medwin made a gesture of realization.

"Where is the Conner boy? I need to speak with him."

"He is gone."

"Gone?" Lolani said exasperatedly.

"Yes."

"Where has he gone?"

"Back to his own world."

"Can you tell me how to find the gate?"

Curiosity and intrigue flooded Medwin's mind as if a mental dam had sprung a leak. For a moment he almost forgot to reply, but then Lolani rustled her wings impatiently and he said, "It's somewhere within the first woods due east of my village."

"Thank you," said Lolani courteously. Without wasting another second, she took flight.

CHAPTER 2

Conner's Return

"Conner, wake *up!*" Mrs. Mathews yelled for the third time. "Your breakfast is getting cold!"

"Okay, Mom," Conner answered drowsily. He didn't want to wake up just yet. He had lost half a night's sleep playing back the scenes from an incredible adventure in his mind — an adventure full of danger and action. There had been strange creatures, cut throat sailors, and a forest of tree-sized flowers. A warrior tribe called the Satria and a wise man named Vivek. A twisted tyrant named Vellix and his Mirthless. A boy named Medwin, who quickly became a great friend, and Zelimir the wolf. And to top everything off, he had seen more beautiful landscapes than ever before in his life.

It was baffling to think that the weeks he had spent in Rohwen had only been hours on Earth. The worlds were clearly on vastly differing timelines. He smiled to himself as a realization set in. He would be able to visit Rohwen for weeks at a time without actually being gone for more than a day in his world.

He lay there, still smiling as images of Rohwen floated across his mind: Mt. Cirrus, the Cliffs of Elders, and the Brio River — with its east and west forks; the Forsaken Desert, Misty Cove, and Botanica.

A thought came to him that caused his smile to fade. How hard might it be to find the gate back into the world he had fallen in love with? He looked over at Zelimir, who was sleeping on his back at the far end of the bed. A sense of relief came over him. The wolf probably remembered exactly where the gate was.

"Conner, seriously, come and eat!"

"Okay, Mom, I'm coming. Come on," Conner said, nudging Zelimir to wake him up. "I'll let you out back. Give me like five minutes to eat, and then I'll be out."

Zelimir barked in acknowledgment and ran out the back door.

"What are you going to do today, honey?" Breanne asked as Conner sat down to a plate of biscuits and gravy.

"Probably just play outside with Zelimir," he answered through a forkful of the breakfast he was eating at record speeds. "Hey, Mom?" he asked, pointing a fork at his plate of food. "Do you think I could get some of this to go?"

Breanne smiled and got up from the table. She crossed the kitchen, pulled a plastic container from the cupboard, and started to fill it with leftovers. "We have a few neighbors down the way you know," she said, clamping a lid down over the container "Mrs. Morris came up to introduce herself yesterday. She said her nephew was staying for the summer. Why don't you go and introduce yourself? You might become good friends."

Conner wanted to say he had already made a good friend in Medwin, but he didn't want his mom to think he was crazy, so he settled for saying, "Sure mom."

He crammed down the last of his breakfast and went out to the garage to look for his dad's old bow and its partnering quiver of arrows. If he had learned anything about Rohwen, it was that having a weapon was vital. Being as he had given Scarlet — his dagger — to Moxie, he didn't have one himself. His dad hadn't used this old wooden longbow for ages. Ever since he got his new compound bow, this old one had been collecting dust. Conner was sure he wouldn't miss it.

He threw the quiver over his shoulder, shrugged it into a comfortable position, and went to find Zelimir. "Zelimir, come on, let's go."

Zelimir came running around the corner at the sound of Conner's voice. A group of birds pecking for worms in the sparkling morning grass took flight, squawking indignantly.

Conner dumped his leftovers out for Zelimir. "There you go."

Zelimir practically inhaled the food, devouring it in seconds.

"Alright," Conner said, his focus set on finding the gate back to Rohwen. "Help me find the pathway, Zelimir." He trudged off into the thick forest of brambles and trees behind his house, Zelimir following in his stride. "The first thing we need to find is a little grouping of rocks that looks like an old fire-pit," he said, remembering that it had been only minutes from the entrance of the pathway.

As they made their way through the forest, it became increasingly difficult to locate the circle of rocks and Conner started to get frustrated.

Zelimir ran up ahead and started to sniff around a cluster of trees. He jerked his head up and bolted off into the thick underbrush.

Initially, Conner felt excited. He assumed Zelimir must have smelled something familiar. He tried to keep up with the wolf, but it wasn't long before he lost sight of him. A few minutes passed and Conner started to worry. "Zelimir!" he shouted at the top of his lungs; apart from the chirps of nearby birds and a light rustle from the branches supporting a few playful squirrels, he got no response. "Zelimir!" he cried again. "Come on, Zelimir. Where are you?" he said aloud, feeling truly nervous now. Just when the weight of what might have happened threatened to crush his spirits, Zelimir barked from somewhere in the distance.

A second later, he came out from between a tangle of shrubbery. He barked and ran down to a path in the thick forest of trees.

"Yes! That must be it," Conner yelled, running down to catch up with Zelimir. A feeling of pure elation swelled inside him as he grew nearer the spot where he knew the gate must be. He stepped through the two trees and his heart sank like a boulder. Nothing had happened. It hadn't worked. What was wrong? Why couldn't he get through? This had to be the right spot. Zelimir's sense of smell was amazing. 'Did the gate close for some reason?' he pondered. He started to drift away from the two trees unconsciously as Zelimir appeared to sniff other possible entrances.

Something lying on the brush-scattered floor caught Conner's eye. He reached down, picked it up, and started to rotate it in his hands. It was a bluish-grey stone with a mildly polished surface and something scratched on one side. It was obvious that the stone must have belonged to someone at some point, but he pocketed it, assuming that whoever it was had been in his family anyway. After all, his grandmother had owned this property since the sixties.

A bird screeched from somewhere nearby.

Conner wrenched his head in the direction of the sound. There she was, her feathers rippling majestically as a short gust of wind blew across them. He had seen this hawk before. It had to be her.

Lolani took off. Conner ran to keep up with her, forcing his way through the forest's thick underbrush. For brief moments, he would lose sight of her, and then his heart would leap when she swooped back into view.

She dove into a pathway of trees with beauty and ease.

Conner knew it at once. This was the *true* pathway; at the end was the gate. He was going back. With Zelimir alongside him, he stepped through a gap between the trees that formed an invisible doorway between two worlds.

* * *

Cheerful afternoon sun gave the faded outline of the Ancient Forest an iridescent glow. A slight breeze from the north swept across the valley of gentle rolling hills. The sky was a stunning shade of azure-blue. It was evident that cars, trains, and other common pollutants from Conner's world had never tainted this atmosphere.

Conner spun around three hundred and sixty degrees and drank in the sights. A light mist of clouds spiraled around Mt. Cirrus and shrouded its jagged peak. In the great mountain's shadow, the Brio River cut through the valley like a massive fork of lightning. A valley stretched to the south for as far as the eye could see, but he knew what lay beyond it: a stone monument to the Satria elders' power, known as the Cliffs of Elders, gazing eternally upon a vast ocean. Conner thought of Ammin, Lenny, and *the Colossus*. A smile spread across his face.

Lolani landed on a branch next to him and Zelimir. "Conner, I am Lolani."

"Vivek's hawk, right?"

"That is correct. Well, I was until he was killed by Vellix."

"I'm … sorry," Conner muttered, realizing how insensitive he must have sounded.

"Do not be sorry. He was well aware that Vellix would win their duel. His intention was to weaken Vellix for the time when you faced him. He left me with instructions for you."

Conner gave the hawk a curious and bemused look.

Lolani ignored Conner's expression and carried on. "He said you wouldn't be ready to hear them until you had faced Vellix. You see, he did not expect you to win the first battle. He just expected you to survive it. There is much about the art of cognition that you have not learned."

Conner continued to look at Lolani quizzically.

"Vivek didn't just live on Rhona to hide from Vellix and make potions, Conner," she continued. "He was searching the island. When he first discovered the scrolls, he realized that there was one missing. Hence, his fear that Vellix had found them first. Although, from what I have heard, you actually defeated Vellix, it was Vivek's last request of me that I make sure you seek the missing scroll. It would be an insult to his memory if I failed to not only relay this message, but to impress upon you how important it was to him."

"So there's a scroll hidden out on Rhona somewhere?" Conner asked, brushing his chin with a finger.

"Yes… and Vivek was convinced that it contains the knowledge which started Vellix down the path of evil. The path that eventually led to his experimentation on creatures and humans."

"Why would he even want to find that scroll then?" Conner asked, confused. "For that matter, why would he want *me* to find it? If it led Vellix to evil, what good is it?"

"He said the information in that scroll is vital to becoming skilled enough to be a true match for Vellix. Don't think he wasn't very concerned about how obtaining its knowledge might affect him, or you. Why do you think he wanted you to wait to read from it until you were ready?"

"I don't really understand," Conner said, now thoroughly muddled.

"Think about the skill level Vellix must have achieved in order to perform the atrocities that he did. Naturally, Vivek felt that you would need to be equally skilled!" Lolani glanced away from Conner, as if to stare upon his ignorance a moment longer would infect her with it as well. She took a deep breath and continued. "You would need to achieve metamorphic cognition — be able to manipulate the atomic structures of all life around you — in order to match his level of proficiency."

"So Vivek thought that the scroll held information for mastering the ability to alter atomic structures?"

"Precisely!"

"And he was certain that Vellix hid the scroll on Rhona?"

"Yes."

"Why?"

"Because Vellix would have felt that only a fool would do that. He knew that Vivek did not take him for a fool. What better place to hide the scroll than right under his nose, stashed near the rest of them?"

"That is actually a brilliant deduction on Vivek's part," Conner muttered, sounding impressed.

"He rather thought so as well," Lolani said bluntly.

Conner looked away from the hawk while he contemplated his next words. "I know that Vivek never knew this, but I'm pretty sure I have already figured out how to alter atomic structures. I gave my friend Medwin wings. I also used it to defeat Vellix. I wiped his mind. All he knows is who he is and what he did to deserve his fate. The creatures of his own creation carried him down to his holding chamber.

I saw —"

"Wait!" Lolani snapped sharply. "You mean to tell me that Vellix is still *alive?* I heard Medwin telling his people that you defeated Vellix!"

"Well, I did. He can't do —"

"Seek the missing scroll, Conner! Go to Medwin. You will need his help. Tell him that I will return shortly with information." Lolani departed quickly, heading northeast.

"What was that all about?" Conner wondered aloud.

"You didn't kill Vellix, Conner?" Zelimir asked, a note of unfiltered concern in his voice.

"No, I thought what I did to him was far worse than death," Conner said, feeling a slight twinge of unease beginning to develop.

"Perhaps it would have been better, except that you're forgetting how many followers he had. People who chose to live under his evil, instead of fighting it. People who chose to take the easy way out. People like the Ryvelians, and I'm sure many others. "What if one of them attempts to rehabilitate their master?"

Conner's stomach twisted nauseatingly, as if he was rolling down a hill at top speed. How could he have overlooked something like this? A thought occurred to him, and the knot in his stomach loosened. "Zelimir, who would have the ability to reverse my cognition? I mean, I put everything I had into that attack."

"Good point. It is somewhat comforting to know that your cognition is very advanced. It would take a master to reverse it."

"Exactly! Vivek is dead, and Vellix is a vegetable!" Conner exclaimed anxiously in an attempt to reassure himself that leaving Vellix alive hadn't been a massive mistake. "Who else would have power on that level?" he asked, hoping Zelimir would have an answer he wanted to hear. An answer that would cause the fear and anxiety that had clamped around his chest to release its grip.

"Who knows?" Zelimir replied thoughtfully. "Vellix has lived for ages… He has had plenty of time to pass his knowledge of cognition on to others…"

Conner went white as a ghost. Zelimir was probably right. Why hadn't he thought about that? It was so obvious now. He punched a tree to release his anger, but all that did was increase his frustration because it tore the skin on two of his knuckles and felt like it almost broke one. "Lolani must have gone to Mt. Cirrus to check. Let's hurry and tell Medwin what's going on," he said, breaking into a run.

Zelimir trotted alongside Conner with ease. It reminded him of how fit the wolf was. He could run considerable distances without a hint of fatigue if he wanted.

After a few miles, Conner tired out and started to walk. He felt bad about this because it forced Zelimir to slow down as well, just as he began to enjoy the run enough to throw his tongue to the wind. "Sorry Zelimir," Conner sputtered, trying to catch his breath. "I just can't run for as long as you."

"You don't need to be sorry. It only makes sense that I would be able to outrun you. I'm a wolf."

"Yeah, I hadn't noticed," Conner said. Zelimir looked at him incredulously, apparently unable to understand his sarcasm.

* * *

As they entered the Ancient Forest, Conner had a vivid image of himself navigating his way through the thick old growth on the previous occasions he had taken the same route. It was almost as if he could see apparitions of himself walking by his side.

"Conner, just so you know, when I went running off — back in your world — I thought I smelled someone out in the forest with us. It was weird, though, because no sooner than I caught the scent, it had vanished."

"That is weird," Conner replied distantly, more absorbed in the forest around him than in what Zelimir was saying. "It was probably a hunter. I did find an old fire-pit out there the first time I discovered the gate… So people must enter that part of the forest occasionally."

"It still doesn't really explain why I lost the scent though," said Zelimir, more to himself than to Conner.

A thin line in the trees revealed the Satria village as the sun started to set. Conner was grateful to have arrived before it got dark. He didn't want to search for the village in the blanketing darkness of night. He pushed through the last of the underbrush encompassing the village. 'Medwin is just through here,' he thought with a smile.

The first to notice that a boy and a wolf had just entered the village was a group of men stoking the evening fire. A few of them pointed. Others whispered to each other.

"Hello," Conner said awkwardly. "I'm looking for Medwin..." No one answered, but they began to whisper more meaningfully. "Is he here?" Conner went on timidly.

"You must be Conner," yelled a man, elbowing past the whispering men. He moved toward Conner and Zelimir and introduced himself. "I am Thane. Come, I will take you to Medwin."

"Thank you. I appreciate your help," Conner said as he fell in step with Thane.

"It's no problem. Medwin told us you had left. Was he mistaken?"

Conner didn't really know how to reply. He settled for shrugging inarticulately.

As they moved through the village, Conner noticed how much attention he and Zelimir were attracting. Many of the villagers were coming out of their huts to watch as they passed. They rounded a corner and Medwin came into view. He was standing out in front of a hut with the little hunchback, Moxie, to whom Conner owed his life.

"Conner! Zelimir!" Medwin cried the moment he realized who was approaching. "How is this possible?" He ran over to Conner and pulled him into a hug.

"Good to see you, Medwin!" Conner said as he released Medwin and moved toward Moxie. "You too, Moxie!" he added, giving him a hug as well.

"Yes, it is very nice to see you both," Zelimir agreed.

"Make sure these two are well fed," Medwin instructed Thane, waving a hand in Conner and Zelimir's direction. "Oh, and see that the wolf gets raw meat."

Zelimir gestured his thanks to Medwin for remembering how he took his meat.

"I didn't think I'd be seeing either of you again," Medwin went on jovially. "How is it that you are together? Last I saw of you, Zelimir, you were a great distance northeast of here! Not to mention headed for a fight you didn't think you would win." Medwin looked to be beside himself with curiosity.

"The answer is quite simple, really," Zelimir replied. "As you will have figured out by now, I won the battle with Rais. I knew that you two would need all the help you could get with Vellix, so I appointed a wolf by the name of Ranulf in charge of the pack. I sped off to Mt. Cirrus, but as I scaled the mountain, I caught your scents from the west. You had already left. I figured you must have been heading back here, so I tracked you. Conner's scent led me to the trees that harbor the gate between our worlds."

"Here you are," said Thane, handing Conner a wooden plate laden with deer, corn, and potatoes. He threw a slab of raw deer meat to Zelimir.

"Thanks," Conner said happily.

Zelimir devoured his venison immediately.

"So tell me, Conner. Why did you come back? You have fulfilled your destiny here." Before Conner had the chance to answer, Medwin's eyes widened with understanding. "Lolani was here nearly three weeks ago! She fought and questioned an owl. But before the owl could answer any questions, someone shot it with a poisonous blow dart. It died instantly. Lolani searched for the attacker, but didn't see anyone. Then she said she needed to talk to you. I told her you had gone back to your world. She asked me where the gate was, I told her, and she left..."

"Well, she found me," Conner said, once again feeling amazed by the vast difference in Earth and Rohwen's timelines. He had only been gone for ten — maybe eleven hours in his world and yet it had been three weeks since he left Rohwen.

"Not only did she find me," he continued, snapping out of his thoughtful mindset, "but she is the reason I was able to find the gate. Vivek left her with instructions for me. Apparently, he wasn't expecting me to win the fight with Vellix. He just expected me to survive it."

"What? He just expected you to survive it?" Medwin replied incredulously. "So he pretty much sent you into a fight he knew you couldn't win?"

"Yep," Conner replied plainly. He told Medwin about the hidden scroll that Vivek had been searching for all the years he had lived on Rhona. And of how he had wanted Conner to be ready to learn the knowledge this scroll would hold: keys to unlocking the ability to manipulate the atomic structures of objects, creatures, and humans.

When he had finished, Medwin was staring at him disbelievingly. "So you mean to tell me that there is a whole other level of cognition, and you've really only scratched the surface of your potential?"

"If Vivek was right about what was in that missing scroll, and I'm sure he was, then yes."

"But why would you need to be any more powerful than you are now? You already defeated Vellix."

Zelimir chimed in. "Actually, I am not so sure about that."

"What do you mean you're not so sure about that?" Medwin snapped, his fear of the idea that Vellix could still be a threat causing him to become uncharacteristically edgy. "What are you talking about? Conner wiped his mind!"

Zelimir shared the thoughts he'd had with Medwin — of how it was very likely that Vellix might have taught cognition to others, one of whom could very well be skilled enough to reverse the cognition attack Conner had used.

Medwin looked sick as Zelimir's theory set in. "*How* could we have overlooked that?"

"That's what I said," Conner mumbled, his expression dire.

"It would seem that a trip to Rhona is imminent," Zelimir observed.

"It would seem," Medwin agreed. "I will need to speak with the elders and appoint a temporary chief. But that will have to wait until tomorrow. It is late. Why don't you guys find a spot in my hut and get some sleep." He gestured them into the hut entrance behind him. "Tomorrow is going to be a long day."

Conner, Zelimir, and Moxie all nodded and entered the hut.

Trying to sleep that night was almost impossible for Conner. He felt like his mind was determined to ponder over a marathon-length amount of worries and wonders. Was Vellix being rehabilitated? Would the missing scroll have the information he needed to truly defeat Vellix?

Would he even be able to improve to the levels that Vivek had been sure he could?

He remembered something that Vivek had said when they met. 'This boy would have the power of cognition without even knowing it, or asking for it. He would be able to use it in ways others have only dreamed of. How exactly, I admit, I do not know.' If Vivek knew about the missing scroll at that time, he would have known it to be essential to Conner's reaching his full potential — essential to his becoming the one to use cognition in ways others had only dreamed of. So why didn't he mention it? Why didn't he at least divulge that such a thing existed?

A stab of anger burned in Conner's mind. 'He thought I was old enough to run off and face Vellix but too young to understand the danger of learning the contents of that scroll...' The longer he thought about it, the more it infuriated him. 'How does that make any sense? I could have been looking for the scroll in the first place! I could have —'

"Mother, I *have* to go. This is my path. I must take it. I am meant to help Conner. I know I am"

"What makes you think —"

"I just know, *okay*." Medwin and his Mother were having a whispered argument right outside the hut entrance.

Conner cupped his ear to hear more clearly.

"How can you be so sure, Medwin? Why can't you just send —"

"I already told you, I am *not* going to send an elder in my place."

"But I already thought I lost you once," Minna sobbed. "I c — can't lose you again."

"Mother, please try and understand. Conner is going to need me. He is the best friend I've ever had. I can't let him down."

Conner felt a surge of appreciation for Medwin sear through him. He already knew that Medwin was his best friend; now he knew that he was Medwin's.

"I'm going to bed," Medwin told his mother to finalize their conversation. He entered the hut, sat down on his bed, and put his face in his hands.

"I'm sorry that this whole thing isn't finished, Medwin," Conner whispered.

Medwin jerked his head up in shock, as if he'd been sure everyone would be asleep by now. "Conner, what are you doing still awake?"

"I can't sleep… Too much on my mind."

"Yeah, I don't blame you."

"What do you think is going to happen? Do you really think Vellix is being rehabilitated?"

"I think that we would be fools not to expect it."

"Almost as big of fools as I was for not killing him when I had the chance," Conner grumbled, harboring tones of frustration and anger.

"Don't be too hard on yourself, Conner. You thought your punishment was worse than death. I thought it was brilliant when you first told me. In fact, I thought it was brilliant up until about three hours ago."

Conner laughed weakly. "Yeah, I suppose that is true. I just can't stand to think of how many people might be affected by my foolishness."

"Don't let it eat at you. You can't change the past. However, you can mold the future like a piece of clay. Stay focused on your goal."

"As usual, you're exactly right. Thanks, Medwin."

"No problem. Let's try to get some sleep."

"Yeah, okay," Conner agreed. He turned over in an attempt to get more comfortable, and within minutes, he nodded off.

CHAPTER 3

Beach Bay

Rays of sun began to find their way through the cracks in the bark covering of Medwin's hut, revealing the small particles of dust that tend to float by unnoticed. Conner, who had been lying awake for the last ten minutes, took to staring blankly at the dust. He wondered what it must be like to have such an aimless existence. How carefree it would be to float along without any worries. That wasn't realistic though; he had plenty to worry about at the moment. Medwin's words from the previous night were like a tonic for his mentality. 'You can't change the past, but you can mold the future like clay.' The words kept repeating themselves in his head.

Zelimir woke up, stretched, and yawned widely.

"Morning," Conner said, still staring up at the peak of the hut.

"Good morning. I am going on a quick hunt. I would like to avoid eating berries and mushrooms if I can. I won't be long."

Conner burst into suppressed laughter, not wanting to wake anyone else. "Okay, Zelimir, see you in a few." He distinctly remembered the last time they left the village. All they had been able to find were berries and mushrooms. They hadn't really had the time to get prepared on that occasion, though. He was sure that Medwin would pack at least enough meat to last them a day, which is plenty of time when a wolf who excels at hunting is traveling with you.

Conner sat up and looked around the hut. Minna was asleep in a bed on the opposite side. She had tearstains all across her cheeks. He felt sick with guilt because of the grief his mistake was now costing her. "I won't fail again," he whispered.

Medwin stirred in his bed, but moments later, his steady snores returned. Conner didn't disturb him. He figured Medwin could use the sleep. For all he knew, Medwin could have been awake for hours after he himself had fallen asleep. If he had been, Conner wouldn't blame him. It isn't easy to watch a loved one endure such misery — especially if it's your mother.

He decided to leave the hut and wander around the village. His mouth split into a broad smile the moment his eyes beheld the vision in front of him. Early morning fog was drifting lazily through the village's web of huts, illuminated by the beaming sun as it pierced the treetops. The pleasant smells of pine and fire smoke mingled as they wandered under his nose. He took a deep breath and continued to survey the village.

Many of its inhabitants were already up. They all seemed to have an agenda of some kind, which gave the place a lively feel.

"Oh, there you are," Medwin said, stepping out of his hut. "Where is Zelimir?"

"He went for a quick hunt. He said he didn't want to be stuck eating berries..."

"What?" Medwin laughed. "Because of what happened last time? I was planning on bringing some meat."

"Yeah, I figured you would. Oh well," Conner said, shrugging.

Moxie stumbled groggily out of the hut and headed over to Conner and Medwin, still rubbing the sleep out of his eyes.

Conner saw Scarlet tucked into his twine belt. He longed to have the blade back, but he would never ask. He really did feel that Moxie deserved it. Seeing the knife reminded him that he needed to get his bow and arrows from the hut. As he went to grab them, Zelimir came trotting back into the village, still licking his blood-tainted muzzle. Conner heard the wolf say, "Are we about ready?" as he headed over to Medwin and Moxie.

Soon they had gathered all they would need for the trip. Medwin appointed the elder, Inoke, as temporary chief, and before long the little group was on its way. The hardest part about leaving was when Medwin said goodbye to his mother. She seemed to put as much effort into not crying as possible; it made things harder for Medwin, as he couldn't rely on being the strong, reassuring one.

Now that Moxie was away from the village and on an adventure, his demeanor changed entirely. He was like a little ball of energy for the better part of the morning. It wasn't until noon that he finally settled down, the original excitement of the journey finally gone.

A thought occurred to Conner. He still hadn't used cognition since returning. He looked up at the line of trees that separated the Ancient Forest from the valley on the other side.

The trees bowed obediently toward one another, forming an archway.

"Show off," Medwin said, smirking.

"That felt good," Conner replied.

"So," Medwin began, "I see that you have a nice longbow there… Are you any good with it?" he asked through a teasing grin.

"Not really," Conner said, glancing at Medwin suspiciously, almost positive that he already knew the answer to his question and was simply being sardonic. "I've only ever shot it a few times with my —" Conner cut himself short. He decided not to bring up his father so as to save his friend the pain, even if that friend had just openly mocked him for being less than talented with his weapon.

Conner pulled the bow from its holster on his quiver, grabbed an arrow and strung it. A mound of dirt and grass spewed up from the ground about thirty yards out in front of him as he used cognition for the second time.

After taking a moment to focus and aim, he fired the arrow. It soared through the air and over the mound of dirt. "Oops. I hope I can find that. Anyway, that's about how good I am... About as good as you expected..."

"I've seen far worse," Medwin said with such encouragement that it was quite plain he felt guilty about giving Conner a hard time. "Just keep working on it, you know?"

Zelimir's ears perked. "Medwin, I believe Lolani is approaching."

"What makes you say that?" Medwin asked curiously.

"She said she would return to you with information. I just heard a hawk screech from a northeastern direction for the second time."

Medwin looked up in search of the bird. "Huh, I don't see anything, Zelimir."

"I wouldn't expect you to be able to see her yet. I can hear for miles — up to six in fact — if the conditions are right, of course…" Zelimir took a moment to calculate. "I would say she is about two miles out at the moment."

Conner and Medwin looked at the wolf in awe. They were both thinking the same thing. Six miles is an incredibly long distance to hear from.

Sure enough, Zelimir was right. Lolani came into view a few minutes later, right as Conner retrieved the arrow he had fired.

Medwin wrapped the leather strap from his pack around his arm and held it out to offer the hawk a suitable place to land, as there were no trees around them. Even though the strap gave his arm some protection, he was relieved that she took extra care when landing.

"I have been to Mt. Cirrus. I was unable to locate Vellix. I fear the worst."

"Did you find the holding chamber down at the bottom?" Conner asked, hoping beyond hope that she would say no, and there would still be a chance that Vellix was down there.

"Yes, I flew down the stairway. When I entered the chamber, I was very careful not to be heard. The cries of the creatures made it quite easy. After I felt I had thoroughly searched the chamber, I left." Lolani turned her attention away from Conner and placed it back on Medwin. "Medwin, it was Vivek's desire that I find ownership in the chief of the Satria — he was always very fond of the Satrian people. When he made up his mind to face Vellix, he told me that he would soon be dead and that I should seek out Nayati as my new owner..."

Medwin kept a straight face at the sound of his father's name, but Conner was sure it took every ounce of his willpower not to let it fall into a heavily grieved expression.

"Due to the unfortunate loss of your father, I offer my services to you instead."

Medwin tilted his head in curiosity. "So, you're saying you would be ... *my* hawk?"

"Yes, if you will take me."

Medwin's mouth broke into a tooth-baring grin. "Of course I will!"

"Very good. I will keep surveillance from the sky. If I see anything suspicious, I will inform you immediately."

Medwin braced himself as the hawk took flight. His arm suffered a few scratches, but none too deep to bother him. "Wow! Can you believe it? Lolani is my hawk now!" he exclaimed as he watched the tiny dot that was Lolani disappear into the horizon.

"Cool," Conner said blandly, staring off into space, a look of disgust plastered to his face.

Medwin scowled at him for not sharing his excitement, obviously assuming that Conner thought Lolani should have offered herself to him instead.

"He's gone…" Conner uttered, not even slightly aware of the look he was getting from Medwin.

"You okay?" Moxie asked, noticing that Conner looked off-color.

"No, Moxie… I'm not okay," Conner replied.

"What is wrong?" Moxie continued sensitively.

"Vellix is gone, Moxie. He is no longer a prisoner in his own prison."

Medwin's scowl melted into a look of pity. Now he understood why Conner hadn't been able to share in his excitement. His mind was sinking agonizingly into the reality of his failure.

Moxie's eyes widened with fear. "Vellix is … back?"

"Thanks to me, he was never really gone," Conner said, full of anger at himself.

* * *

The hours passed without conversation. It seemed that no one had much to say. They walked along in silence, deep within their own thoughts.

Medwin, however, was still glowing with an apparently irremovable smile. Conner wasn't surprised, of course. The young chief had attained ownership of a magnificent red-tailed hawk.

If it hadn't been for the beauty of the land around him, Conner would have been completely depressed, but something about the green rolling hills eased his mind. It was as if each hill was an example of life's ups and downs. Every time he would get over one, it made him feel like he had completed a task.

Rushing water met his ears as they approached the west fork of the Brio River.

The tree Medwin had cut down to use as a bridge was still lying there.

'That's where I did cognition for the first time,' Conner thought as he stepped carefully across the bridge. The last time he crossed felt like a lifetime ago. Everything was so different now. Last time, his mind had been exploding like a box of firecrackers with curious questions: am I really in another world? Where is Medwin taking me? What do they want with me?

Now, his mind was fuming with anger, like a volcano long overdue to erupt.

A gentle fade of colors ranging through yellow, orange, pink, and lavender caressed the western horizon as a tired sun settled down behind the distant tree line. Shadows cast by the long blades of field grass danced playfully on scattered patches of dirt, making it seem like they were listening to the soft song of the wind.

Conner could always count on this time of the day to rejuvenate his confidence. There was perpetual beauty and peace to balance evil and aggression; infinite reasons to fight, so long as they were for the right reasons, and he could think of no reason that meant more to him than the freedom of all who honored Rohwen.

"I think we should call it a day," Medwin announced. "It will be dark very shortly. Plus" — he jerked his head in the direction of Moxie, who was looking extremely worn out — "I think our friend is a bit exhausted."

'His little legs must be burning like crazy,' thought Conner, who suddenly realized how much his own were. 'What a trooper.'

Medwin created his underground room, and after a quick dinner, they all drifted off to sleep.

CHAPTER 4

Within the Chamber

"Master, I was able to dispose of Nikkos before he could reveal any information to the hawk," said a gray-skinned, dark-haired man, projecting his voice over an echoed chorus of pitiful, mourning cries.

"Very good, Adrial," replied a hooded man, his voice dim yet powerful.

"Sir, if I may ask… How did you know that he would need to be followed?"

"I never really trusted Nikkos. I warned him that impatience could hold severe consequences. Told him that it would be wise to bide our time. That to allow the Satria a chance to settle was not only prudent, but also pertinent. He was an impudent fool. He thought he could impress me if he provided information ahead of schedule. He was overeager and irrational. Because of his mistake, the Satria will be aware that something isn't right. They will, of course, come to no logical conclusions, thanks to your efforts." The hooded man gestured his thanks to Adrial.

Adrial bowed. "You know nothing pleases me more than to serve you, Master."

The hooded man waved away Adrial's sentiments of dedication as if they went without saying. "The hawk came here searching," he said, sounding grim. "Why didn't you kill her when you had the chance?"

"I tried Master..." Adrial muttered shamefully. "She took flight the moment my dart hit Nikkos... It made her very difficult to hit. And —"

"— And with the entire Satria tribe so close you didn't want to do anything to reveal yourself."

"Yes Master."

"Fortunately," said the hooded man, "when she searched the chamber, she wasn't thorough enough. However, I feel that she could easily become a thorn in my side." Something covered heavily in shadow moaned, like a hungry baby too helpless to feed itself. "Shhh. Quiet now," coaxed the man with tones nearing mock sympathy. He returned his attention to Adrial. "Inform Katina that she is to seek out and kill the hawk."

"Yes, Master," Adrial replied with a low bow of his head.

CHAPTER 5

Symbolism

"What time is it?" Conner asked, waking to find all three of his companions up and looking as if they had been for some time.

"A few hours past sunrise," Zelimir replied without looking away from the paw he was cleaning.

"Here, eat some breakfast," Medwin said, offering Conner a small plate.

Conner ate quickly, feeling that they should have already been on their way.

The full night's sleep had given Moxie a fresh supply of endurance. Using his blade, Scarlet, for leverage, he clambered out of the underground room. "Come on! It's a good day!" he called lightheartedly down to the others.

Radiant sunlight blinded Conner's pale, blue eyes as he stepped up to Rohwen's surface, but once they had a chance to adjust he saw that Moxie was right. Light puffs of cloud floated by idly, throwing their shadows upon the valley below. The breeze was light and refreshing, just enough to give pleasant contrast to the sun's comforting warmth.

Medwin and Zelimir came up to the surface together. Zelimir's nose twitched as he sniffed the many scents that hung on the breeze. Medwin took a long, deep breath of air and released it with satisfaction.

"Are we ready?" Zelimir asked, surveying Conner and the others.

They nodded, and the four of them set out for the day's travels.

As the hours passed, an emotion other than fear and guilt started to take charge of Conner. It was joy. He was with the three people he cared for the most. 'Well, Zelimir's not a person. Technically, he's a wolf, but close enough,' he thought, laughing to himself. It was little thoughts like these that forced him to realize how fortunate he was to have them at his side and enabled him to find enjoyment in the otherwise dark climate of his mind.

His thoughts turned to Ammin, Lenny, and the crew, and before he knew it, a sense of adventure had started to come over him. He wanted to set sail, feel the spray of the ocean. He wondered again if the crew had voted Ammin captain of the *Colossus*. If they hadn't, what would the new captain be like? Would he be like Bellamy had been: loud and jolly, full of enthusiasm? Or would he be hard and stern, unable to find humor in things? Whoever it was, he hoped they would treat him with the same kindness and respect as Bellamy had.

Daylight started to fade. Conner was shocked that it was already getting late. He had been so absorbed in thought that the day felt as though it passed much quicker than usual. He turned to ask Medwin how much longer he wanted to carry on, only to find the young chief absorbed in conversation with Zelimir. Conner focused on what they were saying.

"...it is. I'm very happy for you."

"Thank you," Medwin said, making an appreciative gesture. "I still feel like it hasn't quite set in all the way. Me, the owner of a red-tailed hawk." He shook his head in disbelief, grinning broadly.

Conner smiled to himself. It was nice to see Medwin in good spirits. The pain of his father's death had changed him. The Medwin Conner had known before Chief Nayati's death had been able to enjoy life's simplicities. But when Nayati died, a part of Medwin died as well: his young heart. He was no longer able to view life from the comforting perspective of a son. He was forced to view it from the demanding perspective of a leader. Every decision he made held a weight that no fifteen-year-old should ever have to bear.

"I think it's about time we stop for the night," Zelimir said, his focus set on the darkening heavens.

Medwin nodded, reaching down to grab a small rock amidst the grassy ground. He pulled up on the rock and the ground around it lifted, revealing a four-foot-by-four-foot opening. "After you," he said, motioning for Conner and the others to enter his underground room.

Conner climbed onto his bed and leaned against the wall. "You need any help with dinner, Medwin?" he asked, watching as Medwin got a fire going.

"No, I'm fine," Medwin replied, pulling the last of the meat he'd brought from home out of his pack. He threw a chunk of it to Zelimir, then stabbed a stick through the two remaining steaks and held them over the dancing flames.

* * *

After dinner, Medwin announced that they would reach the Cliffs of Elders before noon the following day. Conner allowed images of the striking view from the cliffs to saturate his mind, and slowly, he slipped out of consciousness.

He was captain of the *Colossus*, taking the helm with one hand, thundering orders at his crew, and waving his free hand animatedly. The scene morphed flawlessly. The wooden deck of the ship eroded, as if doused in corrosive acid. Heavy, toxic fumes weighed down the air. The light all around him decayed slowly and seamlessly into a sheet of black. Something distant spoke. It sent him into an instant panic. He couldn't make out what the voice had said, but its tones sent electric chills shooting down his spine. As he tried to shake the unnerving feeling the voice gave him, it spoke again, this time more clearly.

"You will suffer, Conner..." it whispered, its tone sharp, icy. "You will suffer for what you did to me..."

An eerie, soft glowing light appeared under Conner's feet, providing only a small circle of visible floor around him. Fear took complete control of his senses. He was helpless as Vellix stepped out of the endless shadows that hung all around them and into the small source of light. Conner started to back away. He stared down at his feet, fearing that stepping into the shadows might mean falling into eternal oblivion. He noticed that the floor was made of crystal. Etched neatly into the center of its surface was a bizarre symbol.

"Did you think you would get away with what you did to me?" Vellix sneered. "You will pay dearly!" Without warning, he began convulsing violently, gnashing his teeth and grunting involuntary cries of pain. He started to change shape. His body contorted repulsively. He grew taller, wider, and stronger. Soon, his dark cloak was tearing at the seams.

"*Conner, wake up!*"

Someone was nudging at him vigorously.

"*Conner wake —*"

"I'm *up!*" he yelled. The scenes from his dream had dissolved, leaving him shaking in cold sweat. He began replaying parts of the dream that were still vivid in his mind as he noticed that Medwin was at his bedside, looking worried.

"It was just a dream," Conner whispered to himself, still trying to shake the feelings of terror the dream had caused.

"Are you okay? You were thrashing around in your bed," Medwin told him seriously. "I've been trying to wake you up for the last minute. What was the dream about?"

As Conner sat up and tried to recall his dream, he noticed a curious Zelimir and Moxie moving closer to his bed. "At first, the dream was just about something stupid" — he didn't really want to say that he'd been dreaming that he was captain of the *Colossus* — "but then it switched, and it was about Vellix. He was telling me that I would pay for what I did to him ... and …"

"Go on," Medwin urged, looking down at him impatiently."

"…A floor made of crystal… There was … some kind of shape thing etched into it."

"Like a symbol?" Zelimir asked.

"I didn't focus on it too much... But yeah, I would say there's a good chance it was some kind of symbol."

"Then what happened?" Moxie asked eagerly.

"Then Vellix started to shake violently. It was like he was convulsing or something. As the spasms reached their peak, he started to change form all together. That's when you woke me up, Medwin."

Medwin, Zelimir, and Moxie were all staring at him with similar looks of confusion on their faces.

"What do you think that means?" Medwin probed. "Or does it even mean anything?" he continued before Conner or anyone else could answer. "Do you think it was just your fears finding their way out?" he wondered aloud.

"Whatever it was, I think we should continue to analyze it while we walk," Zelimir suggested.

They discussed the dream for the first few hours of travel. Each of them with their own idea of what it could have meant. In the end, they came to the same conclusion: all the dream had been was an inner projection of Conner's greatest fear.

If it hadn't been for the fresh smell of sea air that reached Conner's senses, he would have continued to ponder the dream. However, he was starting to be excited again.

It wasn't long before they reached the cliffs. The stunning sapphire-blue water was just as beautiful as Conner remembered. He saw the shadowy shapes of the coral reef that flourished just off the coastline, on which birds flew effortlessly with the various wind currents. They seemed to welcome the newcomers with happy, playful squawks.

"Look! There's the *Colossus*!" Conner exclaimed, pointing enthusiastically.

Medwin smiled broadly in reply.

The huge sixteenth-century warship, *Colossus*, was harbored in her usual spot along the shores of Beach Bay: the most cutthroat city that Conner had ever set foot in. Last time he had been here, he thought he observed at least three murders. To top it off, when he reached his destination he had definitely witnessed a murder as Captain Bellamy slayed a man for the money he owed his first mate, Ammin.

"How are we getting down?" Moxie asked, looking distressed.

"I am going to carve a stairwell into the cliff using cognition," Conner reassured him

"Good! I didn't want to climb down."

Conner smiled reminiscently. His memory of fearing a climb down the intimidating cliff-face was still sharp and vivid. He redirected his focus to a large section of the cliff-top, well inland of the dangerous ledge. The stone exhaled a loud sigh as the sound of breaking rock rang out to the horizon and echoed back. The cliff-top started to carve itself away in a clockwise direction, exposing the first step of a stairwell.

Soon, Conner and the others were standing on the threshold of a hole, looking down and watching the spiraling stairwell carve its way deeper and deeper into the cliff. It was almost hypnotic watching it spiral on what felt like an endless journey to the sandy floor below.

"I think it is safe to say we won't catch up with it at this point," Zelimir observed.

"Good point," Medwin said. He started down the stairs and was followed by the others, Conner at the back. "That was good thinking to make the stairs completely enclosed," he yelled back to Conner. "It is much safer this way."

"That's what I was thinking," Conner replied. "I have to admit, I also thought it would look cool to make a spiraling stairwell..."

"Definitely!" Medwin replied enthusiastically. He seemed to be more impressed by this stairwell than many of the other acts of cognition Conner had done. His fingers skimmed over bumps and abrasions as he caressed the enclosure's stone wall, and his head never stopped turning, for fear he would miss a single aspect of the structure.

They were quickly closing in on the bottom of the stairs. Conner suddenly realized that there was no way out of his enclosure. A spider web of tiny cracks erupted out from a central point on the outer wall of the well and the rock crumbled, allowing a flood of dazzling sunlight to pour in.

It took no time at all for the sounds from the nearby city to reach Conner's ears. Whoops, jeers, and yells, accompanied by the occasional gunshot, became audible before he and the others had even made it halfway across the sandy beach.

"Sounds like Beach Bay to me," Conner said with a glance over at Medwin.

Medwin gave him a serious nod. He had switched his mindset from carefree to on guard with the snap of a finger. "Zelimir, be prepared for the worst. These people shoot first and ask questions later. Seeing a wolf stroll into their city will be sure to scare them."

"Agreed," Zelimir replied pensively. "I feel that we would do well to stick to back alleys until we find Ammin. He will provide enough protection for me to feel safe out in the open."

Medwin gestured his agreement as they reached the outskirts of the city.

CHAPTER 6

Moxie's Sacrifice

"Oi! Louie! I said secure tha' bowline! Righ', now grab tha' brail line. Wha' are yeh waitin' fer? Ter see if molasses can bea' yeh in a foo' race…? 'Urry up abou' it! Oi, Felix, grab tha' other brail line! Today, yeh bleedin' loafer! Righ', hoist the sail. Now tie those lines off to the central bitts… Okay you lot, tha's it fer now. Go 'ave a drink or summat." Lenny wiped the sweat from his brow and turned to face his captain. "Tha' fresh blood's comin' on alrigh', eh?"

"Not too shabby…" Ammin replied thoughtfully, "not too shabby at all... I reckon they're ready to sail," he continued, stroking the scruff on his chin.

"Should be proud, you should," Lenny said. "Yer firs' real act as Cap'n." Lenny grinned heartily.

"Aye," Ammin replied, attempting to return Lenny's good-natured smile, but only managing a weak curl of his lips. It wasn't that he didn't feel proud to have been voted captain of *the Colossus*. It was just that, under the circumstances, he wished he hadn't been. Bellamy's death was a loss that he still mourned greatly. He would have given up his newfound captaincy in a heartbeat if it meant getting Bellamy back.

Lenny read Ammin's pained expression accurately and decided to forge a new path in their conversation. "You know wha' we need?" he said lightly, clapping Ammin on the back. "We need a real reason ter set sail! A good lead ter go on, like… My share o' tha' gold from the las' mission is nearly all in Osman's till a' this poin'!" he laughed boyishly. The fact that he had tossed away a good majority of his gold on drinks and gambling in the local pub amused him greatly. This was the life of a young sailor with the respected title of 'first mate' aboard a greatly regarded warship.

"I admit, I am running short on gold myself," Ammin replied. "The crew will start getting violent amongst themselves if they run out of money for drinks."

"Yeh mean, *more* violent," Lenny chortled through a cheeky little grin.

"Yeah, *more* violent!" Ammin laughed, a true grin unfurling across his face. "But seriously," he continued, putting a hand out to silence Lenny's laughter. "I can't afford to lose men over pointless fist fights that turn into sword fights and escalate into gun fights. It is hard to find good sailors..."

"True enough, Cap'n. Well, speakin' o' Osman's... Yeh fancy a drink?" Lenny gave his captain a "why not" sort of look and shrugged.

"Ah, why the hell not. The whole bloody crew is over there anyways."

They crossed the gangplank to the docks and headed for the pub.

* * *

"Give us the usual, Osman," Ammin ordered as he and Lenny sat down at the grimy, dirt-stained bar.

The majority of Ammin's crew was gathered around nearby tables playing a game called bone-ace. A stale plume of lingering tobacco smoke hung heavily around their heads.

"Tha' don' add up ter thirty-one, Dale! Yeh bleedin' duffer!"

"Like 'ell it don'!" Dale spat. "Look again, Landon!"

Landon made to reach for Dale's little pile of gold, stirring the thick smoke into spiraling swirls.

Dale reached for his cutlass.

"Bloody 'ell! Tha's a wolf!" bellowed a sailor close to the front door. He drew his pistol and shot without hesitation.

A deformed silhouette launched itself into the bullet's path and was pelted in the stomach.

"No!" Medwin cried, running to Moxie's side.

"The wolf is harmless!" Conner screamed at anyone who would listen.

"What the hell is going on?" Ammin interrogated as he elbowed his way to the front of the pub.

There was Medwin, nursing a blood-soaked Moxie. Conner to his right, staring down at the scene through tears glistening in the light that shone through the open pub door.

"Whoever fired that bullet will pay dearly!" Ammin thundered.

"Lenny, help them to the ship. I believe Grayson is still aboard."

Lenny wasted no time in carrying out his orders. He didn't even take the time to react to the oddness of Conner and the others' random arrival. "Come on, mates! 'Urry up!"

Conner and Medwin picked Moxie up and followed Lenny out of the pub.

"Moxie, you're going to be okay," Conner said, placing as much hope in his voice as he could muster.

"You're a trooper, Moxie!" Medwin shouted desperately. "Just hang on!"

Moxie gave them a pitifully weak smile. His eyes started to roll back.

Zelimir jogged alongside them, looking on with great sadness.

'He's going to die!' Conner thought, despair welling up inside him. He stared intently at Moxie's wound, trying with all his might to heal it with cognition. But his focus was scattered with emotion. 'Please let me be able to heal him!' he pleaded with himself. 'I need to be able to heal him! I owe Moxie my life!'

The skin around Moxie's bullet wound started to repair itself crudely. The blood stopped gushing profusely, but the wound still looked horrific.

Conner's cognition had been poor, yet effective. At least Moxie wasn't losing fatal amounts of blood. However, he was completely delusional, saying things that made it obvious he thought he was back in Vellix's holding chamber. "Must find a way... Must... Got to be a way out."

"Do you think your cognition will be enough to save him?" Zelimir asked hopefully. "I can't help but feel responsible for what has happened. If it were not for my appearance, Moxie would be okay."

"You didn't tell that sailor to fire his weapon so hastily," Medwin said distractedly, his focus still on getting Moxie to the ship.

"You also didn't ask Moxie to jump in front of the bullet for you," Conner added.

"You are right — both of you," Zelimir admitted. "Thank you for your reassurances."

Lenny boarded the ship and led them down to the medical quarters. "Grayson ain' 'ere!" he exclaimed when they entered the room and found it empty. "You guys ge' 'im on tha' bed." Lenny gestured wildly to a bed in the center of the room. "I'll go an' look fer Grayson." He took off up the stairs and was quickly out of sight.

"Errgh... Find way... Ughhh," Moxie moaned lamely.

"We can't let him die like this," Conner said desperately. "Mentally, he's back in the holding chamber."

Medwin's features fixed themselves into an expression of immense pity as he watched Moxie writhe around in pain. "I don't think he's going to make —"

"Where is 'e? Ge' ou' the bloody way!" demanded a stressed-looking man, bulldozing his way past Conner and Medwin to see his patient. He ripped Moxie's shirt off. "What is this sorcery? How has his skin healed in this fashion?"

Conner gasped at Grayson, horrified at the thought that his cognition might have done more damage than good. "Sir," he said timidly. "I was just trying to stop the bleeding… I thought we were going to lose him."

"Firs' off lad, don' call me sir. The name's Grayson. An' second, 'ow am I spose ter ge' the bloody bullet ou' now? I'm gonna 'ave ter slice the poor bloke back open, tha's 'ow! Lenny ge' me supplies. Yeh know where they are?"

"Aye, Grayson. I got 'em 'ere," Lenny replied rushing back from a chest of drawers, laden with surgical instruments.

"Bloody well figured 'e'd know where they were," said Grayson, smiling up at Conner and Medwin's gaping faces. "I've 'ad ter patch 'im up more'n once."

'How could he be making jokes at a time like this,' Conner thought, trying to wrap his head around what mindset it must take to be a doctor.

"Go on then. Ge' ou'. Le' me work in peace," Grayson commanded. He started pulling out the tools he would need, muttering things under his breath that sounded a lot like, "Shoulda lef' it ter me," and "'Ave ter bloody slice the poor bloke back open."

Lenny met Conner's eyes with a look that said, "We better do what he says."

"Come on, Medwin. Let's give the doctor some space," Conner said. Lenny gave him an approving nod.

Medwin shifted his feet, reluctant to leave Moxie's side, but he conceded as Grayson glared at him severely.

Zelimir had concealed himself in a shadowed corner of the room the moment Grayson entered it, for fear of his reaction. He moved quietly along the far wall until he reached the door and slipped out unnoticed. He couldn't risk exposing himself again, not until Ammin had informed the crew that he was of no threat to them. His appearance had already done enough damage.

Ammin walked straight over to Conner and the others the moment he noticed them on the main deck. "How is he? Whoever that was..."

"His name is Moxie," Conner said. "Medwin and I owe him our lives."

"Poor bloke," Lenny muttered, staring off into space.

"The man who shot that bullet is in the brig," Ammin said, his tone severe. "He will be punished. You can be sure of that."

"It is my fault that the bullet was even fired," Zelimir confessed. "I should have kept to the shadows until you were able to let your crew know what was going on."

Ammin contemplated Zelimir. "What was your name again?" he mused.

"Zelimir."

"That's right," Ammin replied reflectively. "I will tell my crew that you are harmless. I don't think they will believe me — not a trusting bone in the lot of them — but they will obey orders."

"Thank you, Ammin," Zelimir said gratefully.

"So, I take it you were named captain then," Conner assumed, glancing up at Ammin.

"That I was, lad." Ammin swelled slightly as he replied. "Captain Ramirez is my title now."

"Captain," Medwin started in a businesslike tone. "We are in need of your services — there will be gold in it for you."

Ammin fixed Medwin with a look of viable interest. "Oh? …And what service is it that you are looking for?"

"Believe it or not, we need to get back to Rhona," Medwin replied, scratching the back of his head absentmindedly.

Ammin looked at Medwin curiously for a moment, his gaze pitying. "You do know that Vivek is dead, right? He won't be there, on the island."

"Yeah, we know," Medwin answered.

Ammin's brow creased with confusion. Apparently, he could see no other reason why they would want to go to the island. He had used all the time he spent there attempting to get off of it. He shrugged and said, "If that's where you want to go... Lenny! Round up the crew. We're setting sail."

"Blimey — really?" Lenny asked with excitement.

"Yeah, we're taking this lot back to Rhona." Ammin jerked his head toward Conner, Medwin, and Zelimir.

"Aye, Cap'n!" Lenny yelled, throwing his captain a backwards glance as he ran off in the direction of the pub.

* * *

.

A few minutes later, Ammin's crew was standing in a group around him — some wobbling more than standing.

"Alright… First things first," Ammin said, glancing around to ensure that he had their attention. They stared back at him through glossy eyes. He continued "There's a wolf what's gonna be sailing with us. He will not harm you… Any man caught so much as looking at him the wrong way will be thrown in the brig!"

…Silence…

"Do I make myself clear?"

A muddle of slurred agreement rang out from the crew. Whatever their doubts may have been, they chose not to express them. They were well aware of the fact that Grant — the sailor who fired his gun so hastily back at the pub — had literally been dragged down to the brig by their captain. No one was at all interested in sharing his fate.

Satisfied that he had been heard, Ammin decided to move on. "Right, our heading is southeast. Destination: Rhona."

The crew shifted slightly.

"*Well?* Are we waiting 'til tomorrow to get underway?" Ammin burst out. "Raise anchors! Man the halyards and lower the sails. James, get up to the forebitts! Those ropes ain't gonna untie themselves! I need eyes in the nest! Look lively, you bilge rats!"

"Well, he sure sounds like a captain," Conner laughed.

"Indeed he does," Zelimir agreed.

Medwin didn't respond. The look on his face was distant and pained.

Conner knew exactly why Medwin looked this way. He was thinking about the little hunchback below.

"I'm sure Moxie will be okay," Conner lied, hoping to bring peace to Medwin's thoughts.

"I don't think so, Conner," Medwin replied, far too aware of the truth to be deceived by Conner's lie. "You're just trying to make me feel better. Lies are for fools and the weak-minded."

"I was only trying to help," Conner said, a little stung by Medwin's reaction.

Medwin showed no sign that he heard Conner's response. He gazed out at the open sea with the appearance of someone who would prefer to be alone.

A strong gust of open sea air lashed Conner's face. He put Medwin's reaction aside and looked up to watch as the ship's massive sails caught the wind. It was just as breathtaking as he remembered. Grinning buoyantly, he decided to have a look out over the starboard railing.

The Colossus' huge bow carved through the ocean with ease, leaving white foaming streaks in its wake. Normally, the evenly timed swells of water would have sent Conner into a peaceful trance. Into a world where nothing could harm him — where the spray of the ocean would remind him that he was free. Liberated.

But visions of Moxie lying in a bed somewhere below, dying slowly, unable to escape the prison of his own mind, weighed too heavily on his heart. They made him feel guilty that he was free to stand around and enjoy a leisurely afternoon boat ride. 'I just wish I knew if he is going to be okay,' Conner thought sadly. 'If only there was a way to find —' He paused in mid-thought, struck abruptly by an idea. He started toward the bridge.

"Captain," he hailed Ammin.

Ammin stuck a hand out at Conner, gesturing for him to wait a moment. He turned to face Dale.

"Cap'n, we're well underway an' traveling 'round twen'y-two knots."

"Very good, Dale," Ammin said. He gave the helm a firm tug, his expression definitive of a man who was truly content.

Conner climbed the few steps up to the bridge. "Captain?" he said again.

"Huh...?" Ammin replied distantly.

"I was hoping to have a word," Conner said, coming to a halt a few feet from the ship's helm.

"What's on your mind, lad?" Ammin asked, pulling his focus in on Conner, as if heaving himself back from a place deep within his mind.

"I was wondering what your medic, Grayson's, track record is like. You know, does he usually save his patients?"

Ammin looked at Conner seriously. "It really depends on how bad the injury is. The life of a sailor is not one with a high expectation of survival." He gave the helm another strong tug. "We are well aware of the risks of our profession. We —" Understanding bloomed across his face. "You are concerned for your little friend."

"Very much so," Conner admitted. "And Medwin is even more worried than I am."

"So you wanted some reassurance to give him? That's why you are asking?" Ammin hit the nail right on the head.

"Yes, sir."

"You are a good friend, Conner. Well, I have to say, Grayson has always been —"

"Cap'n Ramirez!" Ammin was cut off by the sailor in the crow's nest. "Cap'n, I've spotted it!"

"So it's true," Ammin whispered uneasily.

"They're approachin' from the southeast," yelled the man in the crow's nest.

"Conner, run to my quarters!" Ammin barked. "There's a spyglass sitting atop the table. Fetch it for me!"

Conner stood there, trying to react, but shock had weighed down his limbs.

"Now, boy!" Ammin thundered.

Ammin's harsh tone brought Conner back to his senses. He ran to the captain's quarters, grabbed the spyglass, and darted back out to the bridge. "Here," he panted, handing Ammin the spyglass.

Medwin and Zelimir came running up to the bridge. "What's going on?" they asked, alarmed by the sudden commotion.

"I'm not really sure," Conner said.

"There's been rumor of a mysterious ship what preys upon other vessels and then just disappears," Ammin answered, still peering through his spyglass. "I haven't had any conformation of this rumor until right now." He handed Conner the spyglass. "Look out past the bow of the ship."

Conner obeyed.

"Now turn ever so slightly to your left. Do you see that ship?"

Conner searched for a moment. "I can't see any — hold on. Yeah, I see it."

"That ship has made an aggressive course change in order to intercept us. We could change course in an attempt to avoid a fight, but I have no idea what speeds that ship can reach. The effort may be a futile one."

Lenny arrived on the bridge, red-faced and pouring sweat. "Cap'n, your orders? Yeh fancy a figh'? I say we show them prats wha' 'appens when yeh tangle with ol' *Colossus*," he suggested passionately.

"Aye, Lenny. I would have to say that whoever they are, they need a wakeup call if they think they're going to run these waters."

"Righ', I'll le' James an' Gavin know wha's goin' on."

"Lenny! Hold up," Ammin said.

"'Old up?" Lenny reiterated curiously, as if he could see no reason to delay the preparations for a fight.

"Tell James I need to speak with him. You and Gavin prepare the cannons. Round up as many men as you think you will need to maintain steady fire."

"Aye, Cap'n." Lenny nodded obediently and ran toward the lower decks.

"Zelimir, would it trouble you too much to stay down below with..."

"Moxie?" Zelimir finished Ammin's question, knowing that he didn't remember Moxie's name.

"Yes, Moxie."

"I do think it would be wise for someone to stay by his side through the fight, and being as I can't really help much, I believe it would be best for me to be the one."

"That's settled then," Ammin said.

Zelimir headed over to the hatch without another word and disappeared down the stairs, leaving a wake of tense-looking sailors behind him

"Conner, Medwin, how well do you swim?" Ammin asked them directly.

They glanced at each other, sharing similarly concerned looks. "Um, well — not too bad," Conner answered first.

"And you, Medwin?"

"I swim okay. I wouldn't say I'm the greatest by any stretch."

"Are you implying that we are going to need to swim?" Conner asked nervously. "Are you thinking there is a good chance they will sink us?"

"No, I have a plan. I've seen you two in battle and I know I could use you, if you're willing."

CHAPTER 7

The Ultimatum for Cassius

"Get those las' three cannons packed, Skylar!" Gavin snarled. "Bloody slackers, the lot of 'em," he rumbled, shaking his head in disbelief.

"Yeh know Skylar ain' never 'ad ter come down 'ere 'afore, Gavin," Lenny reminded him.

"I don't care if 'e's never even set *foot* on a ship! I ain' in the market fer dyin' today!"

"I ain' neither! All I'm sayin' is ter encourage the bloke, mate. Yer sure ter ge' better results tha' way." Lenny looked through the cannon hatch nearest to him and saw that the enemy ship was only minutes from firing range. "'Ere they come, Gavin."

"Gawd I wish James was down 'ere with us!"

* * *

"James, do you still have a good supply of waterproof fuse?" Ammin asked urgently.

"Aye, Cap'n."

"Good! Go fetch it. While you're down there, tell Gavin to watch for my signal. When he sees the sun reflected back at him off my cutlass the first time, it will mean cease-fire. When he sees it for a second time, he is to signal back."

"Aye, Cap'n!"

"And bring Lenny back up with you."

James waved a hand to signal that he heard Ammin before disappearing down the hatch.

Ammin turned to face Conner and Medwin. "You two had better bring a sword and a pistol," he said rather nonchalantly, considering the content of his statement.

"I have my hatchet," Medwin said, patting his pack confidently.

"Whatever you're more comfortable with," Ammin replied with an unperturbed shrug. "Here, Conner, take these," he said, offering him a pistol and a cutlass. "Your bow and arrows won't do you any good in close combat. You can stow them in my quarters for now."

Feeling nervous, Conner took the gun and sword from Ammin. He glanced over at Medwin, who gave him a look that seemed determinedly fearless.

Ammin cranked the helm in order to position *the Colossus* for battle. "Quincy! Get up here and take the helm!"

"Aye, Captain," replied a short and stocky sailor as he ambled up to the bridge.

"Cap'n, wha's goin' on?" Lenny yelled from a distance, running toward them — James right behind him.

BOOM! BOOM! — BOOM! BOOM! — BOOM!

The enemy ship fired and hit *the Colossus*' starboard railing. Large shards of wood scattered across the upper deck. Conner watched in revulsion as a dozen shards of wood struck a man. He fell to the ground with a thud, yelping in pain and clutching the shards nearest to his heart.

"Come " — *BOOM!* — "on" — *BOOM!* — "lads!" *BOOM! BOOM! The Colossus* returned fire, forcing Ammin to scream his orders. He ran over to the port side railing and dove off.

Lenny followed without hesitation, then James.

Conner and Medwin exchanged looks of hopeful bravery.

"Let's go," said Medwin.

Summoning courage from the depths of his core, Conner jumped. Seconds later, the choppy waters of the ocean were all around him. He quickly located Ammin, Lenny, and James as they swam directly under the *Colossus*. He kicked like mad to keep pace with the three highly advanced swimmers.

Ammin swam up to the surface as soon as he had made it to the opposite side of the ship's keel.

Conner was extremely grateful for this because he needed air desperately. He fought his way up to the surface and James grabbed him the instant he reached it.

"Don't move," James hissed with intensity.

BOOM! — BOOM!BOOM! BOOM! — BOOM! The enemy ship fired again.

Medwin popped up.

Ammin grabbed his arm and gave him the same warning James had given Conner. "Okay guys, this is going to be a big swim. We need to reach the portside of their ship before we can come back up for air. The second you come up, take a few quick breaths, dive back under, and head for the starboard," he whispered, purpose and command striking every word.

Everyone quietly nodded their understanding of his orders.

Conner took the deepest breath he possibly could and dove back under, following Ammin once more. A loud melancholy cry echoed throughout the water. Conner looked to his right; Medwin was wearing a wide-eyed expression. A blue whale was cruising by just beneath them. Rays of sunlight, dissected by the choppy peaks of the ocean above, swayed hypnotically across its gigantic body. Conner knew that the whale was harmless, but being this close to a creature so incredibly large and powerful still doubled his heart rate. He watched as the whale blended into the haze of water in front of him and disappeared, its sorrowful wailing still audible.

The moment the whale was out of sight, a new feeling came over Conner. He was getting dizzy from lack of air. The blurred forms of his companions headed for the surface. He had to keep pushing. 'Think positive thoughts,' he told himself. 'Just keep going... keep swimming... keep...' A strong hand clasped around his arm and tugged.

Next thing he knew he was drawing deep breaths of air. His head was buzzing. "Thanks, Ammin. I — I..."

"Catch your breath, and *keep quiet!*" Ammin warned him. The captain took a few revitalizing breaths and dove back under the water, which trembled in the shockwaves of fresh cannon fire.

Conner dove back under and pursued Ammin. The swim from port to starboard side was far easier than the last one had been.

"Okay, first things first," said Ammin as his companions resurfaced around him. "We take both of the gun decks. After that, I will give you your next orders. Understood?"

They nodded assuredly.

Ammin began scaling the side of the ship. Conner quickly understood the great skill this climb would require. He couldn't seem to get a foothold on anything. He looked over at Lenny and James. They were using the barnacles that clung to the ship's hull in order to reach the anchor. From there, they climbed the anchor chain up to a thick wooden piece of trim that ran the length of the ship.

Ammin was already up. He moved down to the fifth cannon hatch.

Conner watched as James and Lenny headed for the third and fourth hatches. And then he understood. The plan was starting to make sense. He climbed over the second hatch followed by Medwin, who stopped at the first.

Ammin drew his cutlass and used the end of its blade to lift the hatch's wooden cover.

Conner lifted the cover to his hatch and climbed through as quietly as possible.

Once inside, he stayed hidden behind the cannon that sat there. He watched the gun crew on the other side of the deck, scrambling like crazy to reload their cannons. Not one of them noticed that five of their enemies had just boarded their ship.

"*Get that barrel of powder over here, now!*" screamed one of the sailors.

Three men hustled to obey their orders.

BOOM — CRASH! A cannonball fired from *the Colossus* came smashing through the gun deck. It claimed the lives of two of the men on deck before its path of carnage was complete.

Ammin decided that this would be the perfect time to catch the gun crew off guard. He charged out from behind his hiding spot, slashing down the men in his path.

Conner watched as James and Lenny did the same.

"This'll bloody teach yeh ter attack yer superiors! I'll kill the bloody lot o' yeh!" Lenny roared as he entered the assault. He fired the two pistols he had and found his mark with both shots, before dropping them to the ground, drawing his cutlass and making good on his threat.

James was savage, showing no mercy to his enemies. He carved through them viciously.

Conner pulled out the matchlock pistol that Ammin had given him only to realize he had no way to light it. 'Wait a second,' he thought, suddenly remembering who he was. A bold, cyan-blue flame burst to life in the palm of his hand. He used it to light the pistol's flint and shot a man that was about to fire a cannon. He reached down for the sword that Ammin had given him; it wasn't there. He hadn't tied it to his belt-loop properly.

Medwin pulled out his hatchet and dove into battle. He was far more agile than the men he fought. They virtually didn't stand a chance against his speed and accuracy.

They had taken the lower deck within minutes.

Ammin looked around the room to make doubly sure there were no survivors. "Alright lads, let's move to the upper gun deck. Don't let this easy victory dilute your focus. This ship's head gunner is sure to be up there. And if he's anything like our head gunner" — he gave James a hardy thump on the back — "then his men will be better trained than this lot was." He looked around at the fallen men that were sprawled across the floor. "Here, Conner, take this," he said, handing Conner a cutlass that belonged to one of the fallen men. "I doubt he'll be needing it."

Lenny burst into laughter. "Yeh don' say?"

James smiled broadly, revealing the fact that his teeth were on the verge of rotting right out of his skull.

"Thanks," Conner said. At that moment, he gained a whole new respect for Ammin's observational skills. Somehow, in the midst of battle, he noticed that Conner had lost his weapon.

"Follow me," Ammin ordered them.

They crept up the stairs until they reached the opening to the upper gun deck.

"What the *hell* is taking them so long to reload down there?" exclaimed a big burly man who looked fanatically stressed out. "I told the captain that Jerome was a worthless excuse for a gunner! But does anyone listen to me? Lucas! Go and check on them down there. Give 'em a hand if they need it."

Lucas obeyed his orders and headed for the stairs.

The moment he rounded the corner, Lenny grabbed his mouth and dispatched him as quickly and quietly as possible.

The gunner lit four cannons in quick succession. *BOOM! BOOM! — BOOM! BOOM!*

Conner heard the distant sounds of two of the cannonballs hitting their marks, followed by the vague cries of several men.

BOOM! — SMASH! "Arrgh!"

Another shot fired from *the Colossus* found its target.

"Nice shot, Gavin," James mumbled.

Conner didn't see what happened, but it sounded as though the cannonball did some serious damage.

"Come on, lads," Ammin whispered. He moved into the room, sword drawn.

Conner allowed James, Lenny, and Medwin to enter before he went in. The fight already looked to be more of a struggle than the one on the deck below as he joined it. Ammin had jumped immediately into battle with the burly gunner.

"So that's why there ain't been any gun fire from down below!" he shrieked furiously. He attacked Ammin with his sword, making wild slashing motions. One of the slashes found its mark and sliced Ammin's left arm wide open.

Ammin glanced at his wound and back to the gunner, his expression furious. A gleam of fear shone in the gunner's eyes as Ammin came at him with twice the aggression, swinging low then high with precision.

The gunner was no match for this increase in skill. He was too slow to recover after blocking the high attack, and Ammin drove his sword through the man's torso. "Should've known you wouldn't get away with that," he jeered, retracting his sword with one powerful tug.

The man made a gurgling noise, dropped his sword, and fell to the ground.

James and Lenny were both taking on what appeared to be highly skilled swordsmen.

"Not bad, mate!" Lenny admitted as his opponent countered what he thought would be a fatal blow.

BOOM! BOOM! — BOOM! — BOOM! The Colossus fired again. One of the shots came smashing through the gun-deck, spraying shards of wood in all directions. A large shard splintered its way deep into James' thigh. With a fierce tooth-gnashing cry, he ripped it out and used it to kill the man in front of him.

A husky man overpowered Medwin and kicked him in the stomach. He fell to the deck with a thud. The man was about to run Medwin through when a ball of flame struck him in the face. His hands moved instinctually to the burn as he cried out in pain.

Medwin seized this chance to act, and slashed his opponent down with a powerful strike. “Thanks, Conner!”

Two more balls of fire came to life, one in each of Conner’s hands.

“I don’ know ‘ow the bloody ‘ell yer doin’ tha’,” James roared, “bu’ yeh must be bleedin’ daft! Yeh migh’ hit a barrel o’ powder an’ kill the lot o’ us!”

Conner disconnected his focus from the flames; they flickered feebly and went out. He drew his sword, took a deep, calming breath, and entered the battle. Two scrawny men charged him, seeing that he had no true form with the sword.

The first came at him with a high powerful attack. Conner dodged and quickly thrust his weapon into the man’s heart; his face contorted with shock. His eyes swept from Conner to his bleeding chest. He dropped his sword to the floor, clutching hopelessly at the wound, and fell to his knees.

The second man became enraged as he watched his friend lie down and die. He flung himself at Conner with a primal look in his eyes and swings of his sword to match.

It was all Conner could do to block the vicious onslaught. Eventually, the attacks overpowered him. Fear flooded his senses as he felt the man’s cutlass slide effortlessly through his side. The wound spewed warm blood, but the laceration felt cold. His vision became distorted and his head felt like it was swimming into a world of delusion.

Something flew across the room and struck the man down before he had the chance to finish Conner.

Next thing Conner knew, someone had sat him up and started wrapping cloth around his wound.

"It's going to be alright, Conner. Just relax," Medwin said. He finished tying Conner's bandages and turned to face Ammin. "He'll be fine." He stepped over the man that had slashed Conner and retrieved his hatchet.

Ammin gave Medwin a nod. He walked over to one of the cannon hatches that faced *the Colossus* and used his cutlass to reflect the sun back at his ship, giving Gavin the signal to ceasefire. "Alright, lads, we've done well so far, but this is where it's going to get a bit tricky. James, can you rig these two cannons here to one fuse? And those three over there to another?"

"Course I can, Cap'n," James answered with a mischievous grin.

"Right, point them two up at the main deck," he gestured toward the canons closest to James, "and point the other three at a downward angle — so if fired, the ship will be sent to the depths. Stay down here and wait for Gavin's signal."

James nodded dutifully.

"When you see it, fire the cannons that you'll have pointed at the main deck."

"Aye, Cap'n."

"Alright, lads, follow my lead — and don't make a sound."

Lenny looked as if he were on holiday; his expression was of pure excitement.

"Are you going to be okay, Conner?" Medwin asked, looking concerned.

Conner sat there and looked up at his companions: Ammin, his arm gashed wide; Lenny, exhibiting scrapes and bruises across most of his visible skin; James, with blood oozing liberally from his leg; Medwin, who showed definite signs of battle. "Yeah, I'll be fine," he answered, using his sword to push himself back up into a standing position. Swaying slightly, he stood and faced his companions, sword gripped tightly.

"There's a good lad!" Ammin exclaimed.

Lenny gave him a smack on the shoulder. "Good fer you, mate! Takes some real spine ter have a row with a wound like tha'."

Conner forced a smile. His state of delusion was making everything around him feel like a strangely realistic dream — a dream he knew was all too real. He drew all the concentration he could muster and willed the skin around his wound to heal. A bizarre sensation followed. He could feel his flesh diligently weaving itself back together under the cloth bandage.

Ammin started toward the stairs that led to the main deck. He gave James one last meaningful glance before he and the others headed up.

The sound of footsteps echoed down the stairwell, followed by a man's voice.

"What the *hell* is going on?"

"I don't know Dominic! If you haven't noticed, we ain't fired a shot for some time! They ain't fired neither!"

"You think both gun crews been killed by enemy fire?"

The two men's voices started to grow louder as they headed down to the gun deck.

Ammin sprang on them the instant they became visible.

Lenny walked a few steps beyond Ammin to make sure there hadn't been anyone else coming. "We're clear, mates."

They reached the top of the stairs and gathered around the hatch, peering over it in four different directions.

There was sheer mayhem on the main deck. Men were scrambling in an attempt to repair the mass damage inflicted by heavy cannon fire. Sails lay in tattered folds around splinters and shards of wood that were once the ship's foremast. Large sections of railing were missing. The broken bodies of fallen men lay all over, some severely wounded, others dead.

"Stay hidden here," Ammin ordered them. "If all goes as planned, you won't need to fight. If it doesn't... Well, you'll know if it doesn't." He grinned boyishly before stepping onto the deck as if he belonged there. He walked straight past groups of men who were all so focused on what they were doing that they didn't realize an intruder was within their midst.

A commanding voice found its way across the deck.

"Aleron! Fetch the grappling hooks!" thundered a large man with short curly hair and a scruffy beard. "I want to board their ship the moment we're in range!"

Ammin knew that this man must be the captain. Only one man on a ship has that voice of authority. Using extreme caution, Ammin moved around behind the captain, stuck the barrel of his pistol in his back, and whispered in his ear, "Move and I'll fire."

The captain remained motionless.

"Tell your crew to stop what they're doing, drop their weapons, and stand in a group over there." Ammin used his free hand to point at the ship's bow.

Still, the captain remained motionless.

"Now!" Ammin demanded, digging his pistol farther into the captain's back.

"Listen up!" roared the captain.

The whole crew turned to face him.

"Drop your weapons and get in a group over there!" he ordered, gesturing in the direction of the ship's bow.

One of the men drew his weapon. "What is this? Who are you?" he spat at Ammin.

"Don't worry about that. Worry about the fact that, if you don't drop your weapon, I will shoot your captain."

"Drop the damn sword, Terrence!" barked the captain.

Terrence reluctantly dropped his sword and joined the rest of the crew at the bow.

Ammin drew his sword and reflected the bright sunlight back at Gavin on *the Colossus*.

Gavin signaled back…

B-BOOM! Two cannonballs came hurtling up through the main deck, narrowly missing the crew.

"Damn you!" snarled the captain ferociously.

"Shut up and listen!" Ammin warned him. "That was just a taste. I have three cannons ready to fire straight into the bowels of your ship. If you value your crew and your ship, you will do exactly what I say."

"And what's that?" asked the captain through grit teeth.

"First off, you'll stop preying upon the vessels in these waters. And secondly, you'll allow me and my crew to dock at your harbor, where *your* men will repair the damage you've inflicted upon my ship."

The captain stood there silently. Finally, he spoke. "It would seem that I have no choice in the matter."

"I rather thought you would see it my w —"

A fireball shot past Ammin and his hostage. It hit one of the men standing near the center of the group. The distinct sound of a gun clanking to the deck rang out through the otherwise silent sea air.

"*Arrgh!* What the hell was that?" shrieked the man, clutching a nasty burn on his face.

Conner stepped out from behind the mainmast. "I thought I might need to keep an eye on them," he said, still staring at the group of sailors at the ship's bow. "That man was about to try and shoot you, Ammin. Does anyone else want to try something stupid?" Conner yelled as two more fireballs materialized in his palms.

The look of fear engraved itself upon the faces of every man standing in the group.

"It can't be," muttered the captain, starring avidly at Conner.

Medwin and Lenny came out of hiding to join Conner. When Medwin saw the ship's captain, his eyes grew wide with shock.

"Cassius?"

CHAPTER 8

The Edelish

"Medwin! What the — why are you — what is going on?" Cassius didn't seem to be able to comprehend the arrival of Medwin on his ship. "What are you doing mixed up with these — these pirates?"

"Pirates?" Ammin flared up. "I believe you are referring to yourself, mate!"

"We're not pirates!" Cassius retorted. "We are doing what is necessary for the survival of our people!" he added passionately.

"So it's *necessary* to kill and steal for your *people* to survive, is it?" Ammin snapped. "Seems to me like we'd all be better off without your *lot*, if those are the stipulations for their survival!"

Cassius was too furious to reply. He clenched his fists so tightly that his knuckles went white.

"I never would have expected you to turn to this way of life, Cassius," Medwin said in disbelief.

"Yeah, well it's not like the Satria were there for us in our time of need. After we came to your aid in battle, you did nothing to stop Vellix and his armies as they scorched our home into a barren wasteland… Edelan was one of the most beautiful and ancient places in all of Rohwen. Everything we knew, our way of life, our families, and our livestock; burned to ash for our allegiance with the Satria! We were lucky to salvage the writings of old, without which all of our traditions, stories, and teachings would have been left in ashes."

"Cassius … I am truly sorry for what happened to your people," Medwin said, his heart wrenched with anguish for the loss Cassius and his people had suffered. "My father felt more sorrow for what happened than you could ever imagine. We had no way of knowing what was going on until it was far too late. Please understand that we would have come to your aid, had we known that we were needed."

"Yeah… Well a lot of good 'would haves' have ever done for anyone!" Cassius scoffed.

Medwin opened his mouth to reply, but at that moment he made eye contact with the captain; the sheer agony that lingered in Cassius' brown eyes made him lose all conviction. He abandoned his argument and shifted his gaze from Cassius to study a coil of rope near his feet.

"Hey, Terrence, get over here," Cassius said to change the subject.

"Hold on!" Ammin yelled. "Do I have your word that you won't try anything stupid?"

"You have the word of Cassius, son of Demetrius, and leader of the Edelish people."

Ammin seemed to be satisfied with Cassius' answer. He removed the gun from his back and stepped a few paces away.

Terrence came to a halt next to Cassius. "Your orders, Captain?"

"We're heading home. Take the helm."

"Aye, Captain," Terrence replied. He left for the bridge.

The rest of the men shifted slightly, as if unsure of what they should do.

"Snap to it!" Cassius yelled to get them moving. He turned to face Ammin. "How many of my men have been slain?"

"We took both of the gun decks," Ammin replied, feeling remorseful at his answer. His feeling of victory was considerably dampened by his understanding of the desperation that had led these men to piracy.

"Those were good men," Cassius uttered, staring blankly out at the vast ocean.

Ammin was left to absorb the impact of those last few words as Cassius headed up to the bridge. He waited a moment and then followed. "Where do you harbor?"

"On the backside of the isle of Ewaun," Cassius replied without turning to face Ammin.

Conner walked over to Medwin and Lenny. "So I guess now you know what happened to the Edelish people, Medwin."

"I can't believe they turned to piracy."

"This, what they been doin', it ain' bloody piracy!" Lenny exclaimed. " Didn' yeh hear wha' tha' Cassius bloke jus' said? It's desperation. Anyone'd do the same fer their families. I ain' sayin' it's righ'. Jus' sayin' it's human nature, tha's all."

Conner looked at Lenny as if for the first time. "That's very insightful of you, Lenny."

"Wha', yeh though' I couldn't make a basic deduction? Yeh think I'm stupid?"

"No no! I only meant that — well, you know..."

"Hahaha! Relax, Conner, I'm only pullin' yer chain! Bleedin' touchy ain' 'e, Medwin?" Lenny clapped Medwin on the shoulder and reared his head back in laughter.

"Very funny," Conner said sarcastically. He turned his attention to Ammin, who had just called over to the *Colossus* in a booming voice.

Skylar called back. "Ahoy, Cap'n."

"Tell Quincy to follow our lead. We're heading for Ewaun."

"Aye, Cap'n."

As day blended slowly into night, the two ships made the short passage to the backside of Ewaun.

In the faded colors of dusk, Conner could just make out the general scape of the island. Its terrain was much rougher than that of Rhona. Mountainous ridges branched like spines from its heart, each of which ran its own course and sloped crudely into the thick jungle of trees that shrouded their roots from view.

Erected within a natural alcove created by two of these ridgelines was a town with beautiful structures. The fact that they were visible from this distance was telling of their extensive size.

"The Edelish people have always been amazing architects," Medwin said, noticing that Conner was gawking at the town. "From what I've been told, the halls of Edelan were some of the most magnificent ever to stand in Rohwen."

Conner looked at Medwin to let him know he was listening intently.

"My father described them to me when I was young. He said that pillars of marble held their roofs, and flakes of gold flecked their floors. Water flowed endlessly from fountains that fed hand-carved streams, creating stunning designs in their gardens and keeping their crops luscious… I wish I could have seen it at least once before it was demolished by Vellix…"

"Sounds like it was absolutely amazing," Conner said with wonder in his eyes.

Lenny had been leaning against the ship's railing, listening quietly. He stood up to his full height and put his hands behind his head. "Kinda makes yeh wan' ter beat Vellix's face in, don't it? Fer bein' such a giant prat!"

"It really does," Conner agreed, his voice distant. His imagination was running wild with images of what Edelan might have looked like. A place so beautiful that he felt to fathom it was most likely impossible, but he didn't mind doing his best to attempt it.

Cassius started giving orders as they drew near the harbor. "Weigh anchor, raise the sails!"

The Colossus pulled up to the opposite side of the docks. Conner could see gaping holes all along the hull where cannonballs had plowed their way through. A loud voice that he recognized to be James' hollered over to the badly damaged ship from the gun deck below.

"Tha' was some bloody fine shootin', Gavin!"

"Learned from the best, I did!"

"Hit me in the bleedin' leg with a shard from one o' yer shots though! Best watch it nex' time!"

"Go an' bury yer 'ead in a bowl full o' leeches, James!" Gavin bellowed, laughing manically.

"Conner, come on. We're going ashore," said Medwin.

Night fell completely and the moon, nearly in its full form, shone brightly, spreading a thin layer of silver light upon the world below. The two crews of men trudged up Ewaun's sandy shores and headed toward the town Conner had seen from out in the ocean. The soft glow of moonlight made it easy to see the detail and craftsmanship that had gone into every inch of each structure. Stilts, carved from top to bottom with intricate designs, held their first levels twenty feet above the ground. A labyrinth of bridges that were lined with torches connected each building to another. They reminded Conner of airfield landing strips, the way the flames formed paths of parallel lines. He went to point out this observation to Medwin but quickly remembered that Medwin would have absolutely no clue what he was talking about. Soft voices drifted back to his ears and redirected his focus.

Cassius and Terrence were having a hushed conversation as they led the group toward a building at the center of town: a huge structure built with more extravagancies than you would imagine to find in the jungle. Blinds constructed from stalks of bamboo covered every window. Large octagonal decks marked its ten stories. Running the vertical length of the building's eight corners, and carved as intricately as the stilts supporting the structure, stood perfectly milled palm tree trunks. They not only increased the building's stability, but also made it more aesthetically pleasing.

Cassius addressed Terrence again.

Conner strained his ears, and was just able to make out what he was saying.

"I told Anthony and Eros to stay aboard and gather the dead. We will give them a proper burial so that their loved ones — if they had any — can say goodbye."

"What will we do now?" Terrence asked, his voice wavering timidly, as if aware that he was flirting with a subject better left unspoken. "Do you remember," he went on, a note of forced resolve beating down his squeamish tone, "what we said about the day when all this must come to an end…?" An awkward pause followed his words. "I feel that what has happened today is as good a sign as any," he finished, shooting a quick glance over at Cassius.

For a moment, it seemed that Cassius had decided not to respond, but then he began speaking slowly. "You are right, Terrence. I have been blinded by greed, and my people have suffered a great loss as a result. It is time that we live as the respected people we once were."

"I am glad to hear you say this, Cassius," Terrence replied, his demeanor that of a man internally sighing with relief. "Our acts of late have been disgraceful. Even desperation does not excuse us."

"…I agree..."

They reached one of the timber stilts that held up the central building. Carved artistically into the stilt was an intricate ladder. Cassius climbed up through a hole in the deck that marked the building's first floor and stood waiting. What was left of his crew followed, Ammin and his crew behind them.

When everyone had gathered on the deck, Cassius led them into a spacious common room.

Fur-swathed couches sat at the center of the room and faced a handsome fireplace, its mantle trimmed with elegantly-wrought spindles of iron. Shelves that bore the weight of many books lined three of the room's eight walls; a few chairs sat flanking the bookshelves to convenience anyone who chose to read. Hangings of magenta silk draped from wall to wall, their languid folds reflecting fragmented rays of moonlight that peeked through the bamboo window shades.

"My men," Cassius said when they had all gathered. "Go to your families. Let them know you are okay. Tomorrow we will bury the dead respectfully." His men obeyed their orders and dispersed. He turned to Ammin. "First off, I believe a formal introduction is in order."

"Oh, where are my manners," Ammin said, extending a hand to shake Cassius'. "The name's Captain Ramirez. Or just Ammin'll do."

"And mine, as you already know, is Cassius… Welcome to New Edelan," he said, making a dismal attempt at a welcoming gesture. "You and your men may stay here in the commons, if you wish. Its upper levels will accommodate your needs comfortably. It will take a week or longer to repair your ship, so make yourselves comfortable."

"Thank you, Cassius," Ammin replied with a formal bow.

Cassius bowed in reply and left the common room, his grief overwhelmingly apparent.

As Conner walked up the stairs to the upper rooms, he felt sick with disgust. How many women would be waking up to find that their husbands were dead? How many children would wake up to find that they would never see their fathers again? He couldn't just bottle up his thoughts, or they would surely poison his mind. "Medwin, I feel terrible about what we did today..."

"I know what you mean. I do as well. There's only one thing that is helping me to cope."

"And that is?" Conner asked, eager to ease his feelings of guilt.

"They would have killed us if we hadn't killed them first. I mean, that was what they wanted to do. They attacked us. We defended ourselves at their great loss."

"That's true," Conner mused. "I guess we did what we had to. I still feel terrible though."

They came upon a room that was still empty. The pleasant scent of fresh wood lingered in the air. Conner recognized it instantly from the projects his father would get halfway through and then abandon, always finding reasons to leave them piled up in the corner of their garage.

Beds rested against each of the room's four walls. Conner crossed the room and lifted the bamboo shade of the single window. The scene that met his eyes was magnificent: a striking view of the moonlit ocean overlapped by the swaying tops of the island's tallest palm trees. He enjoyed the view briefly before the sound of footsteps pulled his attention back to the room.

Lenny strode in. "Oi, mates. Don' suppose I could bunk with you lot, could I? Everywhere else is fillin' up. Yeh don' mind, do yeh?"

"Not at all," they answered.

"Thanks, mates. Didn' really wan' ter sleep in Ammin's room. Bloody snores like a bulldog, 'e does!" Lenny laughed heartily at his own statement, as he commonly did.

Conner and Medwin laughed as well, more at Lenny for finding himself so amusing than at his joke.

Lenny chose a bed and got comfortable. Within minutes, his breathing became heavy. In his exhaustion from the day's events, he passed out almost immediately.

Conner sat on his bed and checked the wound under his bandages.

"How does it look?" Medwin asked kindly.

"Not too bad," Conner replied, pulling away the bandage so Medwin could get a good look. A scar at least a foot in length wrapped the right side of Conner's waist. It looked as though an amateur physician had tended the wound.

"I take it you used cognition to try and speed up the healing process?"

Conner nodded absentmindedly, still investigating his wound.

"Well, you'll probably have that scar forever," Medwin told him seriously, "but other than that, it seems to me that you're fine. I don't see there being a need for you to rewrap the bandage."

"Yeah, I agree," Conner replied. He fluffed his pillow and lied down.

Medwin crossed the room and got in bed as well.

A long hour passed and Conner's mind was restless. "You still awake, Medwin?" he asked, knowing Medwin to succumb to a low steady snore when he was asleep and noticing that he hadn't yet started.

"Yeah, I'm awake," Medwin said quietly.

"I can't get the images out of my head. Every time I close my eyes I see flashes of the men I killed, making exaggerated expressions of pain…"

"You have a strong conscience, Conner. It can be a burden at times like these, but you should cherish it. Many men would have no pity for those they killed in a kill-or-be-killed situation. Take James for instance. Do you think he feels badly about what we did today?"

"No, I *highly* doubt —" A thought occurred to Conner so suddenly that it was as if a light had switched on in his head. "I hope Moxie is okay," he whispered anxiously. "For that matter, I hope Zelimir is okay."

"Me too," Medwin replied, his voice sharing similar tones of anxiety. "I've been thinking about that for a while now. I just didn't want to say anything. I figured you had enough on your mind without worrying about them as well."

"We should go to the ship and check on them!"

"I don't know, Conner. I don't want to look suspicious."

"What do you mean, 'look suspicious'? What is suspicious about going down to the ship?"

"I don't know."

"I'm going. You can stay if you want," Conner said firmly.

"Oh, alright, let's go." Medwin got out of bed reluctantly.

* * *

The silhouettes of two men became visible in the distance as the *Colossus* came back into view.

As Conner got closer, he noticed that they were lining the beach with the dead. "Those guys are going to see us," he said, a hint of concern scratching the surface of his voice.

"I thought you said there was nothing suspicious about going back down to the ship," Medwin said.

"Yeah, well that doesn't mean I wanted to run into anyone," Conner snapped, noticing the gloating tone Medwin had used.

"I'm sure it will be fine," Medwin assured him. "Just act natural. We aren't doing anything wrong."

One of the two men noticed them as they approached the docks. "What are you two doing?" he asked harshly.

"I forgot something on the ship. That's all," Conner answered with a casual gesture toward the *Colossus*.

"If you try and bring any weapons ashore I won't hesitate to shoot you. You understand, boy?"

"Yeah, I do."

"Alright. Go on then."

They boarded the ship and quickly headed for the room where they had left Moxie. Conner pushed the door open, and Zelimir growled aggressively. "Oh, it is you two." He sighed with relief and trotted back to the center of the room. "I am glad to see the both of you."

Medwin moved over to Moxie. "How is he, Zelimir?" Before Zelimir could reply, Moxie started to stir.

"Medwin is here?" he muttered frailly.

"Yes."

"And, Conner?"

"I'm here, Moxie," Conner said, his voice full of warmth and compassion. He moved over to stand next to Medwin at Moxie's side.

"The man, Grayson, said he would be laid up for at least a month," Zelimir said. "Shall we discuss the situation in another room?"

"Good idea," Conner answered.

They left the room and headed down to the hold.

"What are we going to do?" Conner asked, switching his gaze from Zelimir to Medwin and back again. "We can't wait a month! What if

Vellix returns to his full power by then?"

"My thoughts exactly," said Zelimir.

"So what do we do then?" Medwin asked, his tone sounding troubled. "We can't just leave him."

"I am sure that Ammin would be willing to let him stay aboard the ship while he heals," Zelimir assumed. "After all, it was one of his men that shot him."

"That seems like the only logical thing to do," Conner said. "I mean, we really have no other choice."

Medwin looked uneasy about the idea. "Why can't you just use your cognition to heal him?" he asked, giving Conner an expectant look. You were able to heal yourself..."

Conner shifted uneasily on his feet. "Yeah, but that was me. I knew exactly what I needed to heal because I could feel it. What if I do something wrong and make the wound worse? Kill him even..."

Medwin studied Conner's concerned expression for a moment. "If you don't feel confident, then there's no reason for you to try. Cognition requires a great amount of self-assurance to achieve..." He met Conner's eyes with an embarrassed look. "...As you clearly already know..."

Conner grinned at Medwin to let him know he hadn't taken any offense.

Medwin replied with a mollified glance and turned his attention to Zelimir. "What are you going to do?" he asked. "Are you just going to stay hidden aboard the ship until it has been repaired?"

"How long is that going to take? Do you know?"

"Cassius said it would be a week or longer," Conner said.

"Who is Cassius?"

"He is the leader of the Edelish people," Medwin replied.

"So that was the Edelish that attacked us?" Zelimir asked curiously.

Medwin nodded.

"I thought the Edelish were peaceful people," Zelimir reflected aloud.

"Technically, they are," Medwin began, "but when their homeland was destroyed by Vellix they became desperate, turning to piracy as a result."

"I see. It never fails to amaze me the atrocities that men will commit in times of desperation… Anyway, to answer your question from before, I think I will stay aboard the ship and sneak off in the night so I can hunt. It seems easier that way."

"Sounds good to me," Conner replied. "Well, if you're alright, I think I'm going to go and get some sleep. I'm starting to get tired."

"Me too," Medwin agreed.

The three of them went back to Moxie's room, and Zelimir curled up in the corner.

"See you tomorrow," Conner whispered, not wanting to wake Moxie back up as he and Medwin left the room.

CHAPTER 9

Adrial's Dark Exploit

Hundreds of miles to the north, a great eagle owl soared smoothly on the wind. She decided it was time to abandon her hunt for the hawk. She would have to put off her search for now. Adrial didn't like to be kept waiting, and she was already late to meet him.

A matt of deep hunter-green, bathed in pale moonlight, told her that Morik — a forest shadowed by the Monzerrat mountain range — was below. She arched into a dive and headed for the forest.

* * *

"You are late, Katina," hissed a grey-skinned man. "What do you have to report?"

"I have been unable to locate the hawk, Adrial," Katina responded as she settled onto a nearby tree branch.

"Well, your search will have to wait at this point," Adrial replied severely. "As you are well aware, there are more pressing matters at hand."

Katina replied with obedient silence, allowing Adrial to continue.

"You will fly up ahead of the group," Adrial went on with a vague hand gesture in the direction they would be traveling. "Stay vigilant for any and all things. I want this to go smoothly."

"Understood. When do we leave?"

"I need to speak with my men, and then it will be time."

Katina took flight with powerful flaps of her wings.

Adrial moved through the trees until he reached a small camp. "The time has come!" He exclaimed to a group of grey-skinned men who had gathered around at his arrival. "Our master desires the warrior captains of the Satria for his purpose. We will accomplish this task, for we are the Bazza!"

The group of Bazza raised their fists and cheered.

"Arm yourselves. We leave now."

The Bazza left their camp and moved swiftly and silently across the plains of Rohwen. Agility, cunning and stealth were like second nature to them. Nothing slowed them when a task was at hand.

* * *

On the eve of their second day of travel, the Satria village came into view through a mesh of branches stemming from the surrounding trees.

A heavily scarred Bazza turned to Adrial. "The plan?"

"Our purpose is not to fight, Izel. Master does not wish us to harm his prize."

Izel fidgeted slightly, as if entering the Satria village with no intention of spilling blood caused him a small amount of pain.

Adrial showed no sign of acknowledgement that he had noticed Izel's obvious disagreement with the terms of their mission. "The master informed me that the captains reside in huts with special markings of red, symbolizing their significance in the tribe. We will go in and seek these huts. I want at least two men per hut. These warrior captains are not to be underestimated. Gag, blindfold, and bind them. Once you have your captive, return to this spot and wait for the rest of the group. Understood?"

Each of the Bazza thumped their chests with clenched fists in response.

They crept as silently as ghosts into the sleeping village in the early hours of the morning and quickly located the marked huts.

Adrial and Izel entered their hut.

Thane lay there in bed, fast asleep, his wife next to him; his son, Luka, asleep in the corner.

Adrial drew his sword and pointed it at Thane's wife. "Okay, Izel, do it."

Izel quickly gagged Thane.

He woke with a start; fear flooded his face and then drained away, removing all the color from his flesh as it went. He reached instinctually for his weapon in the corner.

"I wouldn't do that if I were you," Adrial whispered. He moved his sword slightly to show Thane the consequence he would pay if he attempted to struggle.

Thane dropped his sword, utterly defeated.

Luka woke up as the sword hit the floor. Someone was blindfolding his father. He gasped with fear, and Adrial turned quickly at the sound.

Luka pretended it had been a snore, and rolled over as if he were still asleep.

Satisfied that the boy had not woken up, Adrial instructed Izel to bind their prisoner and they left the hut.

Luka got out of bed as quietly as possible and followed them. He watched as the Bazza pulled the rest of the captains from their huts. Fear and anger overwhelmed him. What could he do? If he tried anything, the Bazza would just kill him. He watched helplessly as his father and the others were dragged from the village and out of sight.

Thane focused intently on the underbrush a few paces out in front of Adrial. Coils of thorny bramble curled to life and bound him at the ankles.

"You fool!" Adrial sneered. "I am practiced in your ancient art. My master has taught me." The thorny stalks released him as he reversed Thane's cognition.

Fully defeated, Thane allowed Izel to lead him through the Ancient Forest without another struggle.

* * *

Luka walked to the edge of the village, wiping away the tears pouring from his eyes. Something caught his attention, a struggle just through the trees.

Lolani seemed to materialize out of the star specked sky as she swooped quickly upon Katina.

Katina rolled in the air and intercepted the hawk. Her talons pierced Lolani's breast. She screeched in pain and retaliated, slashing Katina's midsection with ferocity.

The brawl intensified. Both birds delivered heavy blow after heavy blow. Finally, the need for air forced them to break apart.

Katina flew toward the treetops.

Lolani pursued with powerful strokes of her wings. The moment she was in range, Katina whipped around and struck her across the face with a devastating blow. She plummeted to the ground, knocked out.

Katina dove down and landed on her, forcing six talons to dig in deep.

Lolani exhaled a cry of pain and lay motionless.

Satisfied with her work, Katina took off and headed northeast.

Luka felt compelled to do something. He ran over to the hawk and bent down to see if she was still alive. He didn't know why, but the sight of her mangled body caused his tears to stream out more profusely than ever. They fell to the forest floor like shimmering vessels of anguish. One of the tears struck Lolani in the face. Her wing twitched feebly.

"Sh — she's st — still alive," he whispered. He bent down to pick her up with a flicker of reluctance. A hawk was still intimidating. Even in this wounded state.

"It is okay," She mumbled weakly.

"What the… You can talk?" Luka's immediate fascination washed away his sadness.

"Yes. Now listen, because this is important. You need to take me to someone that you know can heal me. I am going to die if I don't get medical attention very soon. And it is imperative that I don't die…"

"Don't worry. I know someone that can help," Luka said enthusiastically. He sniffled, wiped the last tears away from his eyes, and set his jaw with determination.

"Very good. What is your name, boy?"

"It's Luka."

"I am Lolani. I will forever remain in your debt."

* * *

Katina caught up with Adrial as he entered the valley north of the Ancient Forest. She landed on a branch and called out to him. "The hawk has been dealt with."

"Excellent! This mission is proving to be most successful. Master will be very pleased. Izel, we will take the mountain pass. It is the quickest route to Mt. Cirrus."

"But, Adrial, the pass is a far more difficult journey. It might be too much for the prisoners."

"Then we will drag them," Adrial said coldly, swatting away Izel's concern like a pestering fly.

Izel shrugged his shoulders, sure that continuing his argument would be a complete waste of breath.

By mid-day, they had reached the Monzerrat pass.

The warrior captains, still bound by rope, struggled to keep up with the relentless pace of the Bazza as the climb became increasingly grueling.

Thane's entire body ached, and his muscles cried out in objection of the abuse they were taking. He heard a man fall next to him.

"Get up you weakling!" jeered the Bazza that held his rope bindings. When he got no response, he kicked his prisoner in the chest.

"Boden! If I see you do that again, I won't hesitate to strike you down! The master wants his prize in tact! Do you understand?"

"But Ad —"

"Do you understand?" Adrial roared.

"Yes, sir," Boden replied, defeated.

Thane fell to the ground, and before Izel pulled him back to his feet, he used his knees to push up his blindfold — just far enough that he could see what was going on. A quick glance told him that the other warrior captains were alongside him. Akamu was directly to his left. Thoughts raced through his mind so fast that he could barely focus. 'What do they want with us? How are we going to get out of this? *Can* we even get out of this? I thought Medwin said that Vellix had been defeated. If that's true then who is their master?' He continued to look around, hoping that something in the landscape would be useful as an aid for escape; to his dismay, he found nothing of the sort.

The hours dragged on. As the sun started to set in the west, Adrial finally decided that he had pushed his prisoners hard enough for one day. "We will set up camp here," he said, surveying the area. "Keep them in separate locations," he ordered his men with a gesture at their captives. "I don't want them trying to communicate. We will take turns with watch duty."

Thane felt like he had just closed his eyes when Izel yanked him back to his feet. The light of the dawning sun shone through his blindfold and caused tears to streak down his face. He wanted to wipe them away, but his bound arms were unable to move more than an inch. The feeling of helplessness struck twice as heavy in that moment. It infuriated him. It scared him. It made him want to weep tears of true sadness, not just the ones the sun had caused.

"Come on" — Izel shoved him forward — "you slouch. Get moving!"

The moment Thane attempted to walk, he realized that the pain was no longer in his muscles alone. Now his bones were feeling the wear of the journey. He forced himself to push on. The sounds of his companions struggling to do the same gave him strength. None of them had given up, so why should he?

* * *

Hours marched on, and still they traveled the Monzerrat Pass. And with each passing hour, Mt. Cirrus loomed ever closer. Eventually they started to scale its jagged slope.

The Bazza seemed to never run out of energy. Their stamina rose to meet the challenge as the climb became increasingly difficult. This made them ruthless to travel with. They had no tolerance for fatigue. If a warrior captain fell behind or dropped to the ground from sheer exhaustion, they would rip on his rope bindings mercilessly, yelling obscenities in his face.

Night had fallen when they reached the cave that led to Vellix's chambers. The torches were no longer burning. Shards of glass were still scattered across the floor.

"Not much farther now!" Boden laughed viciously. "Soon you will meet your new master."

They headed down into the depths of the mountain.

Mournful cries rang ominously off walls of stone and found Thane's ears. He had entered Vellix's holding chamber. The cries struck indescribable fear into his heart. It was fear of the unknown. 'What do they want with us?' he thought again. 'Obviously they aren't going to kill us, or they wouldn't have gone to the trouble of bringing us all this way.'

"Master, we bring before you the eight remaining warrior captains of the Satria, as you desired," Adrial announced proudly.

"You have done well, Adrial," whispered a dark voice, somewhere above.

One of the chamber's many rock protrusions shuddered; its rough underside started to melt. A loud crackling sound filled the chamber as the liquid rock hardened in the shape of a step. And then another. Another.

A heavily cloaked man got to his feet and started to walk down the stairs as they continued to form a path to the chamber floor. "So," he hissed, a tone of twisted pleasure alive in his voice. "The time has finally come," he said, his lips curling to form an evil smirk that went unnoticed in the nearly pitch-black chamber. He lifted his hands in the direction of the warrior captains.

Thane tried desperately to get a glimpse of the man from under his blindfold, but it was no use. The chamber was far too dark.

Something about the man's voice felt… It felt…

His conscious thoughts started to ebb away. He couldn't control the loss of them. He tried with all his might to hang on to some shred of himself, but found that he didn't know who that was, as if the neural pathways in his brain were being forcibly altered. Pain shot through his entire body, like a powerful surge of energy. It was a pain like he had never felt in all his life. He fell to the ground, screaming and convulsing. It was agony beyond comprehension, beyond description. His bones broke and separated, grew and reformed; his stature changed to a size substantially larger than it had been moments ago. Simultaneously, his skin stretched unnaturally to accommodate his new skeletal structure. Its color drained away, leaving it a dull shade of grey. The white markings on his arms and legs slowly saturated with the shade of blood red.

Still on their hands and knees, the eight captains gasped for the air they had lost screaming.

Seeing that their transformation was complete, the cloaked man lowered his hands. “Rise,” he ordered them.

Each of the warrior captains got to their feet and stood facing the man.

“Welcome Ivan, Sava, Alrik, Olof, Soren, Damek, Niran, and Razill, to the band of elite fighters known as the Bazza. I am your master now; my word is law.”

The man once known as Thane, now to be known as Razill, bowed deeply alongside the others. There was no longer a single memory of his former life in his mind. The fact that only moments ago he had been a proud warrior captain of the Satria tribe, a husband, and a father was no longer of consequence. All he knew was that the man standing before him was master, and that his only objective was to obey.

CHAPTER 10

A Mutinous Plot

Conner awoke on the fifth day of their stay with the Edelish to find that Medwin's bed was already empty. He stretched gratefully and surveyed the rest of the room. Lenny was still fast asleep on his bed, his mouth gaping. Conner grinned, climbed out of bed, and headed for the stairs.

The torches that lit the staircase looked as though they had burned out some hours ago. Conner strained his eyes to see the steps in front of him as he made his way down to the common room. He reached the landing and rounded a corner to find Medwin deep in conversation with Cassius.

"I see," said Cassius. "I am very sorry to hear that. So it would seem that I am speaking with the chief of the Satria."

"It would," Medwin replied. "Morning," he said, noticing that Conner had entered the room.

"Morning, Medwin," Conner replied. "Cassius," he added formally.

"Good morning, what was your name again?"

"It's Conner."

"I am sorry that I haven't found time to get to know you in the last few days," Cassius admitted, looking a little sheepish. "I've been very busy with everything, and —"

"It's fine," Conner said. He didn't really feel as though he needed an explanation.

Cassius considered him for a second. "Anyway, I was just telling Medwin that I would like to introduce you to my wife. Would you be willing to come with me and meet her?"

"Um, okay," Conner replied with a glance over at Medwin. It seemed strange that Cassius would go out of his way to introduce them to his wife.

As they walked along the wooden bridge connecting the central building to the houses on the east side of town, Cassius began to question Conner. "What was that I saw you do back on the ship? How did you do that? You know, when you had flames burning in your hands?"

Conner looked at Cassius for a moment in an attempt to see the intent in his question. His expression of curiosity appeared to be genuine, so he decided to answer. "I was using a power called cognition. It's —"

"I knew it!" Cassius exclaimed triumphantly, cutting Conner off. "I knew it must have been cognition. What else could it have been?"

"You know about cognition?" Conner asked, a little taken aback.

"Of course! The Edelish people are keepers of ancient lore. My ancestors were awed by the Hylan, and their art of cognition. I mean, I don't blame them. To be able to bend the world around oneself is truly amazing. The reason I want you to meet my wife is that she is a master of lore, and descendent of the woman who spoke to the last Hylanian to bear children into the world."

Conner's mind started to race. Was he about to meet the woman who could answer the question that Vivek had never known the answer to?

They turned a corner and Cassius gestured them into a house more elaborate than its neighbors. "Odriana… Odriana, my love, where are you?"

"I'm in my study, dear," she called from a room near the back of the house.

Cassius led them down the hall into a room on the right. The smell of old parchment and light perfume hung gently on the air. "This is the boy I told you about. I was right. He does know cognition."

Odriana was a kind-looking woman with soft features. Dirty-blonde hair rested gracefully upon her shoulders. She had dazzling blue eyes that sparkled with life. Her expression lit up at the words her husband had just spoken. "Would you care to sit down?" she asked politely.

"Thank you," Conner said as he took a seat. Medwin pulled up a chair and sat to his left.

Odriana didn't start speaking. She just stared intensely into Conner's eyes. Conner stared back for a short time, but soon found that her gaze made him feel uncomfortable, as if she was attempting to bore into his mind.

Finally, she said, "Your name is Conner?"

Conner nodded slowly. How did she know his name? Cassius hadn't, so he couldn't have told her. Did this woman know who he was?

Odriana remained silent for another moment, this time looking as if she had entered a deep state of thought. Conner sat, watching her, feeling a sense of unease coming over him.

"Have you met Vivek?" she asked, breaking the silence.

Conner glanced over at Medwin; they exchanged expressions of shock. He looked back at Odriana. "Yes, I met him."

"And…"

"And what?" Conner replied. He hadn't been expecting the conversation to go in this direction. What was Odriana getting at?

"And what did he speak to you about?"

Conner's mind relaxed. Now he knew what was going on. Odriana didn't want to reveal anything Vivek hadn't already told him. She didn't feel it was her place. So that must mean that Vivek had told her. She knew everything.

"He told me that I'm the one to have cognition without knowing it or asking for it." Odriana nodded and gestured for Conner to continue. "He told me that I was destined to befriend the lone wolf … and that I would have to face Vellix…"

"Do you know of the scrolls?"

"Yeah, Vivek said that all he knew of my destiny came from reading the scrolls."

"So he told you everything..." Odriana uttered to herself. She looked up at Conner. "There is a story I wish to tell you, but it must wait. At the moment, I have things to tend to. Meet me in the Common room just after sundown."

Conner made a polite gesture of acknowledgment, and he and Medwin left the room.

* * *

They stepped off the jungle path they had been traveling down and strode onto Ewaun's sandy beach shore.

Ammin and Lenny were standing by *the Colossus*, overseeing the reconstruction of its heavily damaged starboard side. Lenny called out as they approached.

"Oi, Medwin! Yeh wasn' jokin'! This lot knows 'ow ter build alrigh'!" He exclaimed. "I mean, blimey! They're on fer havin' ol' *Colossus* looking good as new!"

"Did they say when they would be done?" Conner asked as he and Medwin came to rest next to Ammin.

"They said it would depend on how their supplies last," Ammin informed him, not taking his eyes off the men repairing his ship. "The lead carpenter told me that they might run out of oakum before they're finished."

"Oakum?" Conner wondered aloud. "What's oakum?"

Lenny opened his mouth, but Ammin was quicker to answer. "It's the lose fiber you get from untwisted rope..." He saw the look of lacking comprehension on Conner's face and decided to elaborate. "You see, once the wooden planks are in place" — he pointed to the timbers that ran the length of his ship's hull for reference — "all of the seams between them need to be packed with oakum in order to waterproof the ship."

"Oh, I see," Conner said, now grasping the obvious importance of oakum for a ship you were planning to sail. "...Well, we're gonna go and see how Zelimir and Moxie are holding up." Conner gestured toward Medwin as he spoke.

They crossed the gangplank to board the ship and headed down to its medical quarters.

"I was wondering when you two would show up," said Zelimir as they came through the door.

"We got sidetracked," Conner replied.

Moxie stirred in his bed. He opened his eyes and gazed blearily around the room. When he saw that Conner and Medwin were there, he tried to sit up. His little body still didn't have the strength to do anything of the sort. He crumpled under his own weight. "I'm tired of lying down!" he grumbled.

Medwin looked at him sadly. "You still have a while before you will be able to get up and move around, Moxie. I know it must be tough, but you have to allow your body time to heal."

Moxie crossed his arms in discontent.

Conner laughed at his reaction because he had never seen Moxie act so ornery. Medwin threw him a dirty look, and he immediately tried to wipe the grin from his face. "I'm gonna go and get my bow and arrows from Ammin's quarters," he said as an excuse to leave the room. He needed to grab the bow anyway. If he didn't get some practice with it soon, he could end up finding himself in a dire situation and still unable to hit a target to save his life. He started to climb the stairs back up to main deck, but before he had reached the top, two whispered voices met his ears.

"'E's too lenient, Felix," muttered a man anxiously, as if the topic he was touching upon caused him some amount of fear or discomfort. "We joined this crew with the intentions o' makin' some real money," he continued hurriedly. "'Ere's the bes' bleedin' chance we 'ad since joinin', an' wha's 'e doin'? 'E's getting' all friendly with the same bloody gits what attacked us."

"Aye, Louie, yeh got a poin' there," Felix replied quietly.

Hardly able to believe what he was hearing, Conner strained his ears to make sure he wasn't misinterpreting the conversation.

The sailor named Louie spoke again. "I'm sure we ain' the only ones what feel this way. I say we ge' as many o' the crew as we can ter back us up, an' overthrow Ammin."

The step under Conner's feet groaned as he shifted from shock. These two sailors were planning a mutiny against Ammin.

"Wha' was tha'?" Felix asked fearfully.

"I don't know," said Louie, his voice exuding the same fear.

The sound of footsteps echoed down the stairs as the two men set out to investigate the sound. Conner's heart jumped into his throat, racing at twice the normal speed. His mind struggled to keep pace with it. Certainly, they would shoot him if he ran now. He'd heard their mutinous plot — they would not risk an early illumination of their plan to Ammin. But if he didn't move now, there was no chance of his going unnoticed. He took a deep breath, inhaling focus and exhaling fear.

A section of wood paneling that ran the length of the staircase dematerialized behind him, revealing a small room in which he could hide. He stepped into the enclosure, willing the wood paneling to reform in front of him. One of the men's faces came into view at the top of the stairs a split second before the paneling sealed shut. Conner heard the men walk a few steps down the stairs, their muffled voices barely audible through the wood that concealed his hiding place.

"I don' like it, Louie," Felix admitted, fear and concern causing his voice to waver.

"Oh, don' ge' all superstitious on me, Felix," Louie replied, obviously exasperated. "There ain' no one 'ere."

"I bloody saw someone. I'm tellin' yeh."

"Yer mind's jus' on edge, tha's all. Come on, le's go."

Conner waited for a minute before exiting his hiding place, then went to retrieve his bow and arrows from Ammin's quarters and headed quickly down to the medical quarters to tell Medwin and Zelimir what he heard.

"Guys!" he exclaimed, bursting into the room.

"Shhh. Moxie's asleep." Medwin gestured toward the corner of the room where Moxie's bed was.

"Sorry," Conner whispered quickly.

"What's got you so riled up?" Zelimir asked with a curious little tilt of his head.

Conner tried to tell them about the plot he had just heard, but he rushed his words so fast that nothing more than an undecipherable jumble came out. Neither Medwin nor Zelimir had a clue what he was trying to say.

"Slow down," Medwin said, thoroughly confused by Conner's behavior.

Zelimir seemed satisfied with Medwin's request because he just sat there, waiting for Conner to retell the story at a speed they could understand.

Conner took a steadying breath and told them about the mutinous plot against Ammin, making sure to speak at a pace they could follow.

"You must inform Ammin straight away," Zelimir said with severity. "Our fate, particularly mine, rests upon his captaincy of this ship. If he is overthrown, and a captain consumed by greed is appointed..." Zelimir knew he didn't need to finish his sentence. Conner and Medwin were both well aware of what that could mean for them.

"Ammin is a good captain!" Medwin pronounced. This time Conner gestured toward Moxie's bed. "Oh, right..." he continued, bringing his voice back down to a whisper. "Do you really think enough of the crew will turn their backs on him to become a threat?"

Conner thought about Medwin's words intently. "You have a good point… But what if they kill him in his sleep or something? They could blame it on the Edelish — turn the whole crew against them. I mean, that's the reason they're upset with Ammin in the first place. They thought he should have taken the Edelish for all they were worth. Instead he let them go, on the condition that they fix his ship and abandon piracy."

Zelimir took Conner's outlook of urgency in the matter. "You need to inform Ammin of what you have learned immediately."

Conner made to leave the room. Zelimir called to him just before he shut the door on his way out.

"Make sure no one overhears you telling him!" he said, obviously less than concerned about waking Moxie at this point. Medwin clicked his tongue in annoyance. Zelimir shot him a look that said he was about as concerned with annoying him as he was with waking Moxie.

"What about Lenny?" Conner asked. "There's no way Lenny would be involved in a mutiny against Ammin. He's his first mate… And besides that — he's Lenny…"

"True. Okay, but make sure it is only Lenny."

"Hold on," Medwin said. "I'm coming with you…"

* * *

Conner and Medwin found Ammin in virtually the same spot as they had left him nearly an hour ago — conversing with Lenny while overseeing the repairs of his ship.

"Can I have a word?" Conner asked as he and Medwin approached the captain and his first mate.

"Course you can," Ammin replied with a jolly tone of voice quite contrary to the way he would be feeling in a moment. He noticed something was wrong almost immediately; Conner and Medwin were both glancing around like birds protecting a recently procured worm.

"What's up?" Ammin asked curiously. "Is everything alright?"

Conner placed his focus back on Ammin, content that no one was within earshot. "No, everything is not alright."

Ammin's expression became concerned. Lenny focused in on the conversation.

Before Conner continued, he lowered his voice a few notches. "There is a plot to overthrow your captaincy."

"What!"

"Shhh!" Conner hissed, batting his hands through the air in a downward motion. "I don't know who all is in on it at this point." He gave the harbor another intuitive sweeping glance. "I overheard two men talking about it just now. They said that they joined the crew to make money, and that you were too lenient."

Ammin looked furious. "And did you happen to catch the names of these men?" he asked in the most hushed voice he could conjure in his state of fury.

Conner had to think. The names were on the tip of his tongue. Finally, they came back to him. "One of them was Felix… and the other … the other one was Louie."

Ammin's normally good-natured appearance was livid. His lips went thin and white. His eyes narrowed to slits. His face flushed to boiling point as he clenched his fists into tight balls. Conner had never seen him so furious and found him quite intimidating.

Lenny looked over at his captain. "Shoulda known it would be tha' fresh blood wha's go' it in there 'eads to try summat so stupid! They mus' be barmy, they mus'! Ter think they could get away with tha'."

"Indeed," Ammin grunted through grit teeth. "Conner, are you sure they don't know that you overheard them? Because if they do know, then your life is in immediate danger."

"No, they didn't see me… Well, actually, one of them thought he saw me, but I was well hidden. The other told him he was just seeing things."

"Yeh bes' watch yer back," Lenny warned him.

Conner nodded his acknowledgement of Lenny's warning.

"What are you going to do?" Medwin asked.

"I am going to make an example of them," Ammin replied. He turned back to face his ship, arms folded.

Conner took this as a sign that the captain was done talking. Deciding that it would be best to end their conversation in a nonchalant manner, he raised the volume of his voice and said, "I'm going to go and get some practice with my bow," hoping to make it appear that their conversation had been average.

Medwin accompanied him up to the jungle. They discussed what Ammin might do to "make an example" of Louie and Felix as they gathered coconuts for Conner to use as targets and searched for a good spot to fire the bow.

"This seems as good a spot as any," Medwin said as they came upon a good-sized clearing in the otherwise thick jungle foliage. He dropped his pack to the ground, pulled out the coconuts they'd gathered and went to place them on top of a boulder.

Conner strung an arrow while he waited for Medwin to finish.

"Okay, go for it," Medwin hollered, moving out from the line of fire.

Focusing in on the middle target, Conner let his arrow fly… "Dammit!" The arrow stabbed the trunk of a palm tree, some fifteen yards beyond his target.

Medwin grimaced, but managed not to make any audible sounds that would reveal his uncertainty of Conner ever being a decent archer. "You just need to warm up a bit…" he invented, figuring encouragement was needed. "You know, get used to the feel of the bow."

Conner glared at him skeptically, as if he should know better than to think his lie would fool anyone. Medwin shrugged innocently.

An hour passed and Conner still hadn't hit a single target. However, he had come much closer with his last few shots.

"You just need to allow yourself more time to progress," Medwin assured him after his most recent miss. "Archery isn't a skill one learns on the back of a single afternoon." He walked up to Conner, straightened his aiming arm for the umpteenth time and reiterated the same few pointers on form that he'd been giving him. "Okay, try again."

Several hours of hard work later, Conner was starting to make notable improvements. At least now he had managed to hit a few targets.

"Nice shot," said Medwin after Conner sank an arrow through a coconut from twenty-five yards.

"I think I've had enough for the day, Medwin. My fingers and forearm are killing me. Plus, it's getting close to sunset. We need to get up to the common room." Conner stashed away his bow and went to retrieve the arrows he had fired.

As they made their way up to the commons, Medwin congratulated Conner on his progress. Conner thanked him, grinning. He felt like the bow had already become more of an extension of his will than he could have hoped.

CHAPTER 11

The Betrayal of Faylinn

Conner and Medwin reached the common room shortly before sunset. Odriana was sitting on a comfortable-looking armchair; gathered around her were at least thirty children. Murmurs of excitement filled the room.

“What story shall we hear tonight?” Odriana asked the children, surveying them with an expression of amusement. She noticed Conner and Medwin standing in the doorway and motioned for them to find a place to sit.

“Let’s hear the tale of Corissa and the secret stairway,” said a girl, sitting close to Odriana.

“You always ask for that one, Elaina!” one of the boys griped. “I wanna hear something different for a change.”

Elaina and the boy started to bicker.

“Quiet, children,” Odriana said, placing a hint of warning in her voice. She got up from her chair and moved gracefully over to the bookshelves along the wall. “What if I pick tonight’s story? Would that be okay?”

“Oh, yes,” Elaina said, glaring at the boy who had complained about her story choice. “You always pick good ones.”

"Thank you, Elaina," Odriana replied as she found the book she was looking for and made her way back to the armchair. She placed the book on her lap and opened it to somewhere near the beginning. The children sat attentively as she began to read.

"Chapter Five: The Betrayal of Faylinn… Now Faylinn saw that the beings she created had brought beauty and life to all she held most dear.

"Neksis raised mountains with one movement of his hands, sent hills rolling fluently into the horizon, and carved deep canyons into level plains.

"Aurya carpeted the rolling hills with blades of lush grass, patterned the mountains with trees and bushes, and sprinkled beautiful flowers across the plains.

"Eryx gouged rivers and lakes into the grasslands, whittled streams through the forests, and surrounded the world with a body of water that was vast and great.

"Nessa, whose imagination was unrivaled, brought into existence the many creatures of the world, filling the plains, forests, rivers, and oceans with a diverse assortment of animals.

"Faylinn congratulated them on their works, for she knew they were great. But she also knew their world was still incomplete. There was a need for change and renewal. And so she created the seasons. Spring: the birth of all things, Summer: a time when life thrives, Autumn: the peak of life's journey, and Winter: a time of death and dormancy, a necessity for change and new life.

"Neksis, Aurya, Eryx, and Nessa bowed to the wisdom of their creator and, for many years, there was peace between the five gods.

"As the years passed, a feeling of emptiness began to consume Faylinn, for as much as she loved her creations, she felt that something was still missing — something that would fill the world with emotion. She told the others of her feelings, but none seemed to share her opinion. They were happy with their world, satisfied.

"Faylinn, however, was not swayed by their contentment. They, after all, did not understand life as she did. She was their creator. How could they understand as she did?

"When the first flowers of spring began to bloom, she set out in search of appeasement for her craving. As she traveled the expanses of Rohwen, enjoying every aspect of its creation, the answer she sought finally became clear. There were none, other than four, to enjoy her world, none to cultivate and care for it. It was then that she brought into existence the first humans of the world, pulling elements from all other creations into one to make a being unlike Rohwen had ever seen. She gave the beings the ability to think and feel and create, and to her, they were beautiful.

"Now Faylinn returned home; upon her arrival, Aurya, Eryx, and Nessa gathered around her, overjoyed to see their creator. But Neksis did not share in their enthusiasm. He was able to view all the expanses of Rohwen simultaneously. He knew what Faylinn had done, and he could see that it had changed her. She no longer cared only for them. She had segregated her love. She had brought other beings into the world, and it planted a seed of hatred within him.

"Faylinn saw that her new creations had hurt Neksis, for she knew him intimately. She assured him that the love she felt for humanity was different; it would never be the same as what she had with him and his brother and sisters.

"Neksis told her that he understood, and that he was sorry for his foolish behavior. But the seed of hate within him had already sprouted. He watched as Faylinn nourished the humans and saw the love and praise they gave her in return. Jealousy began to fill his heart. He attempted to make humans of his own, but he did not have Faylinn's ability to create. His creations were crude, unhealthy and deformed. They shunned from light and beauty and felt no true longing for love or friendship.

"Infuriated by his failure, Neksis sought to destroy humanity. But he knew if he wasn't careful, Faylinn would see his intentions and never let him close enough to achieve his goal. He put together a well-constructed plan. He approached Faylinn with a request: that she allow him to know humanity, allow him to be a part of the creation he knew she loved, as it would bring them closer together.

"Faylinn smiled upon Neksis because his idea brought her joy. She introduced him to the humans and told them stories of his greatness.

"Neksis gained their trust with deeds of compassion and love and they let him into their hearts. It was then that he turned them. He brought bitterness, discontent and anger. He brought hate, jealousy and arrogance.

"By the time Faylinn realized what had happened, it was too late. Her creations had changed. The humans were no longer trusting and innocent. They resented everything she said and did. They blamed her for their discomforts and turned their backs on her. But even though they turned against her, she still loved them. And so she created a rift between the existence of gods and men, hoping to stop Neksis from reaching them.

"She banned Neksis from her home for his betrayal and, for a great many years, she mourned..."

CHAPTER 12

Xellore and Areona

Conner and Medwin made their way toward Odriana as the children dispersed. She smiled as they approached.

"Was that the story you wanted to tell us?" Conner asked.

Odriana laughed. "No, that was a story from *The Coridon.* I try to read from it often, so the children will have some knowledge of our history and beliefs."

"Ah," Conner replied. He thought about how important it was to the people of his world to understand their history, and it made complete sense that Rohwen was no different.

Odriana watched as the last of the children were met by their parents or older siblings before she gestured for Conner and Medwin to follow her.

When they arrived in her study, she invited them to sit. She went over to an antique mahogany chest and bent over to dig through its contents. Something dangling from her neck reflected the light and caught Conner's eye: a large chunk of crystal with an odd symbol embedded at the center.

"Ah ha, here it is," Odriana said to herself, struggling to pull a heavily deteriorated book out of the chest. She blew a plume of dust from its cover and read the title aloud, "The Lore of Hylan... I wish to read to you the last Chapter of this book. Not only is it the last Chapter of the book, it is also the last Chapter of Hylan's existence."

Conner felt himself edging forward in his chair. He was immensely curious to know what could have wiped a race as seemingly powerful as the Hylanians from existence.

Odriana cleared her throat and started to read...

"Chapter Twenty-Two. Of Xellore and Areona..." She paused for a moment to let the chapter's title sink in; then continued. "Never in this world has there been a love like Areona had for Xellore, and never again will there be. She took delight in his brilliance and passionate outlook on life. From her childhood, she had eyes for no one but him. He was achieving feats of cognition that astonished his elders by age twelve, creating delightful things just for the fun of it, or perhaps just to show off. Either way, Areona loved him more than anything. But much to her dismay, he did not seem to notice her at all, for he was the son of Jedrek, lord of the Hylan, while she was a mere commoner.

"She would go out of her way just to get one glimpse of his attention, but her efforts were always in vain. Four years passed in this fashion, and Areona grew weary of the feelings that were obviously felt by her alone. Her heart grew cold and bitter, finally sustaining what felt like the final blow on the day her closest friend informed her that Xellore was leaving their great city to seek a higher knowledge of life.

"Now it is said that Xellore traveled the expanses of Rohwen for seven years, studying its wonders and increasing his skill level all the while. His thirst for knowledge was unquenchable and unwavering. He studied all aspects of life, keeping a detailed journal of his discoveries and experiences. Among his favorite forms of life were the trees and flowers. His value for trees was in his knowledge of how vital they were to the land. Their production of oxygen was one of the sole reasons that the world was a sustainable place for all other forms of life. He enjoyed flowers for their immense beauty and delighted in their many forms, each with an appearance that fit the climate in which they belonged.

"Toward the end of his travels, he brought into existence a beautiful forest of tree-sized lilies, giving each his undivided attention, as not to miss one aspect of detail. He spackled the fields around his forest with a wide assortment of wild flowers, adding not only balance, but contrast in color to his masterpiece of cognition. Once he was satisfied that the forest was complete he gave it a name that he felt was fitting, and henceforth, the place has been called Botanica.

"He then traveled north of the forest to continue his studies. He found a grove that moved him beyond anything he had yet seen upon his travels. It was a wonder to behold, with grass of the most pleasant shade of green and an arrangement of wild flowers that made his creations pale in its existence. He decided to make the grove his temporary home, for he could think of no other place he would rather be.

"As time passed, Xellore's longing for companionship began to overwhelm him. He had been alone for so long that just to have a simple conversation would have been marvelous. On a summer's evening, in his desire for company, he created something that changed his outlook on the boundaries of cognition forever. He brought into life a great weeping willow tree, raising it from a sapling to an elder in a brief frame of time. He poured his heart and soul into the creation of the tree, and what he got back in return was a direct result of the devotion that had driven him. The tree had conscious thought. Not only did it have conscious thought, but it was in tune with the land that Xellore loved so much in ways he never would have thought possible. The moment he stepped under its umbrella of branches, it greeted him. His first thought was that he had finally gone mad from the years of solitude. But he soon learned that the tree was merely speaking to him within his consciousness.

"Over the course of the next year, Xellore became aware that the knowledge this tree had to offer about the land, cognition, and the future was far too important to be left undocumented. And so he began writing the scrolls of Hylan: a full documentation of his travels, a guide to the art of cognition and its true potential, and the prophecies of the future, which the tree assured him were not to be taken lightly.

"After the scrolls had been completed, Xellore felt a calling to return to his home. He vowed to visit the willow tree every summer on the anniversary of its creation. The tree bid him farewell, and he left.

"Before he traveled back to the city that he had left so long ago, he went and hid the scrolls where no one but those worthy to study the documents would ever find them. He was sure that the information he had amassed would be catastrophic in the wrong hands.

"Upon his return home, he went straight to his father's chambers to share the story of his great adventure. But much to his dismay, he learned that his father had taken very ill and passed away three years prior to his return. His elder brother, Varick, was now the ruler of Hylan. Xellore mourned the loss of his father greatly. The fact that he had been unable to get any closure caused him to grieve for far longer than was healthy.

"Areona, who had learned of Xellore's return, became hopeful again for the first time in years. For, in spite of her own self, she still loved him as she had when they were children. In order to help support her family she had taken the position of a maid in the house of Varick. She was the eldest daughter in her family, and her father had no sons, so it was necessary that she made money as her father became old and unable to support his children any longer. Her mother was also employed by the house of Varick, for she was much younger than her husband.

"Every morning when Areona arrived at the manor, she would see Xellore sitting in his greenhouse. He never seemed to notice her as she bustled past tidying up the place, watering the flowers and trees. Again, her heart began to grow cold with bitterness.

"Little did she know, Xellore had noticed her, and it was in those brief moments that she came to tidy up the greenhouse that he found any joy. He had never seen such a beautiful creature in all of his life. The way she carried herself was elegant, yet there was not a single trace of arrogance in it. Graceful, yet unforced. She had an aura of subtlety and kindness that was unlike any other woman he had ever encountered. His thirst to see her more often than once a day became a driving force in his life.

"Finally, on a cold fall afternoon, he found the fortitude to approach her. She was tending to the watering of the greenhouse flowers. He noticed that she seemed to be fond of the Gardenias.

"'Do you know what the meaning of this flower is?' he asked as he moved toward her.

"Areona turned to look at him. 'No, I don't,' she answered shyly.

"'It means secret love,' he said simply. And in his voice, there was unmistakable longing. 'Even their petals are white, symbolizing the purity of love.'

"The eye contact they made after those words was electrifying. Xellore fought the urge to kiss her in that moment, afraid that he would be moving too fast. Unbeknown to him, Areona wanted nothing more than for him to kiss her, and so she took it upon herself to do what he would not.

"The world seemed to dissolve around them. Time itself felt as though it stopped in that moment. The passion that Areona had felt for so many years poured out uncontrollably. The intensity with which she kissed Xellore overwhelmed him, and in that moment, he knew he would never be able to live without her. She was the woman to which he wished to devote his life.

"The following summer they united as one before all of Hylan. Xellore hadn't forgotten the promise he had made to the willow tree, and so Areona accompanied him to Willow Grove.

"Upon reaching the grove, Xellore spent three days in commune with the willow tree. And so became his tradition for years to come.

"Now Areona became expectant of child, and when it was time for Xellore to make his journey to the willow tree, she was unable to go. He said he would stay with her, but she was a strong woman. She insisted that he live up to his word. And so Xellore made the trip alone. When he returned, he told Areona of the conversations he and the tree had had. About how the Hylanian people were in grave danger, for a deadly drought would soon be upon them. This drought, according to the willow tree, would be the end of Hylan. He told her that he would never let that happen. He would use cognition to solve the problem.

"The city of Hylan was very near the eastern coastline. The answer was simple. He would carve irrigation inland from the ocean. Once his irrigation was in place he would increase the timeline of the ocean's tides to produce enough water for the city to survive the drought.

"Areona saw this as extremely dangerous. She warned him that to tamper with a power like the ocean could be much more devastating than the drought itself, but Xellore was too proud to heed her words of wisdom.

"As the summer progressed, the weather became incredibly hot and dry. Indeed the willow tree had been right. The drought began to take a hold of the city relentlessly. Xellore went forward with his plans. He carved multiple streams into the land using cognition, each ending at the bottom of a well, which he had placed at all the points in city where water was needed most desperately. Under each well was a furnace that heated the water into steam. The steam traveled into a large tube, where it collected and turned back into cured, drinkable water.

"The whole city praised him for his skill and genius — all but one. His wife, Areona, saw that he had become arrogant. Drunk with the power he had once respected. She warned him again not to underestimate the power of the ocean, but he told her that she was just being foolish because she knew she had been wrong.

"That night, driven by the fear of losing her unborn child, Areona left the city and headed west. She didn't know where she was going. All she knew was that it was as far from that city as possible.

"The following morning, she heard the faint yet unmistakable sounds of massive stone structures crumbling into nothing more than rubble as a colossal tidal wave struck its vengeance upon Xellore and the Hylan. She walked on, blinded by tears that flowed endlessly from her eyes. The love of her life was dead, along with everything and everyone she had ever known. Her only drive to stay alive now was the child inside of her.

"After days of travel without the slightest sign of another civilization, she came upon the vast fields that fringed Edelan. A woman harvesting wheat saw her stumbling wearily. She raced to Areona's aid and took her to Evelina: a gifted woman in many areas, including childbirth. Areona insisted that she give her life's accounts to a scribe, as so her story not be forgotten.

"Two days after her story was complete, she gave birth. To her surprise, she gave birth to twins. Both were boys. She named the first Vellix, and the second was to be called Vivek. She died shortly after that, leaving her two boys in the care of Evelina, along with the one other possession she had — a necklace bearing a large crystal that contained the Hylanian symbol within its core. She said it had been a wedding gift from her love, Xellore."

Odriana closed the book and looked up at Conner and Medwin. Each of them held the expression of grief they felt after hearing such a sad story.

"Vellix and Vivek were brothers," Conner said slowly. "Did they know?"

"Yes, they knew," Odriana said. "...What do you mean, 'were brothers?'"

Conner felt an uncomfortable sensation move through him. Odriana didn't know. But that made sense. How could she know? He looked into her sparkling eyes, wishing he didn't have to say what he was about to say. "Vivek is dead."

"...I see..." Odriana's expression became forcibly business-like as she attempted to conceal her grief. "What happened?"

"Vellix killed him," Conner answered sadly. He saw Medwin's head bow out of the corner of his eye.

Odriana remained quiet for a moment before saying, "He will be missed."

Conner nodded. A pained silence crept into the room. It made him feel uncomfortable. He searched for a different path to take their conversation. "So you are related to Evelina?" He tilted his head with curiosity.

"Indeed, I am the direct descendant of Evelina," Odriana replied. She looked pleased to change the subject.

"May I have a look at the necklace?" Conner asked, his tone sounding blunter than he had meant it to be.

Odriana's hand went to the necklace instinctually. She gazed down at the ornate chunk of crystal, caressing it with her thumb and forefinger.

Conner shifted uneasily in his chair, painfully aware of how blatantly he had just asked to get his hands on what must be the most sentimental object Odriana owned. "Sorry, I noticed it earlier when you were grabbing the book," he said quickly.

Odriana pulled the necklace from around her neck, unable to conceal her feelings of reluctance, and handed it to Conner.

He took it from her carefully to show his understanding of how precious it must be to her and examined the strange symbol in the middle of the crystal. The memory of his dream came back to him. In the dream, he had been standing on a floor of crystal with that very same symbol etched upon it. He held the necklace up for Medwin to see. "Remember my dream?"

Medwin's eyes widened with comprehension. "Yeah," he answered slowly.

"Dream? Did you have a dream about this necklace?" Odriana asked, moving forward in her chair.

"Not exactly," Conner said. "In my dream I was standing on a floor made of crystal, and that symbol was etched on it."

"That is very interesting. What happened in this dream?"

Conner paused before he answered. He remembered the image of Vellix stepping out of endless shadows and had to shake the feeling of fear the image gave him. "Vellix spoke to me."

Odriana's face grew, if possible, even more attentive the instant she heard Vellix's name.

"He told me I would pay for what I did to him. That he would make me suffer…"

Odriana searched Conner's face. "And what was it you did to Vellix? Why do you think you would have a dream in which he wanted to get to you specifically?"

Conner suddenly realized that, although Odriana knew who he was, she had no idea that he had already faced Vellix once. It was his actions in that fight that would cause Vellix to desire nothing more than to get revenge.

"The reason Vellix would want me to suffer is because I fought him and obliterated his mind," Conner answered. Cassius gasped from over in the corner, and Conner realized for the first time that he was in the room with them.

"You fought Vellix?" he asked, taken aback. Clearly, Cassius was impressed that Conner was even still alive to tell the tale.

"Yes, I fought him," Conner answered, remorse for his own stupidity drowning his mind once more. '*Why* didn't I kill him when I had the chance,' he thought, completely infuriated with himself.

Medwin, who had been deep in thought for the last few minutes, finally chimed into the conversation. He addressed Odriana. "Do you think there is some significance to Conner's dream?"

"It does seem strange that he dreamt about the Hylanian symbol," Odriana replied thoughtfully, looking up at Conner. "It is a symbol that virtually has not been seen by more than a few eyes in the last two-thousand years… And surely hasn't been seen by yours, prior to the dream."

"I think it must mean something," Medwin said seriously.

Conner turned to look at him. "Yeah, but what?"

CHAPTER 13

The Cave

Conner felt that they had already gone in enough circles trying to get to the bottom of the meaning of his dream. He got up and told Medwin that he wanted to get some sleep.

Medwin nodded. He got up and said he would join him.

They said goodbye to Cassius and Odriana and headed back in the direction of the commons.

"Well I have to say, that story about Xellore and Areona was really depressing," Medwin said to break the silence.

"Yeah it was," Conner agreed. "I remember when I spoke with Vivek. He said it wasn't until he found the scrolls that he learned the truth — that he was Hylanian..." Conner paused, feeling the weight of Vivek's tragic life upon his own heart. "...Descendent of a people who no longer existed."

"So that means that Evelina must have kept their true lineage a secret to spare them the pain of that knowledge," Medwin said. "Personally, I would rather have known the truth." He put a finger to his lips thoughtfully. "It must have been hard for them to understand why they had a special power that the rest of their 'people' didn't have."

"Especially growing up," Conner replied. "Can you imagine how much they must have been bullied for being freaks by all the other kids?"

"That must have been really horrible for them."

They climbed the stairs until they reached the fourth landing, went down the hall, and entered their room. Lenny wasn't there.

"He must be with Ammin somewhere," Conner said.

"Yeah, probably down at the ship."

Conner nodded as he got in bed. The two stories he'd heard that evening swirled around his head, and slowly, he entered a world of dreams.

* * *

The days melted by in pleasant succession, and with each one, Conner was quickly becoming deadly with his weapon. Medwin was extremely impressed with his vast improvements, yet still able to find little flaws in his form that he could work on.

"You're doing great, but you should widen your stance just a bit. It will ensure that you have the proper balance when firing. I also noticed that most of the times you've missed, you were over-anticipating your shots."

Conner nodded and went to string another arrow.

"Hold on a second," Medwin said. "I've got something for you. I'm sure it will help." He walked over to Conner and pulled something leather out of his pack.

"What is that?" Conner asked curiously.

"It's called a vambrace — an armguard for archers," Medwin answered while gesturing for Conner to hold out his left arm so he could fasten it on.

"Where did you get it?"

"I made it."

"You made it?" Conner echoed, tilting his head to one side.

"Yeah, I've been working on it for the last few days."

Conner looked more closely at the armguard. It had an elegant design etched onto its surface, greatly adding character to its appearance. For a moment, he was speechless. "Thank you," he muttered, finding his voice. "This is amazing craftsmanship. Where did you get the leather?"

"Cassius gave it to me."

"Wow! I can't thank you enough for this."

"You're welcome," Medwin replied. He grinned and finished fastening the armguard's buckles. "Why don't you try it out?"

Conner strung an arrow, drew it back, locked onto a target, and let the arrow fly. He hit his target squarely, strung a fresh arrow, fired, and hit the same target mere inches from his last shot. The fact that he hadn't felt the need to flinch as the bowstring rubbed across his forearm improved his confidence greatly. "That really does make a difference," he said, giving the vambrace an appreciative stare.

Medwin laughed. "Of course it does. Who wants to be in pain while they try to concentrate? Come on. Let's go down to the ship. I think Ammin said it's supposed to be ready to sail by midday."

Conner leaned in closer to Medwin and whispered, "I wonder if he has dealt with Louie and Felix?"

"I don't know," Medwin whispered back. "Seems like something would have happened by now though… Don't you think?" he added, almost as if he had become suddenly uncertain of his own opinion.

"He probably threw them in the brig," Conner said thoughtfully.

As they reached the ship's gangplank, the first group of sailors they saw proved Conner wrong. Two of the men were none other than those whose plot he had overheard. He nudged Medwin and pointed the men out to him subtly. The fact that they were still walking about freely came as a complete shock, but he settled to assume that Ammin had it under control.

They boarded the ship and searched for Ammin. He wasn't anywhere in sight.

Medwin approached a sailor that he must have recognized because he guessed the man's name. "Hey, Quincy is it?"

"Aye. Wha' can I do fer yeh, lads?"

"We were just wondering if you know where Ammin is?"

"Aye, 'e's in is quarters."

Conner and Medwin thanked Quincy for his help and headed for

Ammin's lodging. Before they could knock on the door, Conner heard someone speak his name.

"Of course I care about what happens to Conner!"

"I just hope you realize the importance of that boy to all of Rohwen!"

"I don't know what you're going on about with this whole 'he's the one' palaver… But I have grown quite fond of the boy. I won't let anything happen to him!"

"You said you met Vivek, didn't you?"

"Yeah…"

"Well, you must have noticed that he had a special power…"

"'Course I did. How could I not have? I watched him bring the bloody forest to life in battle!"

"Conner has the same power. He has the power of cognition. He faced Vellix and lived! Don't you realize what that means?"

"What? He never told me that he fought Vellix! I mean, I obviously noticed that the boy has some special power."

"Cognition."

"Whatever. Don't worry about him. I will take him to Rhona, back to the mainland, and from there we will go our separate ways."

"Oi, sorry ter interrupt, bu' shouldn' we be gettin' underway?"

"No, you're right, Lenny. We need to go."

Conner heard footsteps moving toward the door. He grabbed Medwin and pulled him back a few paces so they could pretend they were just arriving.

The first to exit the room was Cassius, followed closely by Ammin and Lenny.

"You lads about ready?" Ammin asked when he saw Conner and Medwin approaching. It was obvious by the look on his face that he hoped Conner hadn't overheard the conversation he and Cassius were just having.

"Ready when you are," Conner said with Medwin by his side, gesturing his agreement.

"It was a pleasure to meet you, Conner," Cassius said as he reached a hand out to shake Conner's. "It inspires me to know that there is hope."

Conner didn't really know how to respond, so he just shook Cassius' hand and smiled broadly. After an awkward moment, in which Cassius seemed to look at him pointedly, they released one another's hands.

"Have a safe voyage," Cassius said with one last wave of farewell. As he left the ship, Ammin started barking orders at a thunderous volume.

Anchors raised and sails lowered as men scrambled to complete their orders. Wind filled the great warship's broad sails to capacity. She started to gain speed. The newly fitted planks of wood creaked and moaned the first few times Ammin forced the ship to obey his directional command, but before long, they settled into position and became one with the rest of the great warship.

"Quincy, take the helm," Ammin ordered.

"Aye Cap'n," Quincy replied. He jogged short-legged up the stairs to the bridge, grabbed the helm with one hand, withdrew a flask from his pocket with the other, and took a large pull from it with a satisfied little shudder.

Ammin headed straight for the two sailors he had been waiting to deal with for days. "Louie! Felix! Choose a length of rope!"

"Now, mates!" Louie yelled defiantly. He charged toward Ammin with his sword drawn — Felix right behind him — and slashed at Ammin in a medieval fashion.

Ammin's skill level was so far beyond Louie's that he didn't even bother to draw his sword in defense — he just sidestepped, stuck out his foot, and tripped the fool unforgivingly.

Felix, seeing that Louie had been no match for Ammin, turned around quickly to make sure he had plenty of back up. To his dismay, he saw that not one other sailor had followed him and Louie in their attempt to overthrow Ammin.

"Oh don' tha' jus' shock yeh!" Dale jeered in a mock tone of curiosity — Landon doubled up with shrieks of laughter next to him. Dale waited a second for his words to sink in before continuing his verbal abuse of the mutineers "Though' we would actually rebel agains' the same cap'n what we jus' voted in! Yer bloody idiots, the both o' yeh! Only reason we wen' along with yer plot, is ter have a good laugh when yer barmy plan backfired!" The whole crew burst into laughter and Dale made to continue his mockery of the two men.

"That's enough, Dale," Ammin advised him, staring down at the two mutinous sailors with a fierce glare in his eyes.

Dale looked as though he had a good many other insults he would have liked to throw at Louie and Felix, but he bit his tongue, knowing that Ammin's mood was venomous.

"*Do you know where greed gets a man in my crew?*" Ammin interrogated brutally — Conner actually saw small particles of spit fly out of his mouth as he barked at the two men cowering at his feet.

Neither Louie nor Felix seemed to be able to find their voices.

"I will show you where it gets you. Choose a length of rope! *Now!*"

Lenny stepped forward with his sword drawn to make sure they obeyed.

Felix grabbed an entire coil of rope; Louie grabbed some and cut it down to a much shorter length.

A chorus of, "String 'em up," rang out from the crew. They surrounded Louie and Felix, tied the lengths of rope they had chosen around their necks, bound their hands behind their backs, and forced the traitors up to the bow of the ship. Dale and Landon tied the other ends of their rope lengths securely to railing posts.

The crew parted out of Ammin's way as he walked up behind his betrayers. He pushed them forward roughly. As they tipped over the edge, he reached out and grabbed the ropes that dangled from the nooses around their necks, leaving them in a flux between falling and standing stably. He allowed them to drink in the fear of what would happen if he let go. "Give me one reason why I shouldn't let the both of you figure out if you've chosen your length of rope wisely!" He gave both men a vicious look and awaited their response.

Louie and Felix were both speechless. They couldn't even mumble a word. Fear had consumed them entirely.

Ammin ripped them back on to the main deck. "You two are hereby disowned from my crew." He circled to stand in front of them. "You will be held in the brig for the remainder of the voyage. When we return to Beach Bay, I will make sure the rumor of your attempted mutiny spreads like wildfire. We will see how long you last…" Louie and Felix peered up at Ammin, their eyes pleading for clemency. Ammin's expression remained cold as a midwinter's night. "I would kill you myself," he said, grabbing the hilt of his cutlass, "but I don't want coward's blood on my sword, my hands or my conscience." He gave the men one last glare of pure loathing and turned away from them. "Dale, take this filth to the brig!"

"Aye, Cap'n," Dale said, obliged to carry out his orders. He dragged the prisoners over to the hatch and disappeared down the stairs, indifferent to the ropes around their necks that were choking them ruthlessly.

Conner nudged Medwin. "I wonder what Ammin meant by, 'chose your length of rope wisely?'"

"I have no idea," Medwin admitted. "It doesn't seem like there *would* be a wise choice in that given situation."

"Actually, mates, there is," Lenny chimed in with a mischievous grin.

Conner and Medwin turned their attention to him. "And what is that?" They asked, unconvinced.

"If yeh choose a shorter length o' rope, yer neck'll break, an' you'll die quick…" He allowed himself a vulgar smirk before he continued. "…If yeh choose a longer length o' rope, yeh ge' ripped under the ship's hull and drown, which I'm sure I ain' go' ter tell yeh, is a much slower death."

Both Conner and Medwin gaped at Lenny with appalled looks.

"Neither option sounds good to me," Conner mused, not finding within himself a desire to contemplate a "better" way to die.

"Well, you won' have ter be worry'n bou' tha' now, will yeh?" Lenny chuckled. "Cause you ain' a mutinous prat!" He exploded into a fit of laughter.

Medwin sniggered, caught up in Lenny's infectious laughter.

Conner tried to look at the young sailor seriously for a moment, but then he burst into laughter as well. "Well, I guess it pays not to be a mutinous prat then, doesn't it!" he exclaimed.

"Tha' it does, mate! Tha' it does!"

* * *

Ammin had returned to the helm of his ship, his crew had gone back to their normal duties, and the faded lines of the isle of Rhona had come into clear focus as the *Colossus* sailed through the passage between the two large islands: Ewaun and Rhona.

"I'm going to pull around to the nose of the island," Ammin said as Conner, Medwin, and Lenny marched up the steps that separated the main deck from the bridge. "That will put you in the same position as you were last time we were here."

"Sounds good," Conner said. He was about to ask how long it would be until they arrived when a thought struck him. How long might it take to find this missing scroll? If Vivek had been searching for it all those years, unsuccessfully, then what chance did they have of finding it in any kind of timely manner? "Hey, Ammin, I hadn't thought to ask until right now..." Conner paused awkwardly, not quite sure how to ask his question without coming across as expectant "...but, um, how long are you willing to wait offshore for us?"

Medwin looked as though his heart sank as Conner's question set in. They never did inform Ammin that it might take a substantial amount of time to find the scroll; that is if they even could find it.

"Well, lads," said Ammin, who appeared to be contemplating his answer. "How long do you think you'll need to do whatever it is you're doing?" he asked, gazing down at Conner with searching eyes. "I don't mean to pry into your business, but a short time ago I was told that you fought Vellix. Is this true?"

"Yes," Conner answered, trying to sound modest.

"Until I heard that bit of information, I hadn't put much thought into what it was you guys were up to. I will admit, I am in this mainly for the gold. It is how I make a living."

Conner and Medwin shrugged, as if to say, "That's okay, we kind of figured as much."

Ammin gave them an appreciative look. "But now I feel that what it is you're doing could be far more crucial than I had previously considered. I want to be of service to you in any way that I can… So you just tell me how long you need."

"That's just it, though," Conner replied. "We have no idea how long it will take. See, we're trying to find something. Something that is vital to my having the skill required to actually destroy Vellix. But we have no idea where on the island it might be."

"We don't even know if it's on the island," Medwin said with a dispirited shake of his head. "We're just going off of a hunch that Vivek had."

"A bloody hunch is better than nothin' though, ain' it?" Lenny stated in a tone only he could invoke in a serious conversation. "I'm jus' sayin', I'd rather have a slim ray 'o light ter go on than ter be in the bleedin' dark altogether."

Conner gave him a hardy nudge in the shoulder and said, "Lenny, only you can take any subject and turn it into lighthearted banter."

"Nah, mate, I'm bein' serious. I can be serious when I need ter be."

Conner gaped, wondering if he would ever figure Lenny out. "…I'm sorry. I just assumed you were joking," he confessed, blushing.

"Well tha'll teach yeh ter *assume* then, won' it? Bloody 'ell!"

Conner looked down at his feet.

"Hahaha! *Blimey,* Conner! Yeh need ter learn no' ter be so *damn* gullible! I'm givin' yeh a hard time."

Conner ogled him. "I can't believe you got me again," he said angrily.

"You'll fig'r it ou', mate," Lenny replied, chuckling in appreciation of his own humorous wit.

Before Conner had a chance to respond, Lenny was hollering at a sailor attempting to secure a rope line" Oi, yeh call tha' tyin' a decent knot!" he snapped before running off to help the apparently insufficient sailor, mumbling under his breath the whole way.

"That's twice he's gotten you now!" Medwin snorted.

"I guess I'm just that gullible," Conner said, a little hurt that Medwin was laughing at him as well.

Medwin noticed that Conner didn't seem as amused by the whole thing as he was. "Sorry Conner. I was just messing around."

Conner tried to make a gesture of indifference and changed the subject. "We should probably go down and get Zelimir. I imagine we'll be dropping anchor anytime."

"Ten minutes," Ammin informed them. He had obviously been unable to avoid overhearing Conner and Medwin's conversation. "Oh, and to answer your question from earlier, Conner, there are enough provisions aboard the ship to last the crew five days. So that pretty much determines how long you will have on the island. I wish I could give you longer, but I can't let my crew starve."

"I totally understand," Conner replied, relieved; he had expected much less time than five days.

They went and got Zelimir from below. Within minutes, the three of them were headed for the shores of Rhona.

Conner rowed the dinghy. He remembered how incredibly scary it was the first time Quincy had lowered him into the choppy ocean on the small boat. Now, after everything he'd gone through, it seemed almost silly to be scared of something so seemingly safe.

As they neared Rhona's shoreline, Zelimir launched himself off the edge of the boat and swam the rest of the way in. He called out to Conner and Medwin happily. "I have always wanted to swim in the ocean!"

Conner rowed the dinghy the rest of the way to shore. He and Medwin dragged it up past the noticeable line that countless high tides had left behind.

"You've never swam in the ocean, Zelimir?"

"Conner, honestly, can you think of a reason why I would have?" Zelimir surveyed him, almost as if pained by his lacking skills of deduction.

"Well, no, actually," Conner started awkwardly. "I guess that's — yeah, why would you have swam in the ocean?"

Zelimir replied with a polite silence. Any other response would have been unavoidably rude.

Medwin drew the hatchet out of his pack. "Come on guys. Let's make this search as efficient as possible. We only have five days, and this island is by no means small."

Conner grabbed his bow and strung an arrow, as to be ready to fire it at any point.

Zelimir's nose twitched restlessly as he searched the land around them before they reached it. He stopped Conner and Medwin on multiple occasions, sensing the presence of a predator. It was for this reason that Conner felt relatively calm as they marched deeper into the jungle. The fact was — with Zelimir's enhanced instincts helping them, there was almost no chance they would enter any unwanted fights.

As the day progressed, Conner felt like time was traveling far too quickly, almost as if it were mocking them for their attempt to beat it. Five days to find something that Vivek had been trying to find for a great many years was starting to feel laughable.

Darkness was approaching. Medwin created his underground room. "Let's call it a day. I'm tired and hungry, and there just isn't enough light to search by at this point anyway."

Conner and Zelimir nodded and followed Medwin into the room. They ate the little food that Ammin had been able to provide them in silence. But silence had never held such volume, or meaning. Each of them read the dismal thoughts of the others. Now that the job of reaching Rhona was complete, the truth of their task was beginning to show itself in a proper light. Did they really expect to find the scroll and make it back to the *Colossus* in five days?

In time, each of them dozed off, feeling as hopeless as the next.

* * *

Late in the afternoon the next day, they came upon a small clearing. A patch of dirt covered sparsely with young foliage lay ahead.

Conner recognized it at once: the grave of the jaguar he had slain. A thought came to him as he walked past the grave. "Moxie!" he pronounced, as if the little hunchback had popped out from behind a nearby tree.

"What?" Medwin said, turning quickly to see what Conner had seen. "What are you talking about?" he asked a second later, realizing that there was no way Moxie could be on the island.

"I know how we can heal Moxie," Conner said excitedly.

For a moment, Medwin's expression was thoroughly confused. He was about to say something, most likely along the lines of Conner needing to rest, that he was suffering from heat exhaustion, but then understanding emerged onto his face. "Conner, I've said it before, and I will say it again. You are brilliant!" he bellowed, beaming.

Zelimir looked at both of their pleased faces ponderously. Medwin, whose spirits had soared at the thought of healing Moxie's gun wound, was positively chipper, and Conner couldn't stop smiling. "Would either of you like to inform me of what it is you are so happy about," he asked shortly. "What do you mean — you know how we can heal Moxie?"

"Vivek's underground room!" Medwin cried, a cheerful gleam in his eyes.

"That doesn't tell me anything, Medwin," Zelimir snapped.

Conner realized that Zelimir was becoming increasingly impatient. He decided that he had better explain. "Vivek has a store of potions that he created during his time on this island." He watched Zelimir, his features caught in a flux between expectant and excited, waiting to see that telltale look of understanding. Zelimir gazed back at him, half amused, half exasperated by his poor sense of how to get to a point — nowhere near the look of understanding Conner had expected.

His excitement abandoned his expectation, his expectation abandoned him, and he was left looking defused. "The point," he went on diligently, "is that all I have to do is locate the entrance to the underground room Vivek lived in… We'll have access to every potion in there. We just grab one of the healers," he snatched at the air as if grabbing the jar, "and Moxie will be good as new."

Zelimir eyed him for a second, his expression unreadable. He started to speak. "I see… There is, however, one major flaw in that plan … and that is…"

Conner barely heard Zelimir's words as he found himself sinking deep into his own thoughts. The idea of going back to the place where he had learned who he was, knowing that the ancient man who had once dwelled there was gone forever, saddened him deeply. He would give almost anything to speak with Vivek again. To pick his brain about the places he had already searched for the missing scroll. To get some real training with his cognition.

There was a feeling he couldn't shake: that Vellix had been toying with him during their duel; that he hadn't even begun to reveal his true potential. The thought was like an irksome wasp, stinging his brain. He tried to swat it away, but it continued to nag him regardless. "And furthermore" — Zelimir's voice became clear again as Conner forced himself to leave the depths of his mind — "I thought our first priority was to search for the scroll."

"It *is* our priority, but —" Conner saw a familiar grouping of trees. He had stood right next to them when Vivek led him and Medwin down into the underground room. "Over here!" he shouted. "Come on guys, this is it. Stand next to me." Medwin and Zelimir strode over to stand by his side. He closed his eyes and formed a picture of Vivek's room in his mind: a magnificent throw rug upon the dirt floor, assorted jars of potions that filled the shelves by the wall, the small bed that sat in the corner.

A sound like ice freezing in fast-forward sprang from the ground as a small crack started to develop in a circle around them. The moment the circle was completed they began to sink into the ground, as if riding a circular elevator.

Zelimir seemed unable to find a good reason why they shouldn't retrieve the potions now that they were so easily accessible. "Well, if I had known it would be that easy, I wouldn't have been so concerned that we were getting sidetracked," he said, looking defeated.

"These come in extremely handy," Medwin said as he held up a jar of the healing agent that had saved his life. He ran his hand impulsively along the spot where a jaguar had swiped him.

"That is what you put on Conner's wound the night we met, and I … attacked him…" Zelimir looked disgusted with himself as the last couple of words left his mouth. "I am grateful that my mistake was amended, and that you were not permanently injured."

Conner gave Zelimir a wide reassuring smile that told him not to be too hard on himself.

Zelimir's appreciation for Conner's ability to see the logical side of things increased significantly in that moment.

"Which ones were the revivers again, Conner?" Medwin asked from over by the potion-filled shelves.

"I don't know. I'd have to look at it again."

"Well then, by all means — come over here and take a look, because I can't decide between these two here. I mean, they're virtually the same." He held the potions up so Conner could get a better look at them. "It's just that this one is a shade darker blue," he added, jerking his head toward the potion in his left hand.

"Medwin, to be honest, I have no idea which one it was," Conner admitted as he compared the two potions. "There's only one of these left," he said, pointing to the potion that was a shade darker, "and Vivek did already give us quite a few revivers… So it's probably that one. But you should grab both, just in case," he suggested lightly.

"Only one problem with that," Medwin said. He glanced up at Conner, concern pulling the strings of his expression.

"What's that?"

"We have no idea what effects the other potion will have." Medwin glanced skeptically at the two potions.

"I can't imagine it would be anything bad," Conner said, his tone light and carefree. He gave Medwin a skeptical look similar to the one that Medwin had just given the two potions. "I mean, this is Vivek we're talking about."

"True" — Medwin closed his eyes and nodded gravely — "but we barely knew him." He looked up at Conner. "Don't you think it would be a bit ignorant of us to assume that all these potions are safe just because he was a nice old man?"

"I agree with Medwin, Conner," Zelimir cut in before Conner could respond to Medwin's statement.

"I never said I don't agree with him," Conner said, feeling like Medwin and Zelimir were teaming up against him for no reason. "I was only saying that it seems strange to me that Vivek would create potions that were harmful in any kind of way."

"Don't you remember the vine with those poisonous berries that he used to attack Vellix during their duel?" Medwin asked realistically. "That alone tells us that he was not only capable of using cognition to physically harm an opponent, but that he was advanced in that form of the art."

Conner looked into Medwin's expectant face, a face waiting to see him accept the truth in reason. "You're right. It was stupid of me to assume that he had only ever created potions for good."

Even though Medwin got the answer out of Conner that he had wanted, he didn't really look happy about it. He hadn't been trying to make Conner feel stupid, just wanting him to be sensible.

"If we have what we came for, then I suggest we carry on with our search of the missing scroll," said Zelimir. Conner and Medwin loaded Medwin's pack with the potions they had decided to take and joined the wolf in the center of the room.

Moments later, dim evening sunlight met their eyes as they resurfaced into the thick jungle of Rhona.

"So, which way now?" Conner wondered aloud.

"I suggest we take this route," Zelimir answered with a jerk of his head in a southwestern direction.

Conner looked at him quizzically.

"For the simple fact that I can smell the remnants of Vivek's scent leading this way," he added. "I hadn't thought about how beneficial it would be for us in our search of the places he's been if I caught his scent first."

"So it was truly a good thing that Conner found Vivek's room before we started our search then, eh?" Medwin chortled.

"Indeed, it was," Zelimir replied, giving Medwin a "thanks for rubbing in the fact I was wrong" sort of look.

With Zelimir leading the way, they followed Vivek's scent for the next hour, until something stopped them from continuing.

They arrived on the edge of a steep drop in the terrain, which led down to a magnificent gorge. Its beauty was immense, leaving the three of them astounded. A large river meandered its way along the floor, finally curving around a cliff edge and out of sight.

The valley seemed to be a sort of oasis for the animals that lived on the island. A herd of antelope grazed on the lush grass that stretched for what appeared to be miles across the expanse of the gorge. Bison, elephants, giraffes, deer, and zebras were all getting their evening drink from the widest point of the river. A flock of flamingos sifted through the shallows looking for a meal.

A sharp screech filled the air as a massive eagle dove straight down at the water. Its talons submerged as it reached the surface; then re-emerged clutching a fish, its shiny scales glistening in the setting sun.

A great commotion came from amidst the herd of antelope. Conner located the source of this upheaval in the otherwise peaceful setting. A cheetah had given chase to one of the younger antelope. Its speed was incredible to witness; within a few hundred yards, it had caught up to its prey, and with one powerful bound, it latched its claws firmly into the antelope and ripped it to the ground ruthlessly.

Zelimir licked at his chops hungrily.

"I suppose we should probably come up with something to eat, set up camp, and call it a day, huh?" Conner presumed when he saw the food lust in Zelimir's eyes.

"I know, I'm *starving*," Medwin grunted as he began gathering wood for the night's fire. "We haven't had anything all day."

"I'll go and see what I can come up with for food," Conner said. He left Medwin and Zelimir to set up camp.

* * *

His bow was poised to fire as he plunged into the jungle. A flock of birds inhabiting the jungle's lower canopy took flight, squawking angrily at Conner for his disruption of their otherwise peaceful evening. He took this as a sign to slow his movements, as not to cause any other unnecessary disruptions.

Soon the amount of light he had to hunt by had diminished so greatly that he considered giving up on his search for food altogether. Just then, the sound of rustling leaves met his ears. It was coming from the other side of a knot of bushes to his left. He crouched as low as possible. Fear knocked at the door of his thoughts. 'This could be anything. Tigers hunt at night… It's not a tiger,' he told himself in an effort to stay calm and focused. The rustling sound rang out again; this time it was much closer to the clearing in which Conner had knelt, breath held and arrow ready to fire.

Something emerged from within the bushes and Conner, being on edge, shot before he knew what he was firing at. His arrow whistled past whatever it was. The creature began to flap its wings frantically. Realizing at once that it was a turkey, he quickly strung another arrow, took a hand steadying breath, and fired upon the bird. This time he hit it directly through its breast. He ran over and quickly put the creature out of its misery.

It was nearly impossible for him to wipe the smile off his face as he headed back to camp. But his elated feeling and thoughts of relishing a delicious turkey dinner dissolved as he noticed he'd been searching for camp for far too long. There hadn't been a single sign of firelight, the very thing he had been counting on to help him navigate his way back.

Dazzling blue flames burst to life in the palm of his right hand, the other holding his kill. He used the light from the flames to search for camp, but to no avail. It seemed that he was thoroughly lost at this point. Nothing appeared familiar in his surroundings.

The brilliant flames lit his way sufficiently. However, in the otherwise perpetual darkness, his vision only extended a short distance. The overwhelming sense that he was in danger came over him, leading to the feeling that something could be stalking his every move. He started to run, but from nothing in particular. His heart pounded as he sprinted through a maze of trees that blocked his way, their lowest branches tearing and scratching his arms and face. The blue flames in his palm flickered as he raced in the direction he desperately hoped was back to camp.

He came upon a rock wall that wasn't at all familiar. Its face ascended so high that in the darkness, he couldn't see the top of it. Evidently, he'd been running the wrong direction. He turned to head back the opposite way and his flames washed over a section of the wall shrouded by a thick layer of plant life, clawing its way upward.

Something caught his eye. The shadow behind the brambles appeared far too solid, as if not just a shadow, but an opening. He held up his right hand. The piercing light of his flames created shadows so deep and highlights so vivid that it became clear he had discovered some kind of gap in the rock, an entrance perhaps. His stomach squirmed with hopeful delight. His mind began to race.

The fear of being lost, hunted, or both, disappeared instantly. He forced his way past the vines and branches that kept the little cave entrance well concealed and entered a small, cylindrical shaft.

After a few minutes of crawling on abrasive furrows of rock, his knees started crying out in objection. But the pain wasn't enough to deter his curiosity; on he crawled. Finally, with a groan of disappointment, he came upon a dead end.

His heart sank as though tied to one of *the Colossus*' anchors. How could this be? He had been sure that this tunnel would lead to something — preferably, the missing scroll, but anything would be better than a cold wall of black rock.

He sat there, feeling letdown and trying to muster the will to leave. He would start his search for camp. The glorious scenes of him showing up with the scroll — Medwin's excitement; Zelimir's admiration — deteriorated into a gloomy fog of disappointment. He should have known that finding the scroll so easily was too good to be true. As he began to crawl away from the end of the tunnel, the unmistakable feeling that he was missing something swept over him. Leaving this tunnel without further investigation was a mistake.

He started to run his hands along the walls, searching urgently for anything out of place: abrasions, cracks, smooth spots — anything. A small voice in his head whispered, 'Use cognition…'

At that moment, a memory came back to him, speaking in the calm, pleasant voice of Odriana. 'Before he traveled back to the city that he had left so long ago, he went and hid the scrolls he had written where no one but those worthy to study the documents would ever find them.'

Xellore had meant for it to be only those worthy to study his scrolls that would be able to find them. Was this the entrance to the cave Vivek had told him about? Conner stared at the end of the tunnel. Focusing intently on the wall removing itself, he whispered, "I am here to learn... For knowledge..."

The wall crumbled away, allowing the light radiating from his flames to cascade into a much larger room on the other side.

Heart racing, he clambered over the pile of rubble and into the next room. He investigated the new chamber, an unfading smile etched upon his face. But when five minutes passed without any sign that this room held anything more spectacular than rock, his smile grew weary and fell to a scowl. Why wasn't anything in here? He was sure he was in the right place. It had to be…

His lust to read the scrolls was so strong that he could hardly stand it. 'I want to know, to learn!' he thought, feeling frustrated. He shut his eyes tight and formed a vivid picture of himself holding the scrolls, reading them.

A four-foot section of the wall shuttered violently and started to move. It receded into the wall around it, the sounds of stone sliding across stone reverberating off the cold walls.

Conner's heart lifted once more as he moved carefully down a short passage and into the next room. Awe overwhelmed him the moment he entered it. He could actually feel the aura of past cognition in the room so heavily that he knew it at once. Xellore himself had created this chamber. None other than a master could have carved rock in the way this chamber had been manipulated. Lines of detail ran the lengths of the walls, adding an appearance of grace and style. At the far end of the chamber, he saw that every carved line came together to form some kind of picture. He moved closer. The light of his flames revealed the image more clearly. It was the Hylanian symbol, and laying in a row directly below it… The scrolls.

CHAPTER 14

Scrolls of Hylan

Conner knew it would be extremely foolish to get anywhere near the scrolls with flames still burning in his palm. However, if he put out the flames, there would be no light to read by. He pondered the situation for a moment before a simple solution struck him.

He held up his hand and started searching. Firelight swept over something protruding off the wall. Conner grinned as he realized it was a torch. 'If there's one, that must mean there are more,' he thought logically. Sure enough, after a short investigation of the walls he had found five torches.

Now well-lit, the chamber was much easier to appreciate. He drank in its beauty again as he realized the designs carved into the rock he first seen were just the tip of the iceberg in comparison to what was actually there.

Lines flowed in parallels and broke off in different directions, forming leaves and blooming flowers. Heading farther along the wall, they came together to form the Hylanian symbol. Conner noticed that five lines extended from the top of the symbol and shot upward toward the ceiling of the chamber. He followed them with his eyes. They formed something else: a great weeping willow tree. After marveling in Xellore's skill and proficiency with cognition, he noticed that the branches of the tree swept back into the designs he had seen originally. Every intricate line in the chamber connected, revealing an immaculate circuitry of images.

Conner allowed himself to appreciate the full loop of creation a few more times before reaching out to grab the first of the scrolls in the row. Handsomely carved pieces of wood held it at both ends. He unrolled it and immediately noticed how ancient and decrepit it was. He finished opening the scroll cautiously, found a relatively flat section of stone to sit on, and started to read.

- To all whom read these scrolls -

In the seven years of my exploration of this land's many wonders, I learned much. Cognition seemed to be an inexhaustible art form. The longer I traveled, the more I realized that what my people had considered to be the limits of the art could not have been further from the truth. The world around me was so striking that I became inspired to push the boundaries of my skill... Slowly, I began to see results. Not only was I able to control the life around me, I was starting to create life of my own. The true impact of what this meant I did not discover until realizing that I had become a master of the very land I loved so much. I began to experiment with various ideas. Some of which included the creation of my own habitats, the blending of existing life with the life I had created, the re-creation of objects in new atomic formats, and the ability to use cognition on living creatures.

When I created Botanica, I thought I had finally achieved my masterpiece. I was wrong to think this, however. For as I write this scroll, I sit under the weeping branches of my true masterpiece. Salix, the willow tree, has something which I never expected to be able to create. I would not have even considered it possible if it weren't for the fact that there is undeniable proof. Salix has conscious thought. The tree taught me a great many things about Rohwen, cognition, and even of the future. It is as if she's on a different plane of existence altogether...

A plane in which she can see beginnings, ends, and all that comes in between. The prophetic nature that she holds is truly mystical. I realized that it would be foolish to leave such knowledge undocumented, so I have decided to write these scrolls specifically for the purpose of making sure her knowledge will be recorded forever.

I would like, now, to address the reader of this scroll. If you read these scrolls that lay before you, which I have written for the love of knowledge, I say to you this: beware the lust of power, as it is the pathway to destruction. The knowledge held within these documents is meant for the betterment of all - not for personal gain or selfishness. Take what you learn and wear it well.

- Xellore -

Conner read and re-read the scroll. The thought that it had been written by Xellore himself; that Vellix and Vivek had both sat here and read from it, possibly even in the same exact spot he was right now, boggled his mind. He remembered something Vivek had said to Vellix before their duel. 'I see you have learned nothing from them.' Now he knew what Vivek had meant by that statement. Had Xellore not made it clear that the knowledge in his scrolls was for the betterment of Rohwen? Not for personal gain...

"Conner! Conner, where are you? Can you hear me?" Medwin's distressed voice filtered in from outside the cave, accompanied by the distinct sounds of someone moving frantically through the thick foliage of the jungle.

"Oh no!" Conner yelled. "How long have I been gone? They must be worried sick." He felt ashamed that he had overlooked the fact that his friends were not only starving and waiting on him to return with food. He had been gone so long that they must be extremely worried about his safety as well.

He bolted back out of the cave, through the other room, and down the small shaft, hoping Medwin was still within earshot. It sounded like he had been sprinting.

"Medwin!" he screamed at the top of his lungs. "I'm over here." Flames erupted in his hands. He waved them frantically, trying to make himself visible. Medwin called back from somewhere in the distance. Relief washed over Conner like warm, soothing water.

Moments later, the two friends were reunited. "Where's Zelimir?" Conner asked, glancing around for any sign of the wolf.

Medwin chuckled. "He said he could no longer wait for you to return with food. Told me he was going to hunt for big game. Then he left, saying it was in everybody's best interest that he found some substantial nourishment … and I believe him."

Conner grinned at Medwin in amusement. He was well aware of how Zelimir could get when he hadn't eaten enough. "So I take it we will just meet him back at camp?" Conner asked. "Speaking of which, I hope you can remember how to get back."

"I left marks on the trees with my hatchet — every hundred yards or so — for that very reason."

It was Conner's turn to tell Medwin that *he* was brilliant. The idea that they wouldn't be searching all night for camp was a great feeling to say the least. Lost in a pitch-black jungle was not his idea of fun.

Now aware that all was well, Conner felt his excitement take over. "I found the scrolls!" he exclaimed, a note of youthful enthusiasm carried in his tone.

"What?"

"Xellore's scrolls. I found them!"

"Seriously?" Medwin asked in astonishment.

"Yeah, seriously! They're in a cave right over here!" Conner led Medwin to the undergrowth-covered cave entrance.

Getting back to the scroll-chamber seemed to take no time at all, now that no obstacles stood in the way.

Pure amazement shaped Medwin's features as he entered the chamber. He stared at the carvings on the walls, his mouth agape.

"This is some of the most beautiful work in cognition I have ever seen." He said. "I mean, it's perfect. Not one flaw in the line work."

"I know. It's crazy." Conner agreed.

"I'd like to have a look at the scrolls," Medwin said as he moved toward the back of the chamber.

"Yeah, I've only read this one," Conner said, handing Medwin the first scroll in the set of four. Quite suddenly, he knew exactly why Vivek had known there was a missing scroll. There were five torches; five lines leading off of the Hylanian symbol up into the willow tree… Xellore had used this number of lines and torches on purpose. Each one represented a scroll.

"Wow," Medwin uttered, submerged in the scroll that Conner handed him, most likely reading it for the second or third time by now.

"I know, right?" Conner replied as he went for the next scroll in the row. He opened it and started to read hungrily. This scroll was of Xellore's travels across Rohwen. As Conner read, he learned that the cognition master had been to just about every area in this world imaginable. He spoke of his visit to Edelan, where he had stayed for a number of months; about his exploration of the ancient forest, although he didn't mention any encounter with the Satria. From there he had headed north and found the Frozen Wastelands, which he named Glacia. He had quickly left the barren land to pursue areas in which he would be surrounded by the life he loved. He traveled southeast, toward a monumental mountain range. Upon his arrival at the Monzerrat Mountains, he discovered that an odd breed of large birds seemed to have made the mountains their home. He studied the birds briefly, intrigued by their abnormal size, eventually concluding that they were not all too different from eagles. He presumed them to be the last of a nearly extinct predecessor to the eagles, which were common in most of the habitats he had discovered thus far.

Conner re-read the last sentence about the large birds, wondering if it had been this very breed of bird that Vellix had used to create his Mirthless. He soon decided that it wasn't really worth the speculation. It wouldn't make much difference if they had been anyway. He continued to read. A few minutes later, he finished the scroll. "Which one have you got there?" he asked Medwin as he rolled up the one in his hand.

Medwin had a cryptic look on his face, which was accentuated by the flickering blue flames that lit the room. "It's the one about the willow tree's prophecies," he said, his face still disfigured by an enigmatic gaze. "That was really weird reading about your prediction… I mean, here I am standing with the person who was written about two thousand years ago. I don't think it gets any weirder than that…"

Conner extended a hand to offer Medwin the scroll he had just finished reading, and Medwin handed him his.

The strangest feeling came over him as he started to read the prophetic scroll, as if he was truly becoming the person that he actually was for the first time. But it was much, much deeper than that. As he read his own name, and that he would possess this incredible ability to perform cognition more powerful than any other written here in the ancient script of Xellore, his whole body started to tingle.

He came to the portion that spoke of the lone wolf. The wolf he was destined to befriend. It was the most inexplicable sensation he had ever felt. Even more so than the first time he had done cognition; he had found that peculiar because doing something he didn't think was physically possible would always seem like the weirdest moment in his life.

But the idea that his existence, *his* name, and what he would arrive in Rohwen to do was all written here made him look at the whole situation in a new light. Reading it for himself had a completely different effect than hearing it from Vivek. "You're right, Medwin… This is definitely the strangest thing … *ever*…"

Medwin agreed with a feverish head gesture.

Conner went back to reading the scroll. The next prediction had been of a great evil that would plague Rohwen for centuries, unmatched and unchallenged. A morbid thought crossed his mind. The evil that Xellore was writing about was his own son. Conner didn't know how to take in the insanity of how disturbing that really was. He thought back to the story Odriana had read, of Xellore and Areona. If it hadn't been for Xellore's arrogance, thinking he could overcome the terrible drought that would threaten Hylan, the city would still exist. His effort to save the city had caused the enormous tidal wave, resulting in the destruction of all he had worked to protect. If he had listened to the wise words of his wife, they could have raised their twins happily, and in doing so, most assuredly prevented Vellix from becoming the cruel and perverse man he was today. It seemed that Xellore had fulfilled Salix's predictions himself. It was as if all the tree's prophecies were predictions of how Xellore would affect his own future, and ultimately the future of everyone who would live in Rohwen for centuries to come.

"Hey, Conner, check this out."

Conner tore himself away from the scroll to see what Medwin wanted to show him. He handed him the scroll he had been reading and said, "Look at the third paragraph."

Salix informed me that to infuse an object with my own power would allow me to call upon that power at a later time, and as a result, my cognition would double in those moments. The object would have harnessed the energy I had given it, keeping it locked within its core, expending it only during times in which I felt it necessary. I have decided to test this theory using a stone, and to my immense satisfaction, Salix was, indeed, correct. My cognition is now substantially greater than what it was before.

"Wow..." Conner whispered, wholly captivated by what he had just read. "He actually created a cognition-enhancing object, using his *own* cognition."

"I thought you would appreciate that piece of information," Medwin said, looking pleased.

Conner read the first part of the scroll, which he had overlooked in order to skip down to the third paragraph. This section's goal was to teach the reader how to refine their cognition: how to stay focused when performing difficult tasks, when to allow your power to take the lead, and how to sense these moments. Why the art only works for the incredibly determined personality; the reasons it is so vital to respect the land; and finally, how to understand and unlock your true potential once you have learned that you possess the gift.

As Conner read the information, it was strange to think how much of this knowledge he had obtained by default. He had learned the essentials that this scroll could tell him on his first adventure in Rohwen. There was, however, still something reassuring about reading it. The fact that he finally had some kind of mentor — even if it wasn't one he could interact with — was like getting confirmation for all the things he had learned. He *had* been doing it right. Luck wasn't what enabled him to achieve his level of cognition. His mindset had been correct every time he had ascended to a new level of skill: full of intent, awareness, and respect. He had to confess, in the beginning it was sheer desperation that allowed him to accomplish cognition, but as he progressed, he became well aware of what he was doing, and why.

His stomach twisted and growled, reminding him how hungry he was. "Hey, Medwin?"

"Yeah?"

"Are you about ready? I'm starving."

"Yeah, I'm ready," Medwin answered as he returned the scroll he'd been reading to its proper place. "We still don't have anything to eat, though."

"Oh, I forgot to tell you" — Conner felt pride creeping into his voice — "I shot a turkey with my bow. It's right outside the cave."

"Nice one, Conner! That's a really good kill! The meat from that should last us for at least a few days. Especially being as Zelimir's gone to get his own food."

"I'm definitely looking forward to a nice hot meal," Conner said, the thought of juicy turkey meat causing his mouth to salivate eagerly.

Medwin was first to exit the cave, Conner close behind.

"Hold up, Medwin," Conner said as he stepped out into the night air. He closed his eyes and pictured the wall at the end of the tunnel reforming; seconds later, crackling noises began to emanate from the mouth of the cave. When the sounds stopped, Conner started surveying the jungle floor. "Ah," he said to himself after a moment.

Medwin turned to watch as Conner grabbed a turkey from near the cave entrance. "That's a nice-sized bird." he said, breathing a low whistle as he started his search for the nearest of many trees he had marked with his hatchet.

Conner gave a quick smile in response and fell deep into thought. The scrolls had left his mind so incredibly full that he didn't even know what subject to ponder first. All of the information had been so enlightening that none of it felt more worthy of his focus.

Medwin located the tree with his hatchet marking, relief apparent in his demeanor. He turned cheerfully to Conner. "I can't believe you found the cave," he said, shaking his head in astonishment. "The odds of that were slim to none."

"I know," Conner agreed. "At first, I came to a dead end," he explained. "I was about to leave when I got the sudden feeling I should try using cognition. If it wasn't for that, I never would've found the scroll chamber."

"Well that worked out," Medwin chuckled.

Conner nodded, grinning.

They began swapping opinions of what they thought were the most fascinating revelations the scrolls held as they followed Medwin's hatchet-marked trees back to camp.

"Could you imagine how Xellore would feel if he knew his son was the great evil that Salix had predicted?" Conner mused. The thought of it made him sick, and he quickly realized that he didn't want to imagine what it would be like for Xellore if he knew.

"No, I can't," Medwin replied, sounding as sullen as Conner felt. "And I thought it was bad enough that he destroyed his own city trying to save it..." Conner didn't reply and Medwin, being intuitive, decided to change the topic to something a little more cheery. "I still can't believe Xellore was able to infuse an object with cognition."

"I know. It must be really difficult to pull off. I wonder if I can do it." Conner looked at Medwin, resisting a hopeful gaze but not doing enough to conceal one.

"Give it a shot," said Medwin, who was so used to Conner breaking all the boundaries of cognition that doubting him felt foolish.

Conner used the light of his flames to search the jungle floor for something worthy of trying on, but all he saw was scattered bits of branch, leaf, and dirt. "I should probably wait 'til we find something worth using," he concluded.

"That's probably a good idea," Medwin agreed. "No point in going through the trouble of infusing a twig with cognition..."

Conner looked over at him, pulling his face into an exaggerated expression of awe, as if Medwin's statement had been an absolute revelation. The look he got from Medwin in response made it impossible not to laugh.

* * *

Zelimir hadn't returned to camp by the time they arrived. Conner got a fire going while Medwin prepared the turkey.

Soon the intoxicating aroma of fire-cooked turkey meat hung enticingly on the air. Neither Medwin nor Conner had much to say. They just gazed hungrily at their soon to be dinner, all other thoughts driven from their minds.

Medwin leaned forward and prodded the turkey, checking to see if it was ready.

"Well?" Conner asked eagerly.

Medwin grinned. Firelight flickered sporadically across his face, making him nearly unrecognizable. "It's ready." He used his hatchet to slice off one of the legs and handed it to Conner.

Conner couldn't keep the smile off of his face as he devoured the turkey leg, and every time he glanced up at Medwin, it was obvious that the feeling was mutual.

After eating their fill, they wrapped the rest of the turkey in large leaves.

Medwin created his underground room. He was about to head down when Conner said, “I don’t know if we should sleep in the underground room tonight.” Medwin looked at him curiously. “What if Zelimir can’t find us?”

“He’ll be able to find us.” Medwin said with a dismissive wave of his hand. “He’ll just track our scents to this spot.”

“Good point,” Conner replied, following Medwin down into the room.

They both went straight for their beds and drifted to sleep without further conversation.

* * *

The boys returned to the surface just after dawn the following morning. Conner built up a small fire and heated some of their leftover turkey, while Medwin went to find water.

The sound of rustling leaves met Conner ears. His heart jolted — the culprit of those rustling sounds could be any of a large variety of predators. He sat motionless and silent, using his peripherals to investigate the sound. A heaved sigh of relief escaped him when he saw that it was just Zelimir returning from his hunt. "Any luck?" he asked, his nerves settling slowly.

"Yes, it was quite the successful hunt… I won't need to eat again for a few weeks after my kill last night," Zelimir replied in a satisfied tone.

"A few weeks?" Conner asked, looking thunderstruck. "Wow, I wish I could eat once and go a few weeks before I needed food again."

Zelimir chuckled lightly and said, "It does have its perks."

"Hey Zelimir," Medwin said as he returned to the campsite.

"Looks like you had some success," Conner said as Medwin offered him an almond-shaped leaf that was brimming with clear water. He took the leaf gratefully and sipped from its contents, then turned to face Zelimir. "Guess what? I found the scrolls last night."

Zelimir looked at him curiously. "Interesting… You mean the other scrolls from the set? Not the one we're looking for?"

Conner felt his excitement drain away. "No, not the missing scroll… I know we weren't looking for the other scrolls, but I just thought you should know that I found them..."

Zelimir nodded. "I imagine you searched the area for the missing scroll?" he asked, looking thoughtful before continuing, "But I hope you didn't waste too much time doing so. To me, it seems clear that Vivek would have searched that region of the island more thoroughly than most. I highly doubt the scroll is anywhere near there…"

"Yeah, that makes sense," Conner replied.

Medwin chimed into the conversation. "So, what's the plan?" he asked, directing his question toward Zelimir.

"Well," Zelimir started, "I was mindful enough to stay alert to Vivek's scent while I hunted, so I am now familiar with many of his old trails." Conner and Medwin cast him an admiring look. "The only problem," he went on, "is that there are so many of them that I don't even know where to start. It leaves us little ground to cover that hasn't already been searched."

Medwin stroked his chin in thought. After a minute, he looked up at Zelimir. "Isn't that a good thing? That means there is less we have to search."

"Yes," Zelimir agreed, "but it doesn't mean it won't take just as long to reach locations that have yet to be searched."

"Well, there's no use standing around talking about it," Conner said. "Let's get moving… Zelimir, lead the way."

* * *

They trudged through mile after mile of jungle, searching areas Vivek hadn't yet been for even the slightest sign of variation in the landscape: something out of place, a landmark, anything that looked out of the ordinary.

The hours dragged past without so much as the slightest indication that they were making progress, and their mood grew bleak. Soon,

Conner and Medwin were bickering amongst one another pointlessly.

"Just hold on," Zelimir said in an attempt to stop their argument.

"I told you," Conner snapped, ignoring Zelimir, "we should be searching the —"

"And *I* told *you,*" Medwin cut in before Conner could finish, "if we don't —"

"*Quiet!*" Zelimir shouted to shut Conner and Medwin up. They stopped arguing and faced Zelimir, sharing equally ashamed expressions. Zelimir waited a moment to make sure they were ready to listen before he started to speak. "I realize that this search feels infuriatingly pointless, but arguing will truly make it a waste of time." The boys exchanged another shameful glance. "We need to keep a positive outlook… Now then, let's —"

"Wait a sec," Conner said. Zelimir's head went down with a sigh of exasperation, but Conner didn't notice. "I think I've found something!" He ran over to a thin opening in the ground, just visible beneath the heavy jungle vegetation and peered down into the cavity. Unfortunately, the fissure was too thin to get a good look at how deep it went. Conner stood up and told Medwin, who had also been attempting to look down the crevice, to stand back.

The ground started to tremor and quake as Conner used cognition to widen the gap. Trees rooted near the fracture shook violently. Something fell from one of them and landed on Conner.

By the time he realized what it was, a dark green pit-viper had already injected his neck with its toxic venom. He flung the snake off and it slithered away, but the damage was already done. The area around the wound started to swell immediately. Blood seeped freely out of the fang holes. He sat down and clutched the wound as Medwin came running over frantically with a glass jar in one hand.

"Here, drink this," he said. Expressions of worry and fear mingled in his eyes and made him look frantic.

Conner drank the potion in one large gulp, and before he had even taken the jar away from his lips, a new feeling swept over his senses. He could no longer feel the snakebite. In fact, he was having trouble feeling anything at all. He sprawled out helplessly as his head began spinning. He fought to hang on to consciousness, but the potion that coursed through him was far too strong. His vision became blotchy; the trees and sky bent as if he were viewing them through a fish bowl. He couldn't fight the power of the potion any longer.

He blacked out.

CHAPTER 15

Salix

Conner came to almost as suddenly as he'd blacked out. He sat up and the most intense and indescribable feeling followed. He felt himself leaving his own body. Looking down, he could see himself lying there — Medwin pouring over him; Zelimir a short distance away, looking worried.

"Conner — *Conner!*" Medwin shook his lifeless body. It flailed around pathetically. "*Conner!*" he yelled again as he put a finger to his neck.

"Can you feel a pulse?" Zelimir asked, his tone riddled with concern.

"He has a pulse," Medwin said, calming down instantly. "But it's weak… We were wrong about which potion was which," he muttered, still gazing down at Conner's limp form, as if Conner's unconscious mind could hear him. He glanced up at Zelimir. "Conner and I assumed that the darker blue potion was the reviver, but it obviously wasn't. We need to get the actual reviver in him right away."

"Medwin… Zelimir…" Conner yelled, as Medwin reached in his pack to grab the reviving potion. They didn't hear him. He'd been sure this would be the case, but he figured it was worth a try anyway. It pained him to look on helplessly as Medwin and Zelimir did all they could to help save him.

He surveyed himself, at least the part of him that was aware of what was going on. His body was translucent, giving off a radiant golden glow. He wondered briefly if he was experiencing what it felt like to be dead, but quickly reminded himself that Medwin had just said he still had a pulse. 'So if I'm not dead — what is happening to me?' he pondered.

'Conner…'

A cool female voice that felt oddly familiar addressed him. He whipped around in a full circle, but saw no one.

'Conner, it is I, Salix…'

With a sudden shock, he understood who was speaking to him. It was the willow tree, and she was speaking within his mind.

'I hear you, Salix,' he said in response. The second he acknowledged her, something invisible tugged him around his mid-section. The next thing he knew, he was hurtling involuntarily across the island.

A cliff was up ahead. He tried his hardest to change course, but it was no use. He threw his extremities out in front of him and braced for impact as he barreled straight toward the jagged cliff-side. His attempt to protect himself turned out to be unnecessary, though. He glided directly through the cliff-face and entered a cavernous recess within the enormous slab of rock.

Stalactites clung determinedly to the roof of the vast cave, for fear of crashing down upon the stalagmite-crowded floor. Veins of minerals ran through the ridged exterior walls, shimmering and sparkling in the golden light that radiated from Conner. Lava shafts branched at random from the main portion of the cave the farther he traveled through it. He flew out the opposite side of the cliff to find that he was directly over the ocean.

Within seconds, he had passed the *Colossus*; it was at that point that he was truly able to appreciate how fast he must be traveling. He knew that the huge warship was at least a half-mile from shore.

He looked down. His reflection bounced back at him off the glistening surface of the water, and he was able to take in the full extent of what he looked like. It was more profound than he could fathom. Just as it was frightening, it was beautiful, and just as it was unbelievable, it was undeniable. He was no longer clothed in his regular jeans and t-shirt. Instead, it looked as if his skin was made of some inexplicable transparent material, wrapped tightly around pure energy. His eyes, nostrils, and gaping mouth blazed a bright white.

The thick belt of trees that bordered the Forsaken Desert drew ever closer as he approached the southern coast of Rohwen. Fear didn't grip him as he zipped into the cluster of trees. He already knew he would pass through them as if he were a ghost. He thought for a second and concluded that he *was* a ghost, just at the moment.

An intense feeling of freedom and joy filled him the farther he traveled, hovering a few feet above the ground.

He was flying over the desert now. Little patches of cacti spackled cascading hill after cascading hill of sand. He remembered the Pons and hoped he would catch a glimpse of them. To his delight, the path he was on journeyed right by the ever-cycling habitats.

As he passed the anomalies, he wished he could have slowed down enough to appreciate their immense beauty and splendor just a little longer. In the time it took him to fly by he was only able to watch as one of them transformed from winter into spring, while another melted from summer to fall, all of its tree's leaves turning a shade of fiery red.

In the hazy distance, towering tree-sized lilies came into view. Minutes later, he was among them as he flew through Botanica. He stuck his hand out to touch one of their massive petals, and watched as his fingers bent over it like a projection.

The intensity of the experience he was having caused him to break into uncontrollable laughter as he entered Willow Grove and landed near Salix. A smile remained upon his face as he surveyed the beautiful grove, its stunning arrangement of wildflowers still as breathtaking as he remembered. As he stepped into the willow tree's shrouding branches, the sight that met his eyes caused him to gasp.

The consciousness of Salix had a form. She floated elegantly within the core of the tree's extremely aged trunk, which appeared to be made of glass, its knots and abrasions engraved artistically into the surface. There was minimal definition to the outline of Salix's body, but you could tell she was a woman. Her long hair, like golden strands of silk, caressed her shoulders and continued to fall until it melded into the wisps of energy that made up her being. Her face was angelic: caring, yet powerful. Young, yet wise. Piercing, yet nonabrasive.

She emitted a dazzling, golden light very similar to that of the light emanating from Conner, and between the two of them, they gave the grass under the tree's branches a cheerful look, as if it were picking up the colors of a beaming sunset.

"Welcome, Conner," Salix said gently, raising her hands in a warm gesture. To Conner's surprise, she didn't speak within his head. Instead, her voice reverberated entrancingly off the surrounding landscape. "I am sure you have many questions," she continued lightly, "but before I grant you the chance to question me, I would like to say a few things."

Conner gave her an understanding nod.

"I am very pleased to admit that you are becoming more than the people of Rohwen could have ever hoped, in character and skill…"

Such a compliment caused Conner to shift his feet uncomfortably.

Salix smiled at his modesty before she went on. "It takes a great deal of courage to do what you have thus far. You have faced the unknown… You have battled grotesque beings… You have even confronted Vellix…

"Your skills have improved vastly since you first arrived here, but I am afraid I must ask more of you. Vivek did not to tell you all he knew of Vellix's true power — mind you, even he was not aware of the full extent. I admit, I also had the chance to inform you. I hope you realize that it was not my intention to keep Vellix's abilities from you. To be overwhelmed by your task would have been a detriment to your accomplishing it. Preserving confidence was essential. Even though you stood no chance of defeating your enemy, you came out alive. You heeded my words of wisdom, and in doing so, befriended the little hunchback, Moxie…" Salix smiled upon Conner, and he could feel the warmth of it filling him.

"Moxie is now *one* of the reasons you are still alive. But there is another reason, a more defining reason for your survival. It is important you know that had you tried to kill Vellix in a physical fight, you would be dead. Disabling the functionality of his brain was the only thing that could have stopped him from killing you. So you see… your decision to let him live a life of suffering, a life in which he could reflect upon his own cruelty, was a decision of true intelligence. Rather than take his life, you hoped to extend it with a punishment worthy of his crimes. However, I am afraid that in the case of Vellix, death is the only option. In the end, you must destroy him." She ended definitively, allowing her words time to sink in — knowing the incredible weight of them.

While Conner comprehended what she had said, she continued. "Now, I welcome you to question me." She gazed into Conner's white blazing eyes, waiting for his first question with a polite and attentive expression.

Conner mulled a few different questions over in his mind. Finally, he asked, "Well, first off, am I dreaming all of this? Because I can't see how else this could be happening right now."

Salix chuckled lightly. "No, Conner, you are not dreaming. That potion that Medwin gave you was created by Vivek for the sole purpose of being able to communicate with me."

Conner didn't reply. Instead, he surveyed himself again — obviously more intrigued than ever by his appearance. Confirmation that he wasn't dreaming made the intensity of the experience that much more astounding.

Salix noticed Conner's state of speechlessness. "Once Vivek learned of me from the scrolls," she said to move the conversation forward, "he was determined to meet me. However, he was afraid to leave Rhona, for the fear that Vellix would confront and destroy him before he could inform you of your destiny. So he developed a potion that would induce an out-of-body experience in order to enter my plane of existence. Vivek was an extremely brilliant man to develop such a substance. I am not sure how many others could have."

"Vivek was *definitely* brilliant," Conner agreed, pondering the other questions he wanted to ask. There were so many that he barely knew where to start. One question in particular insisted on flashing across his mind, so he decided he might as well ask it first. "How do you know those details about my fight with Vellix?"

Salix gave him an approving smile. 'Ah, Conner, you don't fail to amaze me. Instead of asking a self-empowering question, you ask the one question that requires me to reveal more of myself than I had planned to. The answer is that *I* am every tree in Rohwen. For that reason, I am able to see and hear life from the perspective of any one of them. In the instance of your duel with Vellix — I learned of it from your conversation with Medwin as you descended Mt. Cirrus."

For a moment, all Conner could do was gawk at Salix. The idea that she could experience the world around her from the viewpoint of every tree in Rohwen staggered him; then a new question materialized in the front of his mind, a question that never would have come to him, had he not asked his last. His heart started to race. "Do you know where the missing scroll is?" he asked, sweat building up in his palms.

Salix smiled again. "…Yes…"

Conner's heart was pounding now. "…And … will you tell me where I can find it?"

Salix nodded. "It is hidden somewhere within the city of its writer."

"Hylan, you mean?" Conner asked hastily. "It's hidden in the city of Hylan?"

"…Yes…" Salix's eyes grinned with amusement as Conner's expression became vacant and perplexed.

"But how is that possible?" he mused. "I mean … the city is gone … isn't it? It was destroyed by a huge tidal wave."

"True — most of the city was destroyed," Salix replied coolly. "However, much of its western border was merely flooded and buried by rubble. Not completely demolished as the rest was."

"So, what you're saying," Conner began, speaking slowly, "is that part of Hylan is still standing?"

"Indeed. But it is buried deep beneath the surface at this point, a ruin of its former glory."

"If it's buried, how am I going to find it?" Conner probed, frowning in thought. "Is there some kind of landmark or something? Something that will help guide me to the right spot?"

Salix pointed in a direction due east of Willow Grove. "The city was built no more than ten miles west of the eastern coastline, and the Vian River, a tributary of the Brio River, runs near its southern border,"

Conner nodded, and started muttering to himself. "If the scroll is hidden in Hylan ... then that means all those years Vivek was searching Rhona were pointless." A terrible feeling of sorrow rose up in his chest and clenched his lungs tightly. Vivek had wasted all that time searching for the scroll in the wrong place. The picture in his head of the poor old man struggling to discover something that was hundreds of miles away made him feel miserable. He bowed his head somberly. Even the golden glow glistening off the blades of grass around him were unable to warm his heart.

Salix broke the pained silence, speaking in a soft, gentle tone. "There is a reason that he never knew the true location of the scroll…"

Conner looked back up at her. "What do you mean, there's a reason?"

"When I learned that he was searching for the scroll, and that he thought it was on Rhona, I allowed him to believe that he was correct."

"Why would you do that?" Conner asked, feeling the grief clutching his chest release its grip as it transformed into confusion toward the great willow tree. "Why didn't you tell him where to find it?" he flared up, feeling himself grow hot with anger.

"Isn't the answer obvious?" Salix asked, remaining cool and composed.

Conner stared at her, curiosity now battling his anger.

"No…?" she queried. "Well then, allow me to explain… I didn't tell him where to find the scroll because it wasn't his destiny to find it. Had he gone looking for it, do you think he would have been on Rhona to tell you of your own destiny when you arrived?" Salix cocked her head ever so slightly to one side and awaited his answer.

"Well, no … I guess not," Conner said.

"Of course not!" Salix boomed as the wisps of energy that formed her body raged up into blinding flames.

Conner took a few quick steps back, looking truly afraid.

Salix became shameful. The flames died away and she regained her previous, angelic form. She beckoned Conner back toward her. "I am sorry," she said, her tone gentle once more.

Conner shrugged off the alarming moment and stepped forward.

"As I was saying…" Salix carried on. "Of course Vivek wouldn't have been there. He would have been dead because had he found the scroll, he would have tried to use the added skill he had obtained from it to defeat Vellix. The problem was that he was never capable of becoming a true match for Vellix. It is *you* who needs to learn the knowledge held in the words of that scroll, Conner; *you* who is capable of gaining the skill necessary to defeat Vellix."

Conner was speechless. It wasn't that this information was new to him — it was the passion with which Salix had spoken. Hearing her speak with such conviction made him feel empowered. It was the feeling of empowerment that only comes when those you respect the most place their faith in you.

"I know the burden is heavy, Conner," Salix said supportively. "It wasn't your choice to become Rohwen's savior, and yet you have taken on the responsibility, not only proudly, but passionately."

"I wouldn't have it any other way," Conner said firmly. "I love Rohwen!" The smiling faces of Medwin, Zelimir, Moxie, Lenny, and Ammin swam across his mind. "And its people!" he added. They had all become closer to him than anyone he'd ever known. "I would die for them!"

"And that, Conner, is why you are the one who is standing before me now. That is why you are the one I predicted to be this land's savior two thousand years ago… Because you have something special. You have the key elements of a true hero: selflessness, love, friendship, passion, integrity, and courage. It is only with those components that you could have become the one destined to defeat Vellix.

"Your selflessness allows you to put your life on the line for what you believe in. Your love allows you to see the world and those within it in the way it should be seen. Your friendship allows you to rely on others, rather than take on your enemy singlehandedly. Your passion allows you to drive forward and never give up. Your integrity allows you to admit when you have made a mistake and, therefore, enables you to rectify it. And your courage allows you to face the daunting evil that has overshadowed Rohwen for centuries." Salix's intense white eyes pierced Conner to his core.

He didn't have a response for the personal praise she had given him, but he felt determined to live up to it. His mind worked frantically to think up some form of response, a decent thank you at the very least. But when he spoke, his words came out stumbling over one another.

Salix raised a hand to silence him. "There is no need for you to thank me. I was merely voicing the truth…

"...Now, I am afraid it is time that I bid you farewell. Your friend, Medwin, gave you a reviving potion, and in just a moment, you and your body will be re-united. I leave you with these words: do not let the knowledge held within the last scroll warp your mind as it has Vellix's..."

* * *

Conner coughed violently. He opened his eyes. The blurred outline of Medwin came into focus.

"Conner!" he exclaimed. "Thank goodness you're alright! For a minute there... Well, I wasn't sure if you were going to make it," he finished lamely, looking much paler than normal.

Zelimir inched forward. "Are you okay? How do you feel?"

"I'm fine," Conner replied casually.

"Those revivers really do the trick," said Medwin, who seemed to be gaining some of his color back now. "That must have been some kind of powerful poison that you took."

"No, it wasn't poison at all," Conner said. "It was some kind of — well — I can't think of a word to describe it... But it just gave me the most incredible experience of my life!"

"What do you mean?" Zelimir asked skeptically. "You've been lying here the whole time."

"My body has, yeah. But I haven't been."

Medwin and Zelimir exchanged concerned looks.

Conner noticed this and decided he had better do a more efficient job of explaining himself before they deemed him insane. Unfortunately, every way he thought of telling them sounded completely insane in itself. Eventually, he gave up on trying to make any sense of it and said, "Look, I just had an out-of-body experience."

Alarm was now apparent in Medwin and Zelimir's expressions.

Conner fought down the frustration he was starting to feel toward them for not believing him, for not understanding that he wasn't just confused in the aftermath of drinking the unknown potion. He looked at them pointedly, hoping his eyes would tell a story, not only of his sanity, but of his honesty as well.

"Go on," Medwin said, understanding the look Conner was giving him.

Conner exhaled a breath of gratitude toward Medwin and started to explain. "That potion" — he pointed at the empty jar lying next to Medwin — "was created by Vivek for the purpose of visiting Salix's plane of existence…"

Zelimir gazed at him quizzically. "Salix?"

"Salix is the name of the weeping willow tree we visited," Conner said quickly to bring the wolf up-to-date. Then he dove back into his explanation. Medwin and Zelimir listened intently as he told them of his journey across Rohwen, both of them with similar looks of wonder in their eyes when he attempted to describe what his body had looked like.

Medwin brought up what Conner thought was a very interesting point. He wondered if everyone would have a golden glow like Conner's had been, or if different people emanated different colors. There was, of course, no way of finding out the answer, but it was still a fascinating subject for speculation.

Zelimir seemed more interested to learn of Conner and Salix's conversation. So Conner launched into a detailed explanation of his discussion with the great willow tree. He skipped over the part where Salix had praised him for having the traits of a hero because he felt his face starting to burn, but other than that, he told them everything.

Medwin felt sympathy for Vivek, just as Conner had when he found out that the weathered old man spent all those years seeking the missing scroll in the entirely wrong location.

Learning that Salix was able to view Rohwen from the perspective of any of its trees intrigued both Medwin and Zelimir. They wondered if she was constantly within every tree, or if she chose the trees in which she would reside at her own discretion.

When Conner came to the end of his story, the three of them went completely silent. They stared off in different directions, contemplating what came next.

There was a thought that Conner couldn't shake. 'Now I have been warned by Lolani *and* Salix about the information that lies within the last scroll. What about *that* scroll could possibly warp my mind in the way Vellix's has been?'

CHAPTER 16

Lolani's Flight

A shrill crashing sound broke the silent air, causing Lolani to jerk her head up from a dead sleep. She surveyed the room and realized that Inoke had dropped his medicine jars to the ground. The impact had caused them to shatter, leaving their contents splattered in different colored puddles across the floor. A large plume of dust had swelled like a mushroom cloud from the point of impact, and was now seeking its escape from the hut through the numerous cracks in its bark coverings.

Inoke stared at the ground in sheer disbelief of his misfortune before turning his attention to the red-tailed hawk perched some four feet above his head. "That was the last of your treatments, Lolani," he said ruefully. "It will take me at least three days to brew fresh batches." Inoke gave Lolani a sympathetic glance.

"I don't *have* three days, Inoke," Lolani said urgently. She tested her right wing to see how much dexterity had returned. Although simple movements still caused her to wince with pain, it felt good enough for flight. She inspected the still very tender puncture wounds that stretched across her breast and torso. The new flesh scarring over the wounds appeared to have healed enough. She made up her mind. "I'm leaving."

"In your condition?" Inoke tittered, as though the very thought was laughable.

"I don't have a choice," Lolani snapped, her face straining as she attempted to conceal the pain that shouting caused her wounds. "Medwin *needs* to know that his warrior captains have been captured!"

Inoke's face fell into a grim frown. "I know that you want this information to reach Medwin as quickly as possible" — Inoke made an understanding gesture — "but if you attempt to find him now... Well, I would give you about a ten-percent chance of survival..."

"I know my own strength, Inoke," Lolani said dismissively. "I respect your knowledge, and I appreciate your concern, but I will decide when I am fit for flight."

Inoke gave the hawk a defeated nod.

Lolani continued. "I will be forever grateful to you, not only for healing me, but for your kindness as well. Medwin was wise to choose you as acting chief in his absence."

A grin flashed across Inoke's face as he walked across his hut, grabbed a small jar and a shallow tray, and returned to Lolani. "If you must go, at least take this," he said, pouring the jar's tea-green innards into the tray.

Lolani bent down over the tray full of pale green liquid and drank.

"This supplement will hopefully prevent your wounds from worsening as you overexert them. I can't guarantee you anything of course. You intend to fly to Rhona, no doubt."

"I do."

"That is a very long journey…"

"I am quite aware of the distance, having lived there myself."

Inoke was silent, but he looked as if he was choking on a retort.

"Do I have your assurances that you are prepared to act when the time comes?" Lolani asked, ignoring Inoke's obvious frustration with her for not heeding his wise words.

"Of course," Inoke said indignantly. "That is *if* the time comes."

"It *is* coming!" Lolani warned him. "I just don't know how soon. We must prepare now!"

"I wish we still had the captains to lead us into battle," Inoke admitted as the nervous crease in his brow wrinkled a bit further. "It was a strange move capturing the captains and not laying as much as a finger on the rest of the tribe. It doesn't make any sense. What good would they be to Vellix? They would rather die than fight in his name."

Lolani's eyes closed and her features screwed up, as if she was at battle with her own thoughts. "…You do know" she began reluctantly, "that Vellix has been using cognition to experiment on humans for hundreds of years … right?"

Inoke didn't reply, or make eye contact with Lolani. Instead, he stared at the corner of the room, displaying an expression that invited Lolani to continue speaking.

"I expect he has perfected the art by now, and it pains me to say this, but… what better human specimen can you think of to use as an elite soldier than a Satria warrior captain?"

Inoke's fists tightened and his face twisted with rage, his fury clearly far beyond words.

"Why do you think I must leave now? I have to go to Medwin. He needs to know what is going on; rally as many of our allies as possible. As it stands, I fear that the Satria will be vastly overpowered."

"It would be nice if we knew who our allies were at this point," said Inoke, breathing deeply to try and keep calm. "I feel that Vellix's deception has closed its grip over all of Rohwen."

"I agree. There are many who serve him hidden amongst us. The time is coming when those who are loyal to virtue and honor will have to stand up and fight to strike down the evil that threatens our land with a vengeful blow."

"Your words are powerful, Lolani. If only there were more with your passion."

"There are more than you think, Inoke. They have just allowed their passion to become dormant over years of oppression caused by a power they had no hope of standing against. There is hope now, and that hope will rekindle the flames in many men's hearts."

Inoke gave the hawk an inspired stare.

"Tell Luka goodbye for me," Lolani said. Inoke nodded silently as she took flight, leaving his hut behind her.

* * *

Lolani beat her wings vigorously as she took flight over the landscape. She searched frantically for a helpful wind current. The constant flexing of her muscles had already started to re-open the wounds across her breast and torso.

By the time she found a current, her injured wing ached, and her puncture wounds were moist with fresh blood. Relief swept over her the instant she was able to keep her wings at full stretch and ride the heavy gusts of wind from the north. The cool air rushed through her feathers and soothed her aggravated gashes.

The way in which Inoke had laughed at the idea of her attempting to make the journey before completing her treatments pestered her mind. For a second she doubted herself and contemplated the idea of returning to finish her therapy, but the drive of pride and purpose pushed her onward. She couldn't stand by and let the evil events that she was sure were taking place go unchallenged. The longer Vellix had to organize his offense, the weaker theirs would become. It wasn't unlike Vellix to create discontent among people through lies and deceit. If Vellix had decided it was time to act, then the more time he had to spread his deception across Rohwen, the harder it would be to form an army strong enough to challenge him.

A thread of brilliant shimmers beaming off the west fork of the Brio River contracted Lolani's pupils for a brief second; the landscape below blurred out of focus, becoming nothing more than a canvas of bluish-green bubbles. Dark green dots regained lines of detail and turned back into trees and bushes as her vision returned. Soon she was able to make out the various shades of jade, olive, emerald, and lime that made up the plains of Mesala.

The wind current she had found turned out to be on a perfect course as it thrust her out over the ocean, took a slight southeastern bend, and shot her straight for Rhona.

It didn't take long before she was within visual range of the island. Her stomach twisted nauseatingly when it became apparent that the *Colossus* wasn't anchored anywhere off shore. Perceptibly this meant that Medwin was no longer on Rhona, but she decided to scan the island anyway, just to be sure. Ammin could have left, on the pretense that he would return at a later time.

After a few passes of the island, during which she saw no sign of the young chief, a frantic feeling of anxiety began to consume her. Medwin could be anywhere at this point. She decided the best thing to do now would be to head back for Beach Bay. At least she would have a chance of finding Ammin there. Hopefully he would be able to point her in Medwin's direction.

Pain shot abruptly through her right wing as she made a directional change that forced her to fight against the same wind current she'd been riding. As she glanced instinctually at the source of pain, a small, opaque speck sitting amidst the vast sparkling ocean caught her eye. Something in Lolani's gut told her that this dot was *the Colossus*. She wasn't sure why, but for some reason her instincts were urging her to investigate. She made a sharp eastern turn and proceeded in the direction of the dot, ignoring the pain that she knew would only get much worse.

Fatigue forced its dominance over her body, sucking her muscles dry of all vitality. She could feel her wounds tearing fractionally from the inside out with each tedious stroke of her powerful wings. And with each stroke, she knew that the scarcely healed bones in her right wing were on the verge of snapping once more.

Just when it seemed that she had reached her threshold for pain, the three towering masts of *the Colossus* became recognizable. She *had* been right, and that knowledge gave her the determination and strength to push on.

* * *

"Medwin, look, I think that might be Lolani!" Conner yelled, pointing enthusiastically at an approaching spot of black in the sky.

Medwin looked up excitedly, his eyes scanning the heavens for a glimpse of his hawk. "Oh yeah, I see," he said, cupping a hand over his eyes to block out the radiant sun. "Yeah, I think that's her," he concluded as the black fleck gained a more distinct shape.

Conner shaded his eyes from the sun as well. "That is definitely her," he agreed as Medwin pulled a leather glove out of his pack that Conner hadn't ever seen. "When did you — Did you make —"

Medwin grinned. "Yeah, I made it at the same time that I made your vambrace," he said. "I figured it would be a whole lot better than wrapping the strap of my pack around my arm."

Conner laughed appreciatively.

Lolani was close now. Medwin put on the glove and held out his arm to allow her a place to land. Not but a second later, he realized she was coming in far too fast to land on him. He stepped out of her way as she attempted to throw her feet out and grip the ship's railing.

Lolani was so delirious from overexertion and torturous levels of pain that her attempt to land was a feeble one. Her legs slammed into the ship-rail and sent her toppling brutally to the deck.

Medwin ran to her, gasping in disgust when he saw the horrible state she was in: puncture wounds peppering her body and bleeding profusely, her right wing sticking out at a disturbing angle.

He bent down and carefully scooped up the hawk before cradling her. "She's hurt *really* bad!" Medwin cried. "Conner, reach into my pack and get out the healing potion. I only had to use half of it on Moxie." He made an instinctual head gesture in the direction of the little hunchback.

Moxie shifted awkwardly at the sound of his name. He was standing next to Zelimir, a short distance away. His already deformed face creased up with pity for the badly-injured hawk, but otherwise he looked as good as new.

Conner reached into the pack that hung at Medwin's side. The sounds of glass clanking together rang out as he searched for the correct potion.

Moments later, his hand emerged, clutching a half-full jar of a green, goopy substance.

"Here," Medwin said, pointing out a few of the feather-covered wounds across Lolani's chest. "Make sure you apply some through there as well."

Conner rubbed a healthy amount of the potion over Lolani's puncture wounds; then he tried to shift her wing, hoping to locate the broken bones. Lolani screeched horrifically in pain. Conner let go of her wing quickly, his face bearing a look of the deepest pity.

Ammin and Lenny, who had been watching from a few feet away with the rest of the crew, edged forward.

"I recognize this hawk," Ammin said as he came to a halt at Medwin's side. His face wrinkled up as if he had smelled something awful the longer he took in the sight of Lolani's mangled body. "She was with Vivek when I met him..."

Conner found Ammin's disgusted reaction strange, considering the acts of violence he had seen the captain achieve. He figured Ammin would be hardened to any and all disturbing visions imaginable.

"Yes," Medwin replied, "she was Vivek's." He gazed down at the hawk, still cradled in his arms. "I am her owner now. Her name is Lolani… Conner, why don't you just try to get some of the potion on her wing without moving it?"

"Right…" Conner dipped two fingers into the healing potion and shoveled some out. Trying to find the best angle to approach the wing quickly became a problem. He was extremely wary of hurting Lolani; every time he got within an inch of it, he retracted his hand swiftly, as if expecting her to screech out in pain again.

Finally, after Lenny said, "Bloody 'ell, mate, yeh wan' me ter do it?" he managed to apply the potion.

Zelimir stepped forward; Moxie inched along behind him. "What do you think has happened to her?" asked the wolf, glancing at Lolani with a grimace.

To everyone's surprise, Lolani answered Zelimir's question herself. "An owl … altered by Vellix… Incredibly strong…" Her voice was pitiful and frail, but the words she spoke were still distinguishable.

"Like the one I saw you fight?" Medwin asked, using a caring voice that would let Lolani know he wasn't pushing her to answer too quickly.

Lolani gazed at him blearily. "Yes… Only much stronger… I was no match for her…"

"So, what happened, exactly?" Conner asked, using the same caring tone that Medwin had. "I mean, did she attack you, or…?"

"No, I attacked her… I wanted information."

Conner could tell that the healing potion was already doing its job; Lolani's voice had returned to a shadow of her commanding tone.

"Medwin" — Lolani spoke with a sudden urgency that hadn't been there moments ago — "your warrior captains, they have been captured!"

"What?" Medwin's face flushed with anger.

Conner gawked at Lolani in disbelief. He had seen what the warrior captains were capable of in battle and could hardly believe anything would be able to overpower them.

"Do you know who is responsible?" Medwin asked, doing his best to remain calm.

"No." Lolani shook her head petulantly. "That is why I wanted to question the owl. I have made my own deductions, though, and I can only think of one creature with the cunning and strength to accomplish such a feat…" Lolani trailed off, allowing Medwin to make his own deductions.

"The Bazza," Medwin uttered darkly; the red flush of anger in his skin drained, leaving him pale.

"The Bazza?" Conner asked with a note of morbid curiosity.

"You've seen them," Medwin said, his tone dark. He glanced up at Conner with one of the bleakest looks Conner had ever seen etched onto his face. "They were the grey-skinned savages wielding a saber in each hand. You saw them in battle."

The veins in Ammin's forehead throbbed with rage as he heard the description of Captain Bellamy's killers.

Conner remembered them distinctly. He remembered the disturbing thought he'd had when he saw them — that the creatures looked like they could have been Satria at some point. Now, with his added knowledge of Vellix's abilities, he was almost certain he'd been right.

He looked over at Medwin and decided that this concept was probably far too disturbing for him to withstand. He wasn't disregarding the idea that Medwin may already be thinking the same thing he was; he just didn't want to be the one to bring it up if he wasn't.

Ammin turned to Medwin. "If your mission is going to take you on a path that leads to these 'Bazza' you can count me and my crew in!" he exclaimed, looking as though he was ready to rip heads off. "I want nothing more than to kill the lot of them!"

The crew threw their fists, swords, and pistols into the air and roared their approval of some good action.

Dale turned to Landon, punched him in the shoulder, and yelled, "Told yeh we'd see some combat 'afore too long with this lot around!" He pointed shamelessly in the direction of Conner and his companions.

Conner glanced at Lenny. To his surprise, the prospect of a good fight hadn't caused him to cheer with the rest of his crew. Instead, he wandered glumly in the direction of the ship's bow.

Feeling interested and concerned, Conner followed him.

Lenny leaned his elbows against the ships railing and gazed out to sea.

"Lenny?" Conner began as he approached the young sailor. "Are you okay?"

"What are yeh on abou'— *am I okay?*" Lenny huffed and clicked his tongue, as to let Conner know he had no patience for such foolish questions.

Conner felt this reaction was far too extravagant for such a simple question. To him it was the telling sign that something *was* actually wrong. "Sorry," he went on, now determined to pry at Lenny until he knew what was bothering him. "I couldn't help but notice that you don't seem yourself."

Lenny didn't reply. Instead, he continued to stare out at the ocean. Finally, he said, "Blimey, Conner… You *do* pay attention ter wha's goin' on, don' yeh? Ammin's always sayin' 'ow 'e thinks yer brigh' fer yer age… Alrigh', if yeh wan' ter *know* wha's botherin' me…" Lenny paused for a moment; then he burst abruptly into his explanation, pouring out more emotion than Conner would have thought possible. "*I miss Bellamy! Bloody good man 'e was! Closes' thing ter a real father I ever bleedin' 'ad! An' — an' 'e's gone forever!*"

Conner watched sadly as tears welled up in Lenny's fixed, dark eyes. He knew that for Lenny to shed a tear must mean that Bellamy had been truly significant to him.

"Took me in, see?" Lenny continued, wiping his eyes and stabilizing his voice. "I never knew me parents. I fig'r I ain' the only one wha's 'ad ter fend fer themself growin' up in Beach Bay, like… Bu', anyway, Bellamy took a likin' ter me, see? Le' me join 'is crew when I was only ten. I jus' always though' 'e'd be — yeh know — be 'round ter ... ter…"

"To make sure you were okay," Conner said, finishing the part of Lenny's sentence that he knew would be too self-revealing of the young sailor's weakness for him to finish himself.

"Summat like tha', yeah…" Lenny bucked himself up and wiped his nose. "Thanks fer the talk, Conner. Means alo' ter me, tha' does." He clapped Conner on the back, walked back toward the crowd of sailors, who were still cheering as Ammin pumped them up for a fight, and joined in with their jeers and yells.

As he watched Lenny draw his pistol and fire a shot at the sky for the hell of it, Conner got the distinct impression that he had just witnessed Lenny's last display of raw emotion for years to come.

He stood there, smiling to himself because he'd gotten a glimpse into what he would deem the 'untouchable' part of Lenny's personality. A glimpse of the hardened sailor that proved he was human like everyone else.

As Conner continued to watch Lenny, some of the words he had spoken really sank in. 'I never knew me parents… I fig'r I ain' the only one wha's 'ad ter fend fer themself…' As those words rang through his head, he gained a whole new level of respect for the young sailor. Lenny had grown up with no parents. He'd never known the eternal love of a mother, or the pillar of strength that is a father. And yet, he still loved life enough to smile. It was inspiring.

Conner thought back to how furious he had been with his parents for making him move to Montana. It made him sick with disgust. 'How stupid and selfish can one person be?' he thought, thoroughly ashamed of himself. 'At least I *have* parents that love and care for me.' No sooner than this thought had crossed his mind, he wished it hadn't. It made him think realistically. By the time he got home — if he got home — he would have been gone for so long that his parents would be worried sick.

"Conner, what's up?"

Medwin had come to see what he was doing standing by himself, looking troubled. "Oh, hey, Medwin," he replied. "Nothing much... I was just thinking about how worried my parents are going to be by the time I get home. I mean, I know it hasn't been that long in my world yet," he added quickly. "But I still feel bad. Especially for my mom — she's a worrywart."

"I know how you feel, Conner," Medwin said, a look of understanding in his eyes as they wandered slowly toward the ship's deck.

The reality of how much worse Medwin's situation was hit Conner in the face like a brick. Not only had Medwin's mother been worrying about her son's safe return for weeks now, his father would never be able to worry about him again. He was dead.

Conner decided to leave the conversation where it was. Medwin didn't appear all that keen on continuing it, and he agreed with his outlook. There was no point in digging up all these emotions. They had a job to do, and nothing was going to change that.

CHAPTER 17

A New Place to Belong

Hours passed on as the sun melted slowly into the ocean, revealing its most vibrant shades of orange just before it vanished entirely. The eternal darkness of night was born, and with it, a regiment of countless stars that burned bright, twinkling at those who took the time to give them a second glance.

Conner gazed up at the sky appreciatively. A faint lilac mist wisped across the heavens like the trailing shawl of a beautiful goddess. Billions of stars laced within the soft mist shimmered and gleamed, giving the appearance that the shawl had been bestowed with brilliant diamonds.

Moxie stood next to Conner, sharing the amazing vision of the night sky. Conner could only imagine how grateful Moxie must be for moments like these. After all those years trapped within Vellix's holding chamber, things like enjoying a vividly starry sky would be far easier not to take for granted.

The *Colossus* made a northern course change. Within moments, the belt of trees along Rohwen's southern coast began to thin. An ominous, fire-red haze became visible through them. Conner's insides squirmed as he watched dark smoke billow up into the atmosphere. The red glow of fire below flickered across each swelling plume of smoke, illuminating its slow, yet unnerving movements.

Medwin and Zelimir walked absentmindedly over to Conner and Moxie, both of them staring at the massive cloud of smoke with aggrieved expressions.

"What the…" Medwin said, gaping at the shocking scene.

Conner turned to him, a dark look drawn across his face. "Vellix has made his fist move."

"And we have not yet even found Hylan," Zelimir exclaimed, as if he could hardly believe they could be so unlucky, "much less the scroll."

"I can't believe this. What are we going to do?" Conner asked, allowing himself to enter a state of panic. "I have to find the scroll before I can face Vellix! If I don't improve my cognition" — he balled his hands into tight fists — "I won't even be a match for him!"

Moxie looked at his three friends oddly. "How do you know Vellix started the fire? I've seen many fires that weren't started by Vellix."

Conner, Medwin, and Zelimir glanced around at one another.

"You have a good point, Moxie," Conner admitted freely.

"Indeed he does," Zelimir agreed.

"Let's just stay focused on finding Hylan," Medwin said wisely, looking at each of his companions in turn; they all made gestures of agreement. "I think we should still assume that Vellix is at work once more, though. We need to stay alert."

Conner waited a moment to make sure Medwin was finished before he chimed in with a response. “Yeah, we really can’t do anything to stop Vellix at the moment. All we can do is stick to the plan and —”

“Get *off! Let me go!*”

“You’ll shut yer mouth if you know wha’s good fer yeh!” Landon spat as he fought to drag a young girl up the stairs from the hold to the main deck. “Dale, ge’ the cap’n over ‘ere!”

As Dale ran toward Ammin’s quarters, Conner moved in for a closer look at what was going on.

Landon finally managed to get the girl up on deck, but not before suffering numerous scratches and a severe head-butt to the eye, which swelled like a balloon.

Her ratty brown hair flailed wildly as she expended every last drop of energy she had in a frantic attempt to escape Landon’s grip.

“What’s going on?” Ammin asked as he arrived on the scene, Lenny stumbling up behind him. Conner had the distinct impression that Lenny had been drinking rather heavily.

“Who are you and what are you doing on my ship?” Ammin interrogated, crossing his arms to wait for an answer.

The girl spat on Ammin’s face in reply. Landon raised a hand to strike her for this act of insolence.

Ammin grabbed his hand out of the air and twisted it hard. “If you ever hit a woman on my ship, I won’t hesitate to keel hall you!” Ammin pierced Landon’s eyes with the same ferocity he had laid upon Louie and Felix. “Do you understand me, Landon?”

"Aye, Cap'n," Landon replied through a grimace, knowing he'd been overpowered.

Ammin released him and faced the girl. "What are you doing on my ship?" he asked again, an implicit warning in his tone.

The girl didn't spit in his face this time, but she didn't reply either. Her chest rose and fell heavily as she stood there quietly, trying to regain the breath she'd lost struggling against Landon.

"Cap'n, she was armed with this," said Dale, handing Ammin a sheathed sword. "Nearly bloody killed Skylar with it, she did," he added, shooting the girl a withered glare.

Ammin's face hardened. "You attempted to kill one of my men?" He waited for an answer, but got none. "If you don't start answering my questions, I'm afraid I will have no choice but to throw you in the brig. At least until we decide what to do with you." Ammin's brow creased with frustration. "What are you doing on my —"

"I'm here to kill all of you bastards!" she roared, her voice oozing with hatred.

The crew erupted with mock laughter. They obviously thought the idea of this young girl being able to kill them all was completely absurd.

Unlike his crew, Ammin looked upon the girl miserably, his eyes shimmering with remorse. "What is your name?" he asked her, replacing his abrasive tone with a soft, gentle one — his crew looked at him disbelievingly, as if they thought their captain had lost his mind.

But if the look the crew was giving him was doubtful, it was nothing compared to the one he was getting from the girl. She didn't seem to be able to comprehend his kindness. She had just said she wanted to kill his entire crew. Her enraged expression melded to one of surprise and curiosity. "My name is Marcella," she answered slowly, eyeing Ammin like some kind of unsolvable mystery.

Conner thought her voice was quite nice now that she wasn't putting as much loathing into it as possible.

Ammin unsheathed her weapon and examined it carefully. "This is a very nice sword." He rotated in in his hands again. "It is a Katana, is it not?"

Marcella nodded.

"I think I know why you've gone to such lengths to try and kill us, Marcella." Ammin gestured toward his crew while studying Marcella's face sympathetically. "And I can't say that I blame you… However, let me assure you that if you were to attempt something so foolish, you would die trying." He handed Marcella her sword and told Landon to release her. Landon looked like his whole world had just been turned upside-down, but he obeyed orders.

Ammin turned to a short, stocky sailor that was standing just behind him. "Quincy."

"Cap'n?"

"Fetch Marcella some bread and water. And some meat as well, if we have any what's still edible."

"Aye, Cap'n," said Quincy, who had enough grey in his hair and beard to know better than to question orders.

"Marcella, would you care to explain why you want to kill us all?"

Marcella fixed Ammin with a gaze of confusion. Words couldn't seem to find their way to her mouth.

Ammin's demeanor was caring, almost fatherly, as he patiently awaited Marcella's response.

Conner had never seen this side of the captain. He wondered if there was some specific reason for his making an exception in this case.

"Should I go ahead and explain why I think so?" Ammin finally said when it became clear that Marcella needed a little push in the right direction.

Marcella remained silent, still gawking at Ammin as if he were something inconceivable.

"Your father was on the ship captained by Cassius, was he not?"

Marcella looked down at the deck, her eyes tearing up as they lingered on nothing in particular.

"And… he was killed," Ammin said hesitantly, pity now drenching his words, "by my crew?"

Tears started to pour from Marcella's vivid green eyes. She covered her face with her hands to hide her misery and started to speak. "Mother's been gone since I was eight… She died in the battle for Edelan. Father was all we had left… He was everything to my brother and I. Always made sure we had what we needed…"

"Your brother?" Ammin asked. "He isn't on board as well, is he?"

Marcella shook her head. "I left him in someone else's care…"

Ammin nodded.

Conner watched Marcella sadly. He knew he was looking at the direct result of what they had done. Here was a girl, around the same age that he was, and she was alone. Her last living parent was dead. All the regretful feelings he'd had after realizing they'd killed men who had families awaiting their safe return came flooding back to the front of his mind tenfold.

Ammin was looking at Marcella pleadingly. "I am sorry," he said. Marcella didn't glance up at him, but it was clear she was listening. "My crew did what we had to do." He opened his mouth as if he were about to say something else, but no words found their way out. His fingers formed a steeple over his lips as his brow wrinkled in thought. "How can I put this?" he said to himself. "…What you have to realize, is that sometimes life requires us to do things we would prefer not to. Sometimes we must make terrible choices… Your father was part of a crew that attacked us." He gestured around at his crew again. "We had no choice but to defend ourselves… It was kill or be killed… I hope you can understand."

The whole crew was dead silent as they waited for Marcella to reply. Sorrowful looks canvased their faces.

Marcella brushed away her tears and nodded at Ammin.

Ammin nodded back. He put his hand on her shoulder. "I know that we will never be able to replace your family. But as long as you are with us, consider yourself a part of ours."

A fresh wave of tears began to flow from Marcella's eyes, and

Conner had a feeling they weren't due solely to grief.

Quincy emerged from down below, one hand carrying a small tray laden with meat and bread, the other clutching a jug of water.

He handed the food and water to Marcella. She took it greedily, and consumed a piece of bread at a ravenous pace. It was as if she hadn't had a bite to eat in her entire life. She couldn't even wait until she'd swallowed one bite before she was cramming a new one in, taking huge gulps of water every time the amount of food in her mouth became too large to swallow.

"*What?*" She said quizzically, looking up and realizing that everyone was watching her like some sort of spectacle. "You'd be hungry too, if you hadn't eaten in four days!"

The whole crew broke into laughter, and the tension around the ship slipped away like the outgoing tide of an ocean.

"She's a real laugh, she is!" James roared.

Lenny was suddenly looking at Marcella as if she were a bar of glistening gold. He stumbled over in her direction, using his shipmates to stabilize himself along the way.

Once within earshot of her, he attempted to say something, but the words were barely decipherable. "Ain' you bou' — mos' — pret' thin'," he stammered drunkenly; then he made the massive mistake of trying to touch her…

Marcella grabbed his arm, flung him to the ground, unsheathed her sword, and pointed it at his throat in one fluent motion. "*Don't — ever — touch — me — again!*" she barked, flinging long strands of dark brown hair away from her face with her free hand.

Lenny didn't move or say a word. Instead, he laid there with his mouth open wide, breathing deeply.

After a moment, Marcella stood up, looking comically around at the crew. "Well, *hell*, he's passed out on me!"

The crew was beside themselves with laughter.

"Bloody knows 'ow ter manage 'erself, don' she?" Dale admitted, still attempting to stifle his laughter.

"Aye!" Landon agreed heartily. "Wouldn' wan' ter 'ave another row with tha' one, I wouldn'!"

Conner couldn't help but laugh with the rest of them. Medwin smacked his shoulder, grinning broadly.

As the commotion died away, members of the crew slowly started heading back to their regular duties.

Marcella stood there beaming all around her. The crew had just accepted her into their ranks. She had found a new family. A new place to belong. A place where people would care about her. And, ironically, she had found it amongst the very men she had wanted nothing more than to kill less than an hour ago.

* * *

Conner woke up the next morning, feeling like he'd barely slept. He lay there, remembering scenes from the previous night. He and the others had stayed up into the early hours of the morning talking to Marcella. She noticed Conner and his companions almost immediately after the whole scene with Lenny had taken place.

Unlike so many others before her, she went straight for them when she noticed that there was a wolf in their midst, saying, "I already knew he was friendly. I saw him sneak off the ship more than once back on Ewaun. He would always return after a few hours, which is not the way a wild wolf would act..."

Zelimir had been grateful for the change of pace, and after all the discrimination he'd dealt with due to his appearance, Conner didn't blame him.

Within a few hours of conversation, Marcella had opened up to them. Conner could still hear her words ringing vividly in his head. 'My mother was a great fighter! I've been training to be just as great ever since the day she died… Father was able to retrieve her Katana during our escape from Edelan, and I practice with it for hours every day. To me, it feels like the best way to show my respect to mother is to be ready to destroy any piece of filth that sides with Vellix.'

He remembered thinking it must take a truly strong-willed person to not only overcome the loss of loved ones, but to allow their memory to burn within you so passionately.

Medwin's features had turned grim as Marcella spoke. Conner knew it was because hearing of Marcella's loss had undoubtedly reminded him of his own. The young chief knew all too well the feeling of hurt and emptiness caused by the loss of a parent. He was able to understand her pain on parallel. Finally, after staring at Marcella sorrowfully for what seemed to be an eternity, he had said, "I am so sorry the Satria were not there to help defend your people when Vellix and his armies arrived..."

To Medwin's surprise, Marcella had seen the situation much more logically than Cassius. Her thought was; there was no way the Satria could have known what was going on, and it was stupid of him to think that they could have predicted such a thing was happening.

Conner remembered the gratefulness in Medwin's expression after he heard this; from that moment on, Medwin recovered his usual demeanor, joining in the conversation animatedly.

Marcella's eagerness to help them in any way she could was avaricious. Conner had never seen more passionate aggression in a person. He smiled reminiscently as he remembered her jumping to her feet, clutching the handle of her sword the instant that she learned of their plan to destroy Vellix and his followers.

Zelimir had chuckled lightly at her for this, and she had responded by shooting him a poisonous look that said he obviously wasn't enthusiastic enough.

If it hadn't been for the unnerving feeling that something terrible must have happened on Rohwen in order to cause such an immense fire, Conner would have wholly enjoyed their conversation with Marcella. As it was, however, he could not help but glance off in the direction of the menacingly dark billows of smoke, which now covered a vast majority of the unforgettable night sky with their threatening expanses.

Conner noticed that the foreboding scene had thoroughly absorbed Moxie as well. He wondered how much of his previous statement — that they shouldn't assume Vellix started the fire — he even believed himself.

Loud yells and cheers reverberated through the ship's many levels and found Conner's ears, pulling him from his memories and placing him firmly back in the present. He got to his feet, stretched indulgently and nudged Medwin to wake him up.

"Let him sleep," said a voice from somewhere above him.

Conner looked up quickly, his eyes wide with shock. He found Lolani perched on a brass candleholder. "Oh, it's you," he said, still clutching his chest from the way he'd been startled. "You're looking a whole lot better," he added, now taking in the hawk's appearance.

And indeed, she did look better. The wounds across her mid-section had healed completely, and her wing was resting in a position that looked quite normal.

"I must ask," Lolani started, a curious tone in her voice. "Why are we headed for the eastern coastline? Have you already found the missing scroll?"

She awaited Conner's reply with an air of hopefulness that made him wish he had a different answer. A stab of anxiety ran down his spine. Not only did he have to find the ruins of Hylan, but he still needed to discover the place in which the scroll was hidden within them. He stalled for a second, thinking of how he might be able to sugarcoat the truth, before concluding that there was no way out of this. He swallowed heavily. "No, we didn't find the scroll on Rhona … because it isn't there."

"What do you mean the scroll isn't on Rhona?" Lolani asked uneasily. "Vivek was positive that it was somewhere on the island." She glared at Conner in a way that suggested she was much more likely to believe the theory of wise old Vivek than the young, less knowledgeable person who stood in front of her.

Conner sighed. He had been expecting this reaction. Of course Lolani would believe Vivek's theory over his. She didn't know he had visited Salix. He looked the hawk in her brown eyes and said, "Vivek only believed the scroll was on Rhona because Salix made him believe that it was." He sighed again, feeling less than thrilled about the idea of having to explain how he had this seemingly random piece of information. He wasn't sure how to make Lolani believe the story of his meeting with Salix, and he hated thinking about the fact that Vivek had expended all his efforts searching Rhona to find something that wasn't there. Every time he did, the pictures in his head became more exaggeratedly depressing.

As Lolani opened her mouth to reply he knew it was no use hoping he wouldn't have to tell her. She would undoubtedly want an explanation. Conner was about to plunge into his story about the potion; about his conversation with Salix, but before he could start, Lolani spoke, a tone of emerging comprehension in her dignified voice.

"You drank a dark blue potion, didn't you? You had an out of body experience."

"I — yeah. How did you know?"

"You may not remember, but I was Vivek's hawk," Lolani said, looking at Conner incredulously.

"Oh yeah… Duh." Conner smacked himself in the forehead, as if punishing his brain for its ignorance.

Lolani appeared to be mildly amused by his reaction before she arranged her face into a serious expression. "So when you spoke with Salix, she told you the scroll was not on Rhona?" the hawk asked, a dismal air of disappointment about her. This new information was clearly upsetting.

Conner didn't blame her for being irritated. She had belonged to Vivek and probably spent countless hours helping him search Rhona for the missing scroll. Ignoring the twinge of pity he felt for her, Conner continued his explanation. "Salix told me that the scroll was hidden in the ruins of Hylan." He hoped his tone had sounded understanding of her viable frustration.

"I see," Lolani replied, looking as though she grasped the reasons for Salix's actions in a way that Conner had not upon first learning the information.

Unsure of what to say next, Conner settled for appearing to be overly interested in a knot-riddled piece of wood on the dingy deck floor. Before the silence had a chance to become overly awkward, the sounds of Medwin stirring saved him from having to break it.

It seemed that Medwin's waking up was contagious. Just seconds after he had yawned, Zelimir and Moxie began to stir as well.

"Ah, you're awake," Lolani said, as if now the day had truly started.

Conner got the impression that this was because Medwin was now the hawk's master. Her sense of propriety was obviously intact.

Lolani allowed Medwin time to rub the sleep out of his eyes before she asked, "Your orders?" in a significant sort of way.

Medwin gazed squinty-eyed at the bird, still half-asleep. "What?"

"What are your orders?" Lolani repeated, a hint of exasperation modifying her courteous tone ever so slightly.

"Oh, right. Um… Well…" Medwin's brain didn't seem to have woken up at the same time he had.

"Might I suggest that you have me send word to those we hope to gain as allies? Surely many will be anxious to join us in our effort to extinguish Vellix." Lolani stared expectantly at Medwin, awaiting his reply.

"Absolutely," he said. "I am grateful for your wisdom." He bowed thankfully toward Lolani and clambered idly to his feet.

Conner noticed that Medwin's brain appeared to have finally caught up with the rest of him. The glossy, hazed look in his eyes had faded away, leaving the grim stare of a person who had just remembered he has countless worries fighting to be the first to force their way to the front of his mind.

Conner was positive that, had he looked in a mirror when he'd woken up, his expression would have been nearly identical.

Zelimir stood up and walked over toward the door. "I expect that we should be quite near our destination by now. Shall we head up and see?"

Conner nodded in agreement.

Medwin did the same as he strode over to the single, circular window on the far wall of the room. He opened it, put on his leather glove, and held out his arm for Lolani to land on. She told him that once she had made contact with all possible allies, she would seek him out; then asked where he expected to be. Medwin informed her of the general area they would be searching for the ruins of Hylan, and she hopped out the small window.

Conner saw her wings flap a few times, in an apparent battle with a strong gust of wind, and then she was gone.

CHAPTER 18

The Parting of Ways

Up on the main deck, the crew scrambled to fulfill the orders Ammin was bellowing at the top of his lungs. "*James! Gavin!* I needed those sails raised yesterday! What the bloody hell is taking so long? You think me supernatural?" He made a wild articulate gesture. "This ain't gonna work if we're pacing twenty-three knots!"

James and Gavin scattered to opposite sides of the ship and untied equally opposing lengths of rope that ran taut to the ship's largest sail. They heaved on the ropes until the sail came to its closed position, before tying them deftly to their respected bitts and moved on to the next in the row.

Ammin gave the helm a few delicate and decisive turns and looked up to the crow's nest. "How'm I doin', Lenny?" he yelled nervously, his voice cracking with strain. "Talk to me!"

"Yer doin' fine, Cap'n." Lenny called back resolutely. "Keep 'er steady!"

Conner ran up to the bridge, hoping it would provide a better view of his surroundings. His stomach churned with anxiety as he realized that Ammin was attempting to direct the *Colossus* into a cove so small it seemed unsuitable for any ship to enter, much less this one.

Medwin, Zelimir, and Moxie arrived on the bridge, coming to rest around Conner. Zelimir looked as alarmed as anyone with a shred of sanity should. Moxie wrung his hands anxiously as his eyes wandered between the two towers of rock that left only a narrow passage to the alcove within. Medwin's brow stretched in alarm. His focus darted frantically from Ammin to the gap in the rocks and back again.

Ammin glanced over at Conner and the others, beads of sweat glistening across his forehead. "Get up to the bow! Lenny could use a second set of eyes guidin' me in!"

Conner looked around for the sailor Ammin was giving orders to. No one else was on the bridge. He pointed silently to himself, then to Medwin, startled and gaping. Ammin had only ever given him one order on his ship, and it had been an incredibly simple task: fetching his spyglass.

This, however, was an order with horrific ramifications. If he gave Ammin one slight misdirection, it would be catastrophic. "Captain," he mumbled tentatively. "You want *me* to —"

"I don't care who! You! Medwin! Whatever! Just someone with eyes get the bloody hell up there!"

Medwin took off at a run, heading for the portside of the bow.

Conner's mind snapped, leaving self-consciousness in a forgettable, easy-to-lose compartment. He sprinted to reach the starboard side.

He heard a fragment of something Quincy was muttering under his breath as he ran by. "…bloody daffed if 'e thinks he's…"

Fighting the pessimistic thoughts slashing their way to the front of his mind, Conner reached the right side of the ship's bow. He peered over the railing. Instantly, his insides were squirming. His optimism laid down its arms and surrendered to pessimism.

Jagged formations of rock protruded up from the depths all around them. The massive slab of rock that formed the right-hand-side of the cove's perimeter looked close enough to touch. This maneuver Ammin was attempting was more delicate than Conner could have imagined. There was zero margin for error. 'This is completely ludicrous!' he thought manically. 'Why are we even doing this in the first place?'

Medwin threw his arm in the air and flagged for Ammin to steer the ship to his right, using his thumb and his forefinger to warn the captain he had very little room in which to operate.

Lenny yelled urgently down from the crow's nest. "Ten degrees right, hold two seconds, five degrees left, hold!"

Conner watched as his side of the ship came within a foot of the towering rock it was cruising past, then crept slowly away by half the distance it had come. He sighed with relief and looked back over the railing, only to realize the *Colossus* would strike a rock barely peeking above the surface within seconds. He threw his arm to the sky and gestured for Ammin to steer them farther to the left, his arm flailing. "Turn lef—"

CRACK!

The *Colossus* struck the rock and jolted violently.

Conner fell to the deck. He felt the long runs of timber under his hands and knees vibrating as the gut-wrenching sound of wood scraping heavily across stone echoed around the cove.

Lenny cursed at the top of his lungs, finding creative new ways to combine words Conner wouldn't dare use in front of his mother.

"*Drop all anchors now, or we ain't gonna have a ship what floats!*" Ammin boomed.

The sailors nearest the anchors wasted no time in carrying out these orders.

Everyone seemed to let out a simultaneous sigh of relief as *the Colossus* slowed and came to a drifting halt.

Lenny shrieked a high-pitched laugh that made him sound slightly unhinged "Bloody 'ell that was close!" he exclaimed, getting out of the crow's nest and scaling down the ratline with the speed and skill of a monkey down a tree. "Yer one 'ell of a crazy bastard, you are!" he laughed, flourishing a pointed finger at Ammin.

Ammin bowed pompously. "And you my friend, have a pair of eyes worth your weight in gold."

Lenny returned Ammin's bow, his more pompous still.

Conner inhaled a calming breath as he watched the captain and his first mate. If the rock they hit was cause for any real concern, they wouldn't be standing idly around. They would be in the water immediately, investigating the damage.

He began to take in the beauty of his surroundings. Green moss covered the rock formations that made up the outer walls of the cove.

Ferns, bushes, and a small assortment of flower-bearing plants grew from every crevice large enough to house their roots. The fresh water flowing through a branch of the Vian River fell sixty feet and met the salt water of the ocean, creating a billowing cloud of mist.

Many of the crew jumped from the ship and swam gleefully over to the waterfall to drink to their heart's content.

Conner smiled as he watched them swim into the center of an ever-changing show of rainbows that gleamed mystically as the sun shown on the thick mist fuming from the water's surface. He licked his lips as he watched them take long, hydrating drinks and realized how thirsty he was himself. He looked around for the rest of his companions and found that they had all gone to congratulate Ammin for his skill in steering the ship so immaculately. "Hey guys," he called as he headed over to them. "Let's go and get a drink from the falls?"

They nodded. Conner noticed Medwin sucking instinctually at his tongue in order to evaluate his thirst.

"Come on lads," Ammin said, setting off at a brisk pace and signaling for them to follow. He strode up to the front of the ship, climbed onto the railing, studied the water below, and dove off without a flicker of hesitance.

Zelimir ran and launched himself over the ship's railing right behind him, knowing the water where Ammin dove off would be sufficiently deep. He swam happily over to the falls and lapped up its contents.

Medwin saw a rope tied to one of the railing posts. He used it to climb down and swam over to the falls — Conner and Moxie followed suit.

Conner felt his mind and body rejuvenate as he drank his fill of cool water.

"So, Ammin, why did you sail the ship into this cove anyway?" Medwin asked, projecting his voice over the splashing sounds of the falls.

"Well, I don't know how long I'll be leaving her, do I?" Ammin replied loudly. "I don't want her messed with while I'm away, so I had to make sure she was well hidden."

Medwin blushed slightly and said, "Oh. Right… That makes sense…"

Conner could tell that Medwin felt stupid for asking such a seemingly obvious question, but Conner had been wondering the same thing and thought the answer only seemed obvious now that they'd heard it.

"You're kidding! I'll have nothing to change into!"

"An' where's the problem in tha', love!"

A heated argument up on the ship grabbed the attention of everyone down at the falls.

Lenny and Marcella were standing about a foot apart, and while Marcella wore a look of deepest disgust, Lenny was sporting the mischievous grin that suited his features so well.

"Oh, and I suppose, by that, you mean that you'd be fine if I was stuck walking around naked?" Marcella spat, looking completely scandalized.

"*'Course tha's wha' I mean, love,"* Lenny replied remorselessly.

Marcella had had enough. She smacked Lenny hard across the face and stalked off angrily.

Lenny looked down at his shipmates. He shrugged boyishly and dove off the ship, narrowly avoiding a grouping of jagged rocks. By the time he re-surfaced, he had swam all the way over to the falls. He popped up, mouth open wide — like some kind of shark — and drank from the falls avidly.

Moxie scrambled up out of the water onto one of the more gently sloped rocks, breathing hard and fast. When he noticed the looks he was getting from everyone he waved his less than lengthy arms and legs as if to say, "You try and tread water with these."

The crew burst into laughter.

Medwin swam over to Moxie, allowed him to climb on his back, and headed for the ship.

* * *

Once everyone had re-boarded the *Colossus*, Ammin held up his hand to call attention. His crew faced him attentively. He locked his hands together behind his back and paced up and down the line of them, making sure each met his eye briefly. "We're going up against some of the most savage creatures I've ever faced." he said, a sense of urgency burning in his voice. He paced silently up and down the line a few more times before continuing. "You need to prepare yourselves *mentally* if you want to live through this. Your wit is all that will grant you success against the Bazza… Their strength greatly exceeds our own. And their cunning isn't far behind." He surveyed his men seriously. "Grab as many weapons as you can carry comfortably and we'll meet back here."

The crew scrambled to obey their captain.

A few short minutes later there was much clinging and clanging as the now heavily-armed sailors gathered back around Ammin. The captain separated his men into four groups; each group loaded themselves into one of the ship's four dinghies. Skylar, who Ammin had elected to stay aboard the ship to recover from Marcella's attack on him, lowered them down to the ocean below.

Soon the cove was behind them. They came around a tree line to find an unforgettable view of the eastern coastline.

It was Conner's first time ever seeing the eastern shores of Rohwen. He turned to look at Medwin and noticed that he seemed to be taking in the sights in the way a person who had never seen them would. "Is this your first time on the eastern coast as well?" he asked curiously.

"Yeah, I've never seen any of this," Medwin replied, not taking his eyes from the view in front of him.

They headed for the mouth of the Vian River. A huge sand bar protruded nearly the width of the entire river, leaving only a small opening where the river could escape into the ocean. Waves pounded tirelessly into the sand bar, sending large amounts of white foam over its expanses and leaving fragments of seaweed and other debris behind as they receded back into the vast ocean.

Conner let his eyes roam up the river until it bent out of view and he was left staring at the horizon. He found himself scowling as his vision came to rest on several pillars of smoke making their way to the heavens, reduced to nothing more than thin streams in comparison with the billowing clouds of the night before.

As they entered the river, Conner was hoping to get a better idea of where the smoke was coming from. But as time passed, he settled into disappointment, realizing the trees that lined the banks on either side of the river weren't going to thin out enough to see anything other than what was right in front of him.

Three hours passed and nothing more exciting than the occasional fish poking its head up to catch a surface-level bug had happened. A flash of color caught the corner of Conner's eye. "What was that? Did you see that?" he asked anxiously, turning to investigate the trees to his left. "Did you see that, Medwin?" he asked again when he didn't get an immediate response.

"What are you talking about, Conner? I didn't see any —"

"I saw it too," Zelimir said. "I can smell them too."

"Them?" Conner asked worriedly.

"Yes, them," Zelimir replied calmly. Conner, Medwin, Moxie, and every other man on the boat looked nervous now. Zelimir decided he'd better explain. "You saw Abram, Conner… I know because I distinctly remember his scent, as I do most people's. He and the other Botanicans are gathered just on the other side of these trees." He gestured in the direction of the southern bank.

It took Conner a second to place the name, Abram, but then it hit him. Abram was the man who had told him to seek out the great weeping willow tree, Salix. But what were he and the other Botanicans doing all the way over here? Unless…

"Ammin, pull over to the bank!" Conner yelled commandingly. He received an uncharacteristically dirty look from Ammin and shifted his face into a pleading expression. Ammin's flash of anger dissolved as he realized Conner hadn't meant to sound so forceful. He ordered James to row their dinghy over to the river's southern bank; the rest of the crew followed in their wake.

"Conner, you don't think…" Medwin asked, looking horrified.

"It would make sense, wouldn't it," Conner replied grimly.

Moxie looked confused, but he kept pace with his companions as they ran up the bank and plunged into the bushes and trees.

The crew followed, keeping their distance. None of them seemed to feel altogether comfortable with the situation.

Marcella, however, ran frantically to catch up with Conner and the others. She jumped over fallen trees in one bound and ducked under branches that would have otherwise smacked her in the face. Before long, she was side by side with Zelimir, who was leading the way.

Conner shot Medwin an impressed sort of look. Medwin started to laugh before returning the same look: a look that said, "This girl is intense!"

Zelimir stopped abruptly and sat down.

People emerged from the trees all around them.

"Conner! Medwin! Zelimir! I can't believe it's you!" Azalea emerged from behind two men. She ran over and hugged them all in turn.

As she flung her arms around Conner, he noticed a pattern of terrible burns across both of her arms. Even though he wanted nothing more than not to believe it, her burns confirmed his fears. "The fire… it wasn't…"

Azalea's eyes became glossy. A single tear trickled slowly down her cheek and came to rest on her chin. Conner followed the tear as it made its course, past her nose, past her lips. He couldn't help but notice how beautiful she was. It made him feel guilty that he was appraising her beauty when he should be evaluating her grief.

Abram strode toward them. His pain in the physical sense appeared to be very little — he was virtually unscathed by burns. But when Conner looked him in the eye, he saw a story of mental anguish far worse than any physical pain a man can withstand. "The Bazza have burned down Botanica." Abram said, his voice pointedly businesslike. "They came to recruit us as their allies… We refused…"

Ammin stepped forward. "Which way did they head?" he asked sharply.

"South," said Abram, turning to look at Ammin. "You're not … going after them?"

"Damn right we are! Ain't we, lads?"

An explosion of "Aye Cap'n!" rang out from the crew, causing a few nearby birds to take flight.

Conner could hear Marcella cheering amongst them.

Abram shook his head skeptically, but his doubts went unnoticed by the cheering sailors.

"Come on then, lads." Ammin gestured for his crew to follow him. "They'll be after Iden next, you can be sure of that." As he led his men away from the gathered Botanicans, he noticed that Conner, Medwin, Zelimir, and Moxie hadn't made any move to follow. "Aren't yeh coming, lads?"

"No, we have a job to do," Conner said, realizing for the first time that his search for the scroll was obviously going to separate him from Ammin and the crew. "We need to head north from here."

"Oh, right then," Ammin replied, almost too casually, as if hoping it would conceal the fact that he was going to miss them. "Well, you lads take care of yourselves, alright?" He gave Conner a significant nod as the rest of the crew murmured their agreement of Ammin's words of farewell.

"Oi, Conner," Lenny yelled as the crew started to head south. "... Good luck, mate..."

"Thanks. You too." Conner called back to him, taking Lenny's well wishes to heart.

CHAPTER 19

Heartache

Conner gave Lenny's retreating figure one last look and turned idly to face his companions. His eyes came to rest on Medwin. The young chief was watching Ammin and his crew disappear through the trees with a pained expression. The lingering smile Conner carried from Lenny's encouraging words faded away, leaving him with a grimace indigenous to the dark climate in Medwin's eyes.

He was suddenly unbearably aware of the fact that he might never see Ammin again. Or Lenny. Or Dale, Landon, James, Gavin, Quincy… The list of names continued until he came to a place in his mind where faces of nameless sailors he'd never known properly were floating by, beaming happily. They had just left to hunt down the Bazza. He couldn't help but feel that the rate of survival for such a mission was bleak at the very best, and virtually none if truth be told. True, the crew was more than capable of holding their own in a fight, but this wasn't a fight with average men.

Conner glanced speculatively at the last spot he had seen Lenny. "Do you think —"

"— We'll ever see them again..." Medwin finished Conner's question, reading his mind like an open book. "I think they have enough passion and a wise enough leader to survive. But I also think that if you expect them to live, you'd only be setting yourself up to be brutally beaten by harsh truths." Medwin didn't stop staring through the trees as he spoke, but when his last words were finished, he faced Conner with a level, yet strained look.

"…I…" Conner realized as he started to speak that he didn't have a reply. What Medwin had just said was the perfect summary of a logical outlook. He had nothing to add.

Zelimir left Conner's side without a word, possibly feeling that his opinion was one too harsh for his friends to bear, and therefore, one better left unspoken.

Moxie looked up at Conner and Medwin. "Sometimes it's the man least expected to succeed who has the upper hand," he said, giving each of them a lengthy, knowing stare.

They gawked at him with startled expressions, as if they had forgotten a world full of people still existed around them.

"A man with passion," Moxie continued, "will always be more powerful than one acting indifferently. He will always defeat a man following orders alone…"

Conner and Medwin were both gaping now. Were these words really coming from Moxie?

"…Love is more powerful than hate… And honor is eternal. Death cannot harm it…"

Moxie's words hit Conner like a series of powerful waves, almost knocking his composure off balance. A feeling of positivity slammed headlong into the misery that had grasped him. He felt his eyes burn for a moment as he suppressed a tear so confused by his mingled hope and hopelessness it lacked true conviction.

"Now I know why you are so quiet, Moxie," Medwin said, reaching out to put a hand on his shoulder. Moxie tilted his head toward Medwin curiously. "It is because you save your words. Build them until they are like unbreakable foundations of truth."

Moxie smiled bashfully.

Medwin nodded. "The words you just spoke were well-thought, and I thank you for them."

Moxie smiled again. "I just speak when I know my knowledge will filter out untruths…"

Conner returned Moxie's smile with a gesture of thanks better than any words he could find. He turned to look for Zelimir and found Azalea approaching him, her eyes puffy and red. A horrible thought struck him like a cracking whip. Where was Flora? He still hadn't seen Azalea's twin sister since they arrived.

Azalea stopped in front of Conner. "Zelimir s-says you might b-be able to help her," she uttered, starting to sob uncontrollably. She grabbed his arm and led him toward a group of Botanicans that were pouring over those with untended injuries.

Heartache pierced Conner like a thousand burning knives as he came upon the blackened form of a girl he barely recognized as Flora. Her once beautiful golden hair now scorched like a field of hay at the peak of summer. Her milky white skin charred and blistered.

A familiar feeling of pure hatred for Vellix and every vile thing he had brought upon the innocent people of Rohwen began to boil-over in the pit of his stomach. It was like his insides had been left over a raging fire. Like the reaction you get when mixing the wrong chemicals. He swallowed heavily, as if to douse the flame, as if it might neutralize the fuming chemicals within.

Azalea knelt down next to her sister. "Flora," she whispered with what Conner thought was an impressive attempt at an encouraging tone. "The Conner boy is here." She gave Conner a quick smiling glance, and some of the kindness he remembered from their first meeting beamed through. "He might be able to help."

Flora coughed and reached for her sister's hand.

Conner knelt down next to Azalea. He took in Flora's appearance with careful scrutiny, making sure he didn't miss a single aspect. After a minute of this, he closed his eyes. The image of Flora was vivid in his mind's eye. He visualized the burns removing themselves from her skin, her hair growing back to its original luster, and the char drawing itself from her lungs.

Azalea gasped and placed her hand on Conner's arm. A smile grew broad across his face. It was working. He concentrated on the images a moment longer before opening his eyes.

The real version of Flora wasn't perfect the way the one in his mind's eye had been, but she was considerably better. Her burns looked weeks old now, well into a progressed stage of healing. He watched her chest swell as she took the kind of breath healthy lungs crave.

"I — I don't know..." Azalea's eyes swept from her sister to Conner and started glossing up again. "I don't know what to say..." She confessed, leaning in to kiss him on the cheek. "Thank you so much!"

Conner felt his face flushing. He fought the urge to touch the spot Azalea's lips had been only moments ago. 'Say something,' urged a voice in his head.

"It was nothing," he replied, instantly blushing more heavily as he realized his response sounded incredibly arrogant. It wasn't the right thing to have said at all. Almost anything would have been better. Other responses, better responses, came to him in quick succession. 'You're welcome. It was my pleasure. Glad I could help...' Any of these would have been just fine. But no, he had to say, "it was nothing," like he was some kind of unsung hero who went around healing people for kicks.

He snuck a quick glance in Azalea's direction. The concern he felt about his less than humble response to her gratitude subsided slightly as he noticed she was still beaming at him.

Looking at her fully now, he said, "I'm glad I was able to help," with the kind of sincerity he hoped would make him appear less conceited.

"You have no idea how much this means to me..." Azalea ran her hand gently down the side of Flora's face. "My sister is everything to me. I couldn't bear to lose her..."

Conner thought of how he would feel if Medwin or Zelimir or Moxie died. "I understand," he said softly, getting back to his feet and brushing the pine needles off his knees.

He looked around to find Medwin and saw him conversing with Moxie, the two of them standing a little ways from everyone else. An awkward feeling came over him as he became aware that Azalea was still watching him, clearly waiting for him to say something conclusive to end their conversation. "Well," he began, already sure his sense of unease was on display, "I have things to discuss with Medwin… So…"

"I know," Azalea said, reaching out to place a hand on his arm. "Thank you again." She turned away from Conner to face Flora with an unmistakable air of conclusion.

* * *

Zelimir and Abram were talking quietly to one another. They peered furtively at Azalea and then went back to conversation, nodding on occasion.

Conner instantly knew the subject of their discussion. He adjusted himself and resettled comfortably against the trunk of a well-aged oak tree. Medwin and Moxie were leaning idly against its two closest neighbors.

Medwin grabbed something from the ground and turned to Conner. "Hey, this is a nice-looking stone. Maybe it would be worth using. You know, to infuse with cognition."

Conner had almost forgotten that he intended to attempt infusing something with cognition. There had been so much on his mind since his conversation with Salix that the thought had completely slipped away from him. He took the small rock from Medwin and studied it for a moment. Its surface layer was clear and glossy, and it was streaked with milky white inside. "Yeah, this is nice," he said, still rotating the stone in his fingers. "I definitely think it's worth using."

Medwin gave Conner an excited look, making his eagerness more than apparent.

Conner closed his eyes and focused on channeling his cognition into the stone. For a solid minute, he sat completely motionless. Finally, he opened his eyes and looked down at the stone in his palm.

"What are you going to try it on? Medwin asked.

At first, Conner wasn't sure how he could test the stone, but it wasn't long before the answer came to him. "I'll do something without the stone. Then I'll do the same thing with the stone. That will give me a good comparison."

"That's a good idea," Medwin replied as Moxie snagged a bug from under a nearby leaf and ate it happily.

Conner formed a picture of an intricate design carving itself into one of the trees across from where he sat. The sound of splintering wood emanated from the tree for a moment, and when it ceased, Conner walked over to investigate his work. It was rather crude compared to the vision in his mind, but not terrible. "Okay," he said with a glance over at Medwin and Moxie, "now I'm going to try it with the stone."

He re-summoned the image of his design, this time focusing on a new tree. The sound of splintering wood rang out again, and as it stopped, he studied the new design; it was nearly identical to his previous attempt. Feeling a bit disheartened, he turned to Medwin. "It didn't work..."

"Well, that's okay," Medwin said, trying to sound as encouraging as possible. "We didn't expect it to be easy. Try infusing the stone again."

Conner nodded, sat down next to the oak tree he'd been sitting next to before, and leaned against its trunk. He re-devoted his thoughts to infusing the stone with cognition. This time, he waited twice as long before breaking concentration. But, when he tested it, the results were the same. He had failed again. Now thoroughly disheartened, he said, "I don't think I'm going to be able to do it."

Medwin didn't respond for a moment — he was clearly thinking the same thing as Conner. However, his reply was still optimistic. "I don't think you should give up that easily. At least try it one more time."

Moxie gave Conner an encouraging nod after Medwin had finished speaking.

It wasn't until he had failed a few more times that Conner officially gave up. He settled for assuming that Xellore's cognition was probably far more proficient at the time he achieved infusing his stone. Conner decided he would keep trying periodically until it finally worked, stuffed the rock into the small pocket of his jeans, and forced himself to forget about it for the time being.

Jonquil, leader of the Botanican's, strode over and came to rest in front of Conner and the others. He insisted they stay and eat before moving on. They didn't argue, as none of them had any clue when they might have another decent meal.

While they waited, the three friends struck up a conversation that turned instinctually to dark subjects. They allowed it to wander from subject to subject: what would Vellix's next move be? Would Ammin and the crew be able to catch up to the Bazza in time to help the Idenites? How hard was it going to be to find the missing scroll?

Soon the conversation had become so depressing that they abandoned it.

As time slipped away, Conner found it harder and harder to sit there, doing nothing. He just wanted to eat and go. Talk of finding the scroll had forced him to make some depressing realizations. He fought to stay positive, telling himself that the information Salix had provided was enough to take most of the guesswork out of their search. But then, as he replayed her words in his mind, his thoughts would grow dark again.

All she had told him was that Hylan was roughly ten miles west of the eastern coastline and somewhere just north of the Vian River. The information had seemed like plenty to go on when he'd heard it. But now, after further consideration, it seemed vague at best. How would they know if they were ten miles west of the ocean? How would they even know what to look for? Was there a secret entrance?

His frustration toward Salix ebbed slowly through him until he was full of resentment. 'She had to have known more than she told me,' he thought furiously. 'She probably saw Vellix when he entered the ruins... She sees Rohwen from the perspective of every tree!' Conner fought the sudden urge to elbow the trunk of the oak he was leaning against.

He tried to steer his thoughts in a more positive direction, but they ignored him and grew darker still. 'We're sitting here, doing nothing but having a nice little break, while somewhere out there' — he looked absentmindedly in the direction of Mt. Cirrus — 'are the forces of evil... And *they* aren't resting.' He thought about the fact that Ammin and his crew were well on their way to risking their lives, and here he was, waiting for a pleasant lunch.

Something caught his eye. He looked up and saw Azalea walking past. Before he knew it, he was on his feet. "We need to eat and get out of here," he snapped sharply. "Whatever it is you guys are giving us, just give it to us so we can go!"

Azalea turned to look at him, a mixture of shock and anger imprinted upon her usually good-natured face.

Conner knew as soon as the words left his mouth that he'd been extremely rude. He wished he had taken more care to speak calmly. It wasn't fair for Azalea to receive the blunt end of his frustration. "Look, Azalea," he said, trying to sound apologetic. "We just don't have time for this."

"I know..."

"Can you just give us something simple, so we can go? Bread and water?"

Azalea nodded politely and scurried off.

Zelimir came trotting over. "What was that all about? Did you just yell at —"

"I already said I was sorry," Conner replied quickly. He looked past Zelimir. Abram was watching him with a puzzled expression. "Just drop it, okay. I'm not in the mood."

Zelimir gave him a jagged look and wheeled around to face Medwin and Moxie.

Azalea returned less than a minute later, breathing heavily. "Here," she panted, handing Conner a chunk of bread and a tin full of water.

He noticed as Azalea handed him the food that she'd brought each of them a small piece of meat as well. "Thank you," he uttered, gazing at the food she'd placed in his hands.

Azalea gave him another polite nod and went to offer the others their shares of food.

Conner watched her, feeling so guilty about his behavior that he almost lost his appetite. She caught him staring and cast a warm, reassuring smile in his direction. He smiled back, and thought to himself, 'her appearance makes her pretty, but it's who she *is* that makes her beautiful.'

CHAPTER 20

The Tantherians

Conner, Medwin, and Moxie split Zelimir's share of food after he reminded them he still wouldn't need to eat for well over a week. They ate hastily, said their farewells, and set off for the Vian River.

Zelimir said he would catch up and stayed behind to have a few words with Jonquil. Only a couple minutes passed before the wolf stepped into stride with Conner and the others.

"What was that about?" Conner asked.

Moxie, who had been staring off into space, something Conner had noticed was quite usual for him, turned to listen to Zelimir's reply.

"I was asking them if they were ready to take up arms against Vellix and his armies when the time comes for battle," Zelimir said matter-of-factly, as if the answer was completely obvious.

"How do you know there's even going to be a battle?" Conner asked seriously. "I mean, if we find the scroll, and if I manage to learn what's in there fast enough —"

"Conner! Listen to yourself," Zelimir barked impatiently. "If this — if that. We *cannot* go on ifs! We need to ensure that we're ready. I will promise you this: you can be sure Vellix *will* be. What do you think he's doing right now?" The wolf waited a brief moment to see if

Conner had a quick answer and then plunged on. "Didn't you hear what Abram said? The Bazza came recruiting... And when the Botanicans refused, they burned down Botanica! We can't afford to —"

"Okay, *okay*! I *get* it!" Conner yelled, making a gesture of distinct frustration. "I don't know what I was thinking. I was being stupid..." He broke off, feeling dumb and defeated. What *was* he thinking, assuming they could avoid a battle? Hadn't he learned anything? Things didn't always go the way they wanted them to. He knew that.

"Don't be too hard on yourself," Moxie said with a brief glance in Conner's direction. He went silently back to his investigation of the treetops, as if hoping to see some kind of bird that only came out if you stared at the trees they lived in without blinking for a long period of time.

"Yeah, Conner," Medwin said in a continuance of Moxie's statement. "It's not stupid of you to want to finish this without a full on war taking place... But..."

Conner had been ready for the "but". He wanted to interject. However, he remained quiet and let Medwin carry on.

"...You have to admit. The chances of avoiding one are slim. It *is* best, I guess to say, to over prepare. Or, at least prepare for the worst. That way we won't be caught off guard."

Although he knew Medwin was trying to console him, Conner wished he wouldn't. The effect it had was to further his own feelings of stupidity. All the things Medwin was saying were so blatantly obvious that the fact he hadn't thought of them in the first place truly made him feel like an idiot. Of course they should be preparing for the worst. This was Vellix they were talking about. Who even knew what the full extent of his armies would be? Had he, Conner, become so deluded by the fact that he was the "one" who would defeat Vellix that he thought himself some kind of singular hero; that he could just march up to this incredibly powerful evil, while a host of his creatures surrounded him, and just take them all on?

They reached the river's southern bank, climbed aboard one of the four dinghies, and rowed across to the northern side.

Zelimir leapt out first. He landed in the river's shallows and lapped up a drink. Medwin hopped out behind him and pulled the dinghy up to the bank. Conner helped Moxie out of the boat, and after a short, investigative look to the north, the group took off, moving at a quick pace.

The sparse arrangement of ancient oaks that thrived near the riverbank thinned as a dense assortment of pine, birch, and maple trees horded the land's nourishment, their sprawling canopy offered an ideal habitat for a wide variety of low-growing plant life. Medwin pulled out his hatchet and hacked a path into the tangle of thorn-riddled vines and bushes.

Their surroundings became darker with every stride they took, and as if on cue, the subtle sounds of the forest became increasingly menacing.

An ominous, threatening feeling came over Conner. He had felt these feelings before, yet it didn't make him any better at dealing with them. They were just as unnerving now as they were on every other occasion he'd dealt with them. He grabbed his bow and strung an arrow.

Moxie pulled Scarlet from his belt and held it at the ready. Conner had never seen him this way. He looked formidable and aggressive.

Zelimir's nose went to work. He seemed to be aware of whatever it was the rest of them had sensed.

Conner slowed his pace to the point that he was literally inching along. He looked around and saw that his three companions had slowed as well.

They reached a small opening in the otherwise thick forest. Millions of tiny yellow particles blew like dust through the trees as they entered the opening, reminding Conner vaguely of some kind of pollen. Before he could form another thought, his vision blurred. He felt fervently hot. His breathing became restricted. As he fell to the ivy-covered floor, he saw Medwin clutch his throat and drop to the ground.

Zelimir tried to run, but he fell to the floor after a few steps, gagging.

Moxie collapsed in a heap. He, too, was clutching his throat, as if unable to breathe the air around him.

And then everything went black.

* * *

"I want the little one! His meat looks the best to me!"

"Ha! Like any of us are gonna get to choose..."

"Hey, we found 'em didn't we? I want the one with these strange garments."

"Oh shut up! All of you! We'll be lucky to get anything and you know it! Oba will decide what we get."

Low gritty sounding voices met Conner's ears. At first, he thought he was having some crazy dream, in which it appeared that he and his companions were on the menu, but as he opened his eyes, he saw a group of spear-wielding little creatures gathered around him. Their dull brown skin looked like weathered burlap. They wore skirts of leaf around their waists, and twig-made headpieces baring sharp teeth rested upon their pointed ears, crowning their heads. They might have been a few inches taller than Moxie but were very short all the same.

Conner jerked violently, trying to move away from them, only to find himself tied firmly to a tree. He strained to think quickly but realized his head was pounding fiercely. It felt like someone was trying to use a jackhammer to escape from within. He looked around and saw Medwin, Zelimir, and Moxie tied to trees nearby.

One of the creatures noticed that Conner had opened his eyes. It walked up to him, cracking a grin that revealed foul, pointed teeth with bits of old flesh stuck between them.

Conner's stomach spiraled with the sickness. These things, whatever they were, were planning to eat them. The creature held out a handful of yellow particles and blew them into his face. The heavy dosage knocked him out instantly.

* * *

As Conner came to, he found the others awake and having a hushed conversation. They were underground now and trapped within some kind of wooden holding cell.

The room outside the cell consisted of dirt. Roots from the plant-life in the forest above stuck out in all directions. Torches that burned along the walls kept the place dimly lit.

"What do you figure this place is?" Medwin asked when he saw that Conner had woken up.

Conner took a deep breath to clear his throbbing head, and the strong smell of soil drifting on the thin, cold air filled him. His head was pounding, if possible, more furiously than before. Whatever toxin the creatures sedated him with still hadn't run its full course. It was hard for him to think straight, but his urge to let Medwin and the others know they were in serious danger overpowered the excruciating pain. "I don't know what this place is," he said, massaging his temples, "but I saw the creatures that captured us. They're foul… They intend to eat us." He surveyed the room and took a few more mind-clearing breaths. "This must be where they live."

Moxie looked scared out of his mind. "I don't want to be eaten!" he exclaimed, getting quickly to his feet and tugging frantically on the sturdy wood bars of the cell.

"Get a grip on yourself," Zelimir said seriously. "None of us are going to get eaten."

Moxie didn't look convinced. He continued to glance fearfully around the cell, as if hoping a way of escape would present itself.

A large section of the wooded bars that made up the enclosure bent obediently out of the way at Conner's mental command. He stepped out of the cell and started investigating the room in further detail.

Zelimir walked by Moxie, striding with an air of smug satisfaction.

Moxie followed him, looking foolish and upset. "You could have just told me Conner would use cognition to get us out."

"I would have thought that much would be obvious," Zelimir replied as he joined Conner in his investigation of the room.

Medwin walked up to Conner. "First thing's first," he said, looking up at the mesh of roots piercing the ceiling. "We need to find our weapons. After that you can just —"

"Shhh…" Zelimir interrupted. "…I hear something."

Excited voices found their way into the room. A segment of the dirt wall burst open. No less than thirty of the little creatures filed into the room, stopping dead in their tracks when they saw their prisoners had escaped. Mingled looks of shock and anger at finding their dinner on this side of the cell distorted their already hideous faces. They pointed their spears aggressively and bared their sharp teeth, hissing and grunting.

The creature at the front of the group blew a cloud of yellow toxin into the air and yelled, "Get them!" in his evil voice.

"Don't breathe in the yellow stuff!" Conner cried. He focused intently on the ground. It came to life and bound the ankles of every creature in the room, a few of whom had just blown more of the toxin into the air.

Unable to escape the cloud of yellow dust, Moxie fell to the ground, clutching his throat. Medwin ran over to him, grabbed his arms, and dragged him away from the creatures.

The roots in the ceiling twisted and turned toward the creatures and tied themselves around their arms. It happened so fast that they had no chance to react. They struggled hopelessly against the bonds, but their efforts brought no reward.

"First of all," Conner said, eyeing the group of creatures with disgust. "What *are* you things?"

None of them responded. They stood silent as a windless night, expressions of fear scrawled vividly across their faces.

"*Well?*" Conner nipped aggressively.

The creature at the front of the group just stared at Conner, his eyes bulging and face trembling with terror. He looked as though words would never form in his mind again for the fear that had taken control of him.

"Conner," Zelimir whispered, "I think they're terrified of you because of your cognition."

This, Conner had to admit, was an almost undeniably true theory. He raised a hand toward the creatures, and they flinched as one.

"Alright," he said, raising both hands toward them now. "If you don't answer my questions, I'll kill you! Now tell me, what are you things?"

The front-most creature started to speak. His voice shook so badly with fear that his words were nearly indecipherable. "W — we — are T — Tantherians, s — sir…"

"Have either of you ever heard of Tantherians?" Conner asked Medwin and Zelimir.

They both shook their heads inarticulately.

Conner turned back to the creature. "Who is in charge here?"

"I — it is Oba, s — sir"

"And what's your name?" Conner asked the recoiling creature. He didn't really know why, but he almost felt a shred of pity for the grotesque being as he interrogated it.

"M — my name's V — Vasska… sir…"

"Okay, Vasska, I'm going to release you." Conner made a hand gesture that mimicked roots withdrawing themselves back to the ceiling. "You will take us to Oba."

The root bonds that had wrapped themselves tightly around Vasska released their grip. The dirt around his feet crept back into the ground. Vasska didn't try to grab the spear that lay on the ground next to him. Instead, he signaled for Conner, Medwin, and Zelimir to follow him.

Medwin slung Moxie over his shoulder. They followed Vasska out of the room and into the dark landing of a stairway.

After marching up two flights of stairs, they entered a narrow hallway. Had it not been for the faint flicker of firelight in the distance Conner would have wondered if the passage was endless.

Eventually, they rounded a corner and came into a spacious room, well-lit by torches. Marking the center of the room was a great cauldron, standing on four-clawed iron feet that held it well above the ground. Its cracked surface was stained black from the countless flames that had licked it. A neat stack of wood sat waiting in the space underneath.

Instruments for preparing food littered workstations that crowded both sides of the room: basting brushes, assortments of knives, peelers, corkscrews, ladles, stacks of bowls, plates, forks, and spoons.

Conner felt sick with disgust as he envisioned himself and the others being prepared as some kind of feast for these repulsive creatures.

Vasska led them through another door that blended almost seamlessly into the dirt wall.

They entered a long corridor. Two guards, armed with shields and spears, flanked an elaborate door quite the contrary to the others that had blended so well with their surrounding walls. The guards' shadows ran nearly the full length of the corridor, undulating unpredictably as torch-confined flames on the back wall danced at random.

As Conner drew closer to the door, he noticed an image painted upon it: a group of Tantherians bowing in a circle around one more elaborately dressed than the rest.

"Hey! *What* do you think you are doing?" yelled one of the guards when he realized that Conner and the others weren't bound.

Before Vasska could reply, Conner had made hand gestures toward the walls on either side of the two guards. Dirt came to life, swallowed them whole, and reformed quickly, muffling their cries.

Vasska gave Conner a terrified glance before turning his focus to the door. He opened it and showed them into the room.

This was a vast hall, far more elaborate than Conner would have expected. The dirt walls eased flawlessly into attractively carved granite. Stylized iron brackets shaped like repulsive, exaggerated faces held the torches that burned along them.

Rows of pillars sculpted to look like extravagantly dressed Tantherians — similar to the one depicted in the painting on the door — stood like monumental statues on either side of the hall.

Conner assumed the pillars were representations of deceased kings.

"What is this, Vasska?" called an ugly, commanding voice from the deepest shadows that shrouded the back of the chamber.

A dozen shield and spear-wielding guards came running out of the shadows to intercept the apparent threat.

"Oba, s — sir… I was ordered to bring these" — Vasska gestured a badly shaking hand in the direction of Conner and the others — "these men before you … sir…" Vasska bowed so deeply that it looked like he was in danger of toppling over.

"And I would be led to believe that it has become practice to bring my meals to me *before* they are ready to eat!" snarled the low, grumbling voice of Oba as he got up and stepped out of the shadows that concealed him.

As the fire light found its way, flickering onto him, Conner saw that he wore a leaf-made skirt similar to the rest of his tribe. But as opposed to his subjects, whose skirts consisted of plain green leaves, colorful variegations patterned his leaves, giving him an eccentric appearance.

His stomach overhung his waist obnoxiously and cast a heavy shadow. Many necklaces of various human bones dangled loosely from his neck and came to rest on his protruding belly.

The headdress that crowned him was elaborate, and in its own way, almost elegant. Along with its many sharp teeth, three ornately cut precious stones had been skillfully imbedded. Firelight shimmered and gleamed on their many reflective faces.

Oba's glare shifted from Medwin, still supporting Moxie's limp form, to Zelimir, growling and poised to lunge, to Conner, who returned his vulgar stare with a gaze like a sharp blade, and finally came to rest on Vasska, who was shaking more violently than the last clinging leaf in a winter storm. "Explain this trespass, Vasska!"

"I — I had no choice, sir," Vasska exclaimed, pointing at Conner and sounding as though he wasn't sure who to be more afraid of: his king or the boy who stood next to him. "He — he has magic!"

"What is this? What do you mean he has magi —"

Bright blue flames roared up in Conner's palms and banished the deep shadows that lurked all around him, casting new ones that spoke of the power their master held. He pelted every guard in the room in quick succession. They fell to the ground, shrieking in pain and grasping their burns. Conner turned to face Oba. He lit a new flame in each of his palms and fixed the Tantherian king with a threatening stare.

Oba jumped back; the blue of Conner's flames washed over his fear-stuck face, making him look twisted and misshapen. Reflections of each flame shone distinctly in his horrified, dark eyes. "How are you doing that?"

"I wouldn't worry about that," Conner said, unable to keep the satisfaction out of his voice. "Worry about what I'm going to do to you… Now, where are our weapons?"

Oba didn't reply, but he gave the shadows from which he had come a nervous glance.

Medwin set Moxie down gently and ran off into the shadows, stepping over a few of the guards still writhing in pain on the cold stone floor. He disappeared for a moment and then re-emerged into the firelight, clutching his hatchet, Conner's bow and arrows, and Moxie's dagger, Scarlet.

Oba started to plead with Conner as Medwin handed him his weapon, all command now gone from his voice. He dropped to his knees and begged pathetically. "Please don't kill me! *Please* don't!"

Conner continued to eye him maliciously, unmoved.

"Take my men!" he offered desperately, making a sweeping gesture all around his underground domain. "There are plenty of them to feed you and your companions! Take them!"

"I don't eat human flesh!" Conner spat in revulsion. "Or whatever it is you filth are," he added.

Oba grunted with aggravation when Conner called him filth, but he didn't say anything. He just knelt there, cowering — waiting.

"So let me get this straight," Conner said, unperturbed by Oba's understandable anger. "You're the ruler of all the Tantherians and you ask me to spare only your own life, while you offer me your people?" Conner awaited Oba's reply, disgusted by his incredible selfishness.

"I — well, I didn't mean —"

"Don't lie," Conner snarled, cutting right across Oba's attempt to back track. "Vasska, is it?" He asked, turning to the Tantherian on his right.

"Y — yes, sir," Vasska replied.

"Grab Oba." Conner pointed a condemning finger at the king.

Vasska didn't take a step, or give any sign of moving. He stood there, looking as though he'd rather lose a limb than approach his king with hostile intent.

"I said grab your pathetic excuse for a king!" Conner yelled furiously. Zelimir and Medwin started to inch forward behind him to exemplify Vasska's predicament. Not only did Conner have "magic," but he also outnumbered Vasska three to one.

Vasska looked as though he would have given anything in the world not to have to carry out this order. His hesitance to move toward Oba was so strong that he appeared to be battling some invisible force field. However, the prospect of Conner attacking him was enough to force obedience.

"Now," said Conner, staring right into Oba's face, "we will take you before your people and let them know how keen you were to save your own skin! And how easily you offered them up to us as food, as if they meant nothing to you. I'm sure this situation will resolve itself from there. Don't you think so, guys?" he asked Medwin and Zelimir, eyeing them with a mock quizzical expression.

"Definitely," Medwin said, unable to conceal a grin.

"I would say that it is very likely, indeed, to resolve itself, yes," Zelimir added happily, his overly pompous use of grammar causing Medwin's grin to break into full on laughter.

"Vasska, lead the way."

Vasska led them out of the King's Hall, back into the corridor, and through the door that lived discreetly in the wall of dirt.

No sooner than they had entered the room littered with cooking utensils and centered by the great cauldron, was Oba crying for help at the top of his lungs.

Conner smirked with satisfaction when nothing came of his cries, but his contentment withered and died as Zelimir took a defensive stance and started scanning the room for something seemingly invisible.

"What is it?" Medwin asked anxiously.

Multiple doors flew open along the walls ten feet above them. A flood of Tantherians poured onto a thin landing that Conner hadn't noticed before. With his focus set upon the cauldron and cooking instruments, his eyes hadn't made a true sweep of the room.

Soon, a hundred or more Tantherians lined the perimeter of the room. They gawked at the scene below with expressions of bafflement: Vasska holding Oba's arms behind his back, accompanied by the prisoners

"Help me you fools!" Oba shrieked wildly. "*Donat!* What are you waiting for?"

The soldier named Donat jumped down to ground level with incredible grace and ease. A swarm of Tantherians rained down behind him, landing as light on their feet as cotton nestles into a field on a midsummer's breeze. They closed in on Conner and the others, pointing their spears aggressively, their eyes flashing dangerously, sharp teeth gleaming in the firelight.

"What do you think you are doing, Vasska?" Donat interrogated, his confusion overshadowed by anger.

Beads of sweat began to swell on Vasska's brow. "I… I…"

"He's doing what he is told," Conner interjected, saving Vasska the trouble of answering.

Donat turned his attention to Conner. "You dare speak to me! You dare speak in place of the one I question?"

"Just kill them!" Oba spat hysterically.

Donat reached for a small pouch tied to his waist. The soldiers behind him did the same.

"You can't use that in here!" Conner pointed at Donat triumphantly, fully aware of what the pouches contained. "There are too many of you. The dosage will knock all of us out."

"We're immune!" Donat hissed. He and the throng of Tantherians behind him blew their pollen-like toxin into the air.

Conner quickly pulled the collar of his tunic over his mouth and nose.

Medwin set Moxie down, clapped one hand over his mouth, and scrambled through the contents of his pack with the other. He grabbed his hatchet but was barely able to lift it as he began gagging uncontrollably.

His free hand moved instinctually from his mouth to his constricted throat. Then, with a few useless swings of his hatchet, he crumpled to the floor in a lump next to Moxie.

Zelimir sneezed and began to choke.

Conner knew it before Zelimir hit the floor: he was going to have to finish this on his own. The shirt covering his mouth was doing just enough to protect him from the full effects of the toxin, but his mind was reeling. He started to lose focus. His thoughts felt scattered, like glass broken over stone.

Tantherians were closing in from all sides.

He had to concentrate. If he didn't get his thoughts in order, there was no way his cognition was going to work.

Closing.

He strained to illustrate a picture of the floor leaping up and grabbing hold of the Tantherian's feet, but the image was vague and blurred. Nothing happened.

Donat's spear was mere inches away now.

Conner's head was swimming. Images of these foul creatures preparing him, Medwin, Zelimir, and Moxie for dinner panned disturbingly across his mind. Then, something even more disturbing forced its way to the front of his thoughts. If he died now, if he didn't find a way to survive this, Vellix would have won. The only other person that had ever stood a chance of defeating Vellix was Vivek, and he was dead. It was up to him, Conner, to stay alive until that time that he would face Vellix. If he died during their duel, at least he would have done his best. But to die here? Like this? To become the meal of these disgusting creatures...

His mind snapped. "*No!*" he cried out, just as Donat's spear sank into his stomach. Time slowed to a crawl as he staggered back a few steps, every moment passing like an eternity of pain. He looked down at the spear protruding from his torso at an angle and mimicking the motions of his heavy breathing.

His head remained clear through the excruciating pain. He grabbed the spear firmly, and the slight motion it caused within his guts caused his teeth to gnash. He ripped it out in one swift motion, and threw it to the floor, screaming in pain. Blood began to gush freely from the wound. A part of his mind, buried deep beneath fear and pain, knew exactly what to do. His wound started weaving itself back together.

Donat backed away, fear stricken. He shook his head quickly, as if flinging away the vision of the boy across the room, whose wound was healing itself. He extended his arm toward the soldier to his right and opened his hand expectantly. The soldier handed him his spear.

With a sharp war cry, Donat charged, aiming his spear for Conner's heart. Dirt spiraled up around his legs before he could take more than a few steps. He crashed to the ground in a heap of tangled limbs.

A unanimous look of fear spread like wildfire across the faces of every Tantherian in the room.

"Drop your weapons!" Conner demanded as flames ignited in his hands.

Clinging and clattering sounds echoed around the room as the soldiers obeyed.

"What do you think you're doing?" Oba thundered. "*Kill* him!"

The soldiers shifted uncomfortably.

"There's a *hundred* of you and *one* of him!" Oba pointed out, his voice drenched with incredulity.

Not one of the soldiers responded.

"You will all follow me," Conner ordered.

Too afraid to disobey, the Tantherian soldiers followed Conner as he led them down to the prison chamber.

Conner opened the door and pushed Oba into the room. He waited in a corner for everyone to enter.

There were murmurs of surprise as the arriving soldiers saw the other group of Tantherians, bound at the ankles by dirt and at the wrists by coils of root.

"Close the door," Conner said as the last few soldiers made their way into the room. He had noticed Oba's beady eyes glancing thoughtfully at the only means of escape.

The few murmurs throughout the room grew to a steady hum.

"Quiet!" Conner snapped. The hum of voices ceased. Conner continued. "Vasska," he said, stepping toward him, "why don't you tell the rest of your people what's going on."

Vasska gaped wordlessly.

"Don't be shy about it now… Tell them how their king was only concerned with saving his own skin… Go on then, tell them."

Every Tantherian in the room scowled at Oba, bearing their formidable looking teeth. Oba looked around at them all, horrified.

Vasska started in a small voice. "The king offered us up as food," he said, cowering away from Oba. But when no repercussions came from his first statement, he gained a little confidence. "And he did it to save *himself!*" Vasska pointed an accusatory finger at the king.

A stunned silence weighed heavy around the room.

Oba fidgeted guiltily and stammered a few poorly chosen words in his defense.

"So it's true then?" Donat moved slowly toward Oba. "You offered us to the human in return for your own safety?"

Oba made a pleading gesture. "I — I didn't mean —"

"Liar!" Vasska exclaimed. "I was there! I heard him!"

"Shut up, Vasska!" Oba snapped. "Clearly the human boy has used his magic to control your mind."

"No," said Donat. "Vasska speaks the truth. You *are* lying. I can see it in your eyes… You will pay for this, *King Oba.* Your rule is at its end, as is your life."

"Wait just a — you can't — I…"

Conner removed the dirt and root bonds from the detained Tantherians and crept, unnoticed, out of the room as Oba disappeared into a swarm of fists, feet, and spears.

Horrific shrieks and ruthless jeers reverberated through the dirt walls as Conner made his way back up the stairs. "Well, that's settled," he said to himself.

* * *

Medwin, Zelimir, and Moxie were still motionless heaps on the floor when Conner re-entered the cauldron room.

He began searching the walls for a door he hoped would lead to an exit. He knew that killing Oba would only keep the Tantherians occupied for a short time. He worried that they might try to rally another attack, rather than let their dinner escape. What if the soldiers he'd faced were only a handful from of a much larger group? What if there were thousands? There was no way of knowing how extensive this underground lair actually was.

His thoughts caused him to speed up his search. At first glance, the walls appeared seamless, but after inspecting each in turn with a careful eye, he found two paper-thin lines on the wall opposite the door he already knew existed. He pushed the section of wall between them. A door swung open into a narrow hall, leading to a set of stairs dappled in natural light.

He moved quickly down the hall and peered up the stairway. Four slender lines shone bright, creating a square silhouette in the ceiling. Conner climbed the stairs, leaping two steps with each stride. When the ceiling restricted his climbing any farther, he dug his shoulder into it and shoved. A door, hinged on one side, flew open.

The purpling evening sky temporarily blinded his dilated pupils. With eyes half-shut and watering, he did his best to look around. A blurred matt of green told him he was still somewhere within the forest. He used his shirt to wipe away the last few tears from his eyes and blinked his vision into focus. A thicket not too far off looked large enough to conceal two bodies while he retrieved a third.

He jogged back down to the others. Moxie was lightest, so he grabbed him first. Even though he weighed less, it was hard work getting Moxie up to the thicket and well hidden.

By the time he managed to carry Zelimir to the surface, his muscles had become infuriated. The prospect of lugging Medwin all the way up was dreadful, but he had no alternative. So he heaved Medwin over his shoulder and stumbled his way down the hall and up the stairs, finally collapsing into the thicket with what felt like the last step he could possibly take.

After a minute's rest, Conner got up and closed the door over the stairwell. For one small moment, he thought of using cognition to crush the Tantherians below. But as he noticed the lengths to which they had gone in order to conceal the entrance to their lair — a few cleverly placed bushes whose branches swept over the four outlining seams — he realized that these creatures weren't just flesh-eating animals. They thought on a deeper level than that. They deserved to live just as much as he did. Killing them would be blatant murder. All that would do is bring him down to the same level as his enemies.

He went back to Medwin and the others to try and rouse them. It was like trying to wake the dead. He yelled in their ears and kicked their legs…

Nothing…

He pulled back Medwin's eyelids to let some light in…

Still nothing…

Finally, after much self-debate, he decided to rip out a tuft of Zelimir's fur. It seemed to hold less consequence than waiting for a huge group of Tantherians to come after them.

The wolf jumped up growling viciously, pure instinct driving him.

"Zelimir," Conner yelled, "it's okay. It was just me. You wouldn't wake up… I got desperate…"

Zelimir took a calming breath. "Conner…" He shook his head in disbelief. "Conner, *never* do that again… I was closer to biting you than you would like to know. Next time you are desperate to wake me up" — he paused, searching for the right words — "just, well just… I don't know, rip out some of Medwin's hair instead."

Conner chuckled and glanced absentmindedly at Medwin. "Okay, I'll remember that. I guess a good punch in the face is better than a bite from a wolf."

Zelimir nodded, smiling in amusement of Conner's reasoning. "Let's get out of here. You carry Moxie; I'll take Medwin. Just lay him over my back."

As the sun sank beneath the western horizon, the amount of light in the heavily wooded forest became nearly nonexistent. Conner lit a flame in his right palm to help lead their way, but Zelimir advised that he put it out, saying that they had no idea what else could be in the forest, and the bright flames would surely attract attention. Conner heeded Zelimir's words. They traveled on in near darkness, trying not to make any noise as they went.

The fact that they had been so vulnerable to capture had baffled Zelimir. He couldn't understand why he hadn't been able to smell the Tantherians. Conner suggested that it was probably because the creatures had lived and hunted in the woods for so long that they'd learned to smell identical to their surroundings. Zelimir didn't disregard his theory, but he still felt that he should have been able to catch a faint scent.

The trees began to thin. Conner was able to see the dim, blue-grey light of the northern horizon through them. Mt. Cirrus was barely visible, its top-most peak enveloped by the ever-enduring wisps of cloud spiraling around it.

A feeling of relief came over him as he exited the forest. He and Zelimir walked on for another half-hour before deciding it was safe to set up camp. Conner created an underground room nearly identical to Medwin's.

Zelimir stayed behind as Conner headed down and laid Moxie on a bed. "I'm going on a hunt," the wolf said, turning away from the room entrance.

"Hold up. I thought you said you wouldn't need to eat again for a few weeks," Conner reminded him.

"I don't need to eat, but you three do, don't you?" Zelimir gave Conner a curt nod and took off at a run.

Conner got Medwin onto his bed, then laid down on his own. It was quite comfortable, especially considering it was made of dirt. Before long, he was deep in thought. The same three questions kept coming up… 'Where are Ammin, Lenny, and the crew now? Are they going to be able to defeat the Bazza? Will I ever see them again?'

CHAPTER 21

Ammin's Revenge

"Aye, Cap'n, I'd say they been 'ere alrigh'," Lenny whispered, crouching over the scattered remains of a fire.

Ammin bent down next to Lenny to examine the area himself. He picked up a charred piece of wood. "The Bazza must not feel they are in any danger of being followed." He dropped the wood to the ground and stood up. "If they were, they wouldn't have been so careless as to leave the remnants of a fire out in the open like this."

"Aye," James said, standing next to Ammin and stroking his chin thoughtfully.

"Tha'll give us the upper hand, tha' will," said Gavin, an air of optimism about him.

"That it will, Gavin," Ammin replied, his grin scarcely visible in the moonlight. "We'll set up camp here for the night. We might as well use the same area for our fire as they did. Dale — Landon, go and see what you can scrounge up for food."

"Aye, Cap'n," they chimed back in unison.

"I'll go with you," said Marcella. She stood up and re-sheathed the Katana she'd been polishing.

"Yeah, yeh know wha', I think I'll go with yeh an' all," Lenny announced, starting after them.

"Lenny, I need you to stay here and go over our plans." Ammin reminded his first mate impatiently. Marcella threw Lenny a suspicious look while Ammin was speaking, but the young sailor didn't notice.

"Oh, righ'," Lenny said, looking deflated as he watched the other three walk into a knot of trees and disappear.

James started a fire. The crew gathered around it for warmth, and Ammin began to go over his plans for battle.

* * *

Quite some time later, Dale, Landon, and Marcella returned with the food they were able to find.

"Ain' much," Dale admitted as he dropped several dead rabbits to the ground and sat down by the fire, "but it's somethin', though, in' it?"

Landon sat down, grabbed one of the rabbits, and got to work preparing it. Marcella sat next to him and went back to polishing her sword.

Ammin watched Landon work for a moment before returning his attention to a crude drawing in the dirt at his feet. "See, if we catch up to them soon enough," he said, pointing a stick at the drawing. "Lenny! Pay attention!" Ammin nudged his first mate in the shoulder.

"Wha'? Oh..." Lenny pulled his gaze from Marcella and turned to

Ammin. “Sorry, Cap’n. Wha’ was yeh sayin’?”

“Ah, never mind. You’re in no fit state to focus.” Ammin gave Marcella a short glance, smiled, and shook his head. “You’re young… I can’t say that I blame you.”

Lenny shrugged impishly, as if to say he couldn’t blame himself either…

A heavy silence fell over the crew as the mesmerizing flames of their fire drew them in one by one, leaving them all in contemplation of what was to come.

The quiet moment was finally broken when Landon announced, “Oi! Serve up if yeh wan’ it hot… And don’t be taking more’n yer worth neither. Like I said, it ain’ much, bu’ it’ll have ter do.”

Soon after everyone ate their meager amount of food, Ammin ordered them to get some sleep. He didn’t have to tell anyone twice. They were all well aware that they would need their energy in the morning.

* * *

Dawn broke, bringing with it a heavy accumulation of morning dew, revealing the many webs that spiders had spun in the nearby trees and bushes. The air was crisp. A gentle breeze blew its way cheerfully through the glade in which Ammin and his crew were just beginning to wake.

It had been a restless night for Ammin. His thoughts kept him awake for far longer than he would have liked, and by the time he had fallen asleep, images of the same thoughts inundated his dreams. They were thoughts of what might happen to his crew. How many of them would have to die before his revenge on the beasts that took his captain's life was secure?

He thought of Captain Bellamy. What would he have done if it had been Ammin killed by the Bazza, and it was up to him to make them pay? 'Bellamy would have stopped at nothing to get his revenge,' Ammin thought, wishing there was even a small chance the answer could be different. His apprehension about leading the crew to their near-certain deaths was almost more than he could bear.

Fortunately, they did have a few things going in their favor. For one, they had the element of surprise. They also had some exceptional fighters in the crew: Lenny, James, Gavin, Dale, Landon, and Quincy were all worth a few men on the battlefield. And then there was Marcella. She seemed to be a feisty one. Although Ammin had never seen her in a real fight, he got the impression that she was more than proficient with a sword.

Knowing he wouldn't be able to fall back asleep if he tried, Ammin got to his feet and brushed the dirt and twigs off his clothes.

"Awake then, are yeh?" Lenny got to his feet as well, not bothering to brush himself off. "Di'ja manage ter ge' a wink?"

"Barely," Ammin said wearily.

"Aye. I've always known I was a bi' o' a tosser, bu' I didn' think I'd 'ave ter deal with it in me sleep an' all."

Ammin laughed and clapped Lenny on the shoulder. "Lenny, you're priceless, you know that? You're absolutely priceless." Feeling considerably better than he had beforehand, Ammin yelled for his crew to get up and get ready to move out.

Much muttering of discontent mingled indecipherably as the crew got up and slowly re-armed themselves with the weapons they had removed before bed.

"You'll all be dead with that lack of motivation," Ammin derided, shaking his head with disapproval.

Marcella took his words to heart. She quickened her pace and was ready before anyone else. "Which way are we headed, Captain?" she asked, looking straight at Ammin and ignoring Lenny, who had made a vague greeting gesture as she arrived next to him.

"Oh go on then," Lenny said, sounding dejected. "Pretend like I don' even exist…"

Marcella didn't acknowledge that Lenny had spoken as she waited for Ammin to answer her question.

"Well, I'd say that Iden is still about thirty to forty miles south of here, so we'll be heading —"

"That way," Marcella said, pointing south.

"Ah, you know your directions." Ammin gave her an approving nod. "That's good. It could save your life someday. As it has mine on more than one occasion."

Marcella beamed and waited silently for the crew to finish arming themselves.

They set out minutes later, leaving the forest behind and entering a vast field, its blades of grass easily reaching their thighs — in Quincy's case, his waist.

The first hours of travel were pleasant. There was plenty of morning shade to keep them cool. Their legs were fresh, their minds clear. But soon, every inch of shade had cowered as the sun poked up over a belt of trees running along the eastern coastline, and their comfort evaporated into its blistering heat.

Lenny stepped into stride with Marcella. She used her hand to shield the bright sun in order to see who it was.

"And what do you want?" she asked, taking no care whatsoever to remove the dislike from her tone of voice.

"Jus' wanted ter walk nex' ter yeh," Lenny said, looking at her hopefully.

Marcella made a huffing sound and sped up her pace.

"Wha' is yer problem with me, love?" Lenny asked as he quickened his own pace to that of Marcella's.

"Um… let's see," Marcella snapped in a mock version of curiosity. "First of all, *you call me love!*"

"Sorry, lo —"

"And secondly," Marcella went on, bulldozing over Lenny's retort. "You are completely tactless, self-loving, cocky, and vulgar. If I felt like I could have a conversation with you without you ogling at me… well, then that would be different. But as it is, I can't."

Lenny looked thunderstruck. He had just been told he was tactless, self-loving, cocky, and vulgar. "Well — I'm — I mean… I — I'm sorry, love, but —"

Marcella shot him a furious look.

"Oh, yeah, right… I mean… I'm sorry, *Marcella*. I didn' mean ter come across like all tha' stuff yeh said 'bout me. I was jus'… bein' meself, like."

Marcella turned away from Lenny to hide her satisfied little smirk before saying, "Well you should try to act a bit more civilized around a lady."

Lenny gawked at her. "*You're* a lady?"

Marcella tried not to laugh, but in her attempt, she let out a little snort.

"Ah ha! Made yeh laugh," Lenny snickered, pointing at her.

Marcella looked at him for a moment, as if she were contemplating whether or not she should give him the satisfaction of knowing he was right. Her furrowed brow slackened a few notches. "Yeah, that was funny," she said, grinning back at Lenny's expectant face. "Can you imagine? *Me*, a lady?"

* * *

As mid-day approached, the sun reached a central point in the sky. The heat it produced was nearly unbearable to travel in.

Ammin stripped off his shirt and used it to cover his head.

Seeing the benefit in this, most of the crew did the same.

Lenny looked expectantly at Marcella, smirking perversely.

She made a loud clicking sound with her tongue, which said he clearly hadn't managed to take a single hint from the conversation they'd had, and stalked off to catch up with Ammin.

The sun's heat persisted as the day wore on. If anything, it grew hotter until finally setting in the west.

Ammin was so exhausted from the combination of lacking sleep and the day's travels that he didn't even notice the stunning sunset that exploded into life, its vibrant medley of yellows, oranges, and pinks stretching artistically over the western horizon. He wanted nothing more than to stop for the day. To sleep. But he knew they would never have a chance of saving Iden from the Bazza if they wasted another night sleeping.

"Uh, Cap'n, yeh think we should stop fer a bit?" Quincy asked, noticing that Ammin had started to stumble.

Ammin slapped himself in the face a few times to revive his focus. "No, it's fine," he said.

"But, Cap'n," Quincy implored. "You're in a righ' state, you are. You need some —"

"I said I'm fine, Quincy!" Ammin bellowed. He wasn't going to let the Bazza slip away from him. He wasn't going to show up in Iden with the place already burnt to the ground and the Bazza long since come and gone. The time for revenge was now. Before the beasts could do any more damage.

"Alrigh', Cap'n, whatever yeh say," Quincy said. He walked off mumbling something under his breath that sounded like, "Bloody fool…"

But Ammin didn't care. He knew he had the energy for this. As soon as they reached Iden and he saw just one of those bastards, he would be more alert than he had ever been in his life.

It wasn't long before flickering lights from the torches lining the northern boardwalks of Iden became visible through the sparse trees.

Ammin and his crew crouched low and cautiously approached the edge of a large marsh.

Marcella quivered with the anticipation of finally using her mother's Katana for something other than practice. Lenny licked his lips, as was usual for him before entering a fight, and quietly awaited some sign of what was going on. Dale and Landon were having a whispered conversation — no doubt betting what little gold they had on who would have the most kills when the fight was over.

James gave them a warning to quiet down, which they heeded immediately. Not because they cared what he had to say, but because two shadowed figures had just become visible across the marsh: one the average height of a man, while the other stood at least seven feet tall. They walked along Iden's perimeter boardwalk. The shorter man spoke, unmistakable fear taking charge of his voice. "I will never serve your master, Adrial…"

"Don't be a fool, Derron," Adrial replied, laughing cruelly. "Think of your people." He gestured toward the city behind them. "You don't stand a chance in battle with my men."

"We are the best arch —"

"Don't make me laugh," Adrial hissed, cutting across Derron. "Your people are great archers, yes. But what good will that do you in close combat?"

"It will do us —"

"No good," said Adrial, interrupting again. "You might kill a few of my men, but we will wipe you from existence! We won't leave one man, woman, or child alive! Do you understand me?"

"Well," Derron said, a new level of resolve in his voice, "you're going to have a hard time killing our women and children, because while you've been blowing hot air at me, they've escaped."

"You're bluffing," Adrial replied, a note of cruel satisfaction in his voice.

"I was counting on you thinking that. It proves that you are just as stupid as you —"

A saber flashed menacingly in the firelight as Adrial drew his weapon and pierced Derron through the heart. "Fool," he sneered. "Come, men, it's time." The marsh surrounding Iden began to stir, sending countless ripples in every direction. A legion of Bazza soldiers rose from the shallow waters, their grey skin gleaming eerily in the moon and firelight as they reached their towering height. "Leave no one alive!" Adrial ordered them viciously.

The Bazza moved swiftly toward the boardwalks. A swarm of arrows filled the night air and struck their front line with deadly accuracy, impaling heads and necks and hearts.

Ammin and the crew slithered through the tall grass that lined the bank of the marsh and slipped silently into the water.

Another surge of arrows found their marks, knocking the second wave of Bazza trying to climb up to the boardwalk back into the marsh.

"They're firing from the trees!" Adrial yelled, craning his neck to try and catch a glimpse of the hidden archers. He lifted a hand in the direction of the nearest trees. They shook violently; men fell to the boardwalk below, crying out with fear and pain.

Ammin swam underwater, searching for the legs of his enemies, his mind so alert that even through the thick and foggy swamp-water the images in front of him were clear. A pair of grey legs came into view. He slashed the Bazza's Achilles tendons and met its throat with one swift slice as it fell forward helplessly.

Lenny gave Ammin a wide-eyed look of admiration and set out to find more of the Bazza before they could reach the boardwalks.

Marcella launched herself sword-first at a Bazza that had spotted Lenny as he sliced behind the ankles of another. The creature swatted her down, turned back to the spot where Lenny unknowingly awaited its attack, and reared its saber to strike. Something plunged through its torso. The beast craned his neck to find Marcella on the other end of the Katana she had just driven through him. He back handed her, ripped the sword out of himself, and turned to use Marcella's own weapon against her.

Lenny shot out of the water and stabbed the Bazza through its neck, then turned back to the one whose Achilles Tendons he had sliced, ran it through, and reached out a hand to help Marcella to her feet. "Stay sharp, love," he said, grinning. Then he dove back under the marshy water and out of sight.

Idenite ground units emerged from the far end of the town and charged the Bazza. They fought courageously, but their skill was primitive in comparison to the enemy they faced. The Bazza picked them off like annoying scabs.

"Now men!" Ammin boomed as he jumped from the depths of the marsh.

"What is this?" Adrial shrieked, realizing for the first time that his men weren't fighting the Idenites alone.

"This," Ammin yelled fiercely, "is what happens when you seek to harm the people of Rohwen!" He drew a sword with each hand and advanced on Adrial without the faintest trace of fear in his eyes. "We will unite! And we will take down whatever *scum* stands in our way!" He sprang toward Adrial with a powerful strike. Adrial blocked and countered in one effortless motion. Ammin dodged, and they began to circle one another.

Quincy gave his captain an inspired glance and dove into battle, wielding a hatchet in one hand and a cutlass in the other. His height made him an incredibly difficult target for the Bazza to hit. He immobilized them with carefully placed slashes to their legs and left them for the Idenites to finish.

Dale and Landon fought back to back, feeding off each other's intensity.

"Top tha', Dale!" Landon yelled chauvinistically as he ripped his cutlass from the Bazza he'd just slain.

"You call tha' an attack, Landon!" Dale goaded over the cries of battle. "Watch this, mate. He ducked quickly as the Bazza he was engaged in battle with swung its saber for his throat, jumped back up, drew his pistol, and shot the beast pointblank in the face.

Landon turned to Dale, roaring with laughter. But instead of receiving a smile in return, he got a frozen look of fear; before he could react, the sabers of the Bazza that had crept silently behind him had slashed through his torso in two different directions.

Dale screamed with rage as Landon's lifeless body collapsed to the boardwalk. He attacked the creature that stole the life of his best mate, blinded by the rage that drove him. Tears poured from his eyes as he slashed aimlessly in the direction of his enemy.

Before the Bazza had a chance to finish Dale as well, Gavin came bursting out of the shadows, slicing the beast just above its calf and bringing it to one knee. James flew in behind Gavin and cut off its head. "Ge' a grip o' yerself, mate!" he warned Dale. "Or you'll be dead an' all!"

Dale gave Landon one last tearstained look and didn't waste another moment in which his sword wasn't striking down any Bazza in its path.

Lenny climbed up to the boardwalk, ducking as three of his shipmate's mangled bodies fell into the marsh below.

The Bazza that had slain them let out a roar of self-empowerment, turned his attention to Lenny, and made a hand gesture that invited him to attack.

Lenny drew his weapon and stared the creature down.

"Razill will destroy you!" thundered the Bazza, advancing on Lenny with a skill unlike any he had encountered. It was all he could do to defend himself, much less mount an attack of his own.

Razill's use of the two sabers he wielded was immaculate. He devoted one to high attacks, while focusing the other on his enemy's legs. Every time Lenny caught on to a pattern, he would switch the objective of each saber.

Lenny — try as he might, and as valiant an effort as he put in — was no match for the skill, speed, and strength of Razill. Soon, the creature's sabers had caught his left leg and mid-section. He fell, no longer able to put pressure on his injured leg, and clutched at the wound on his side to slow the loss of blood.

Razill moved in for the kill, a twisted smirk of pleasure warping the network of scars across his face. Lenny swung his sword uselessly. Razill knocked it from his hand; it plunged into the marsh with a small splash.

Realizing he was about to die, Lenny spat on his enemy and cursed obscenities at him, which went unheard over the yells and cries of the battle around them.

A flash of shimmering steel streaked through Razill's waist. The sound of metal clashing with bone rang though the air. Razill's eyes grew with shock.

Lenny backed up a few inches.

The top half of the beast fell grotesquely from his lower half, splashed into the marsh, and sank out of sight, the look of shock still glued to his scarred face.

Marcella's head and shoulders were visible behind Razill's legs. She kicked them aggressively into the marsh, and the rest of her body came into view. "Come on then," she said, helping Lenny back to his feet.

"Yer wonderful, you are," Lenny said weakly as he clambered to his feet.

"Yes, well, now we're even, aren't we?" Marcella replied in a business-like tone. "You saved me and now I've repaid you. She helped Lenny away from the action and into one of the nearest huts. "Stay put."

"Bu', I've go' ter help," Lenny said. He sat up slowly, a grimace of pain distorting his face.

"You won't be any help to anybody in your state," Marcella told him apologetically, knowing it would pain Lenny to accept the truth of her words.

Perhaps her voice carried more affection than she had been aware of, because after she spoke, Lenny looked into her eyes with a smile. "You're righ'. I'll jus' stay put 'til the bat'le's over then, shall I?" he said, basking in the moment in which Marcella had spoken to him tenderly.

* * *

Adrial raised a hand toward Ammin; the planks of wood at his feet rose up and snatched at his ankles. Ammin dove in time to evade, got to his feet, and started to jump erratically in different directions, knowing it would make it incredibly difficult for Adrial's cognition attacks to find their mark if he was never in one place for more than a split-second.

"You are incredibly skilled," Adrial admitted after Ammin's most recent evasion of his attacks. "Our master could use you."

"I would never serve your master!" Ammin replied, seizing his chance to stop and catch his breath.

"You wouldn't have any choice," Adrial scoffed, his lips curling to form a horrible smirk.

"Then I would die!" Ammin exclaimed. He charged Adrial ferociously.

Adrial laughed maniacally, as though enjoying himself immensely. He blocked Ammin's attack and countered with a strong kick to his side.

Ammin cried out in pain as he felt a few of his ribs break. He crashed down to the boardwalk.

"Bet that hurt," Adrial said, his voice full of conceit, his smile broad — teeth glistening in the firelight.

Ammin struggled back to his feet, gasping for air and nursing his side. "Not as bad as this is going —"

"*Kreeee-arrrr!*"

Lolani dove from out of the darkness and pierced Adrial's neck with her sharp talons. He let out a shriek of pain that nearly rivaled Lolani's as she shrieked hatefully back into his face.

Ammin couldn't see what Lolani was doing to Adrial, but based on his morbid cries of pain he could only guess.

Adrial dropped his sabers and attempted to rip Lolani off. Ammin seized his chance and drove his swords through Adrial, wincing in pain because of the strain this put on his broken ribs.

Lolani took flight. As Ammin withdrew his swords from Adrial and saw what Lolani had done to his face, he closed his eyes, not wanting to allow the image to imprint itself upon his mind permanently.

He turned away from his dead opponent. What remained of his crew stood in a small group, gazing at him with expressions of respect and grief for the many who had fallen. The battle was won, but victory came at a heavy price. Many of the crew lay slain upon the boardwalk, or were otherwise unaccounted for.

Ammin gave his remaining men a nod that spoke of the admiration he felt for them and of the sorrow he felt for the men they'd lost. The crew nodded back and, as if a frozen moment in time had thawed, they made to busy themselves with the dead and wounded.

James started kicking dead Bazza into the marsh. He was nursing a few wounds but appeared to be okay.

Gavin joined the Idenites in moving their wounded to the nearest huts.

Dale moved drone-like to where Landon lay motionless, pulled him into his arms, and began sobbing uncontrollably. It wasn't until one of his shipmates rested a hand on his shoulder and spoke a few well-chosen words of condolence that he got up and carried Landon's body over to the group of dead awaiting burial. His demeanor was that of a man who had suffered the greatest loss.

Quincy sat on the boardwalk breathing hard. He finished tying his shirt around his stomach, its once cream coloring now drenched in crimson. He placed two bloodstained hands on the planks of wood below him and attempted to push himself to his feet. "Bloody *hell!*" he groaned, falling lamely back to his knees.

Ammin limped over and helped Quincy up. He was in bad shape, but with medical attention so readily available, Ammin didn't fear that he would lose his life. "You gonna make it, Quincy?" he asked to lighten the mood.

"Aye, Cap'n," Quincy replied feebly. "Jus' as long as I can manage ter save some o' me blood, I should be all righ'."

Ammin looked down and saw that Quincy was cradling a stomach wound far more horrific than he had guessed. “You need immediate medical attention,” he said with a grunt of pain as he pulled Quincy to his feet and felt the weight tug at his broken ribs. He helped him to one of the nearest huts and asked if there was anyone available to treat his wounds immediately.

“I’m a damn shade busy at the moment,” said a flustered-looking man who appeared to be more than overwhelmed by his workload. He only had a few men helping him, and the amount of wounded entering his hut was increasing at an alarming rate. “Set him over there.” He pointed the sharp instrument in his hand at the far corner of the room. “It should just be a moment before the women arrive to help out.”

Ammin laid Quincy gently on the floor and stayed by his side to make sure he didn’t pass out.

The minutes crept by like hours. When five had passed without any sign of the reinforcements the doctor had spoken of, Ammin began to panic. Quincy wouldn’t last much longer.

The captain’s spirits rose as muffled voices drifted into the room.

One of the doctor’s aids perked his ear at the sound. He dropped the sponge he was holding into a bucket, walked casually to the back of the room, and slid open a false panel in the wall, revealing a small recess. The man went back to the doctor’s side as if he hadn’t done anything more interesting than open a window to let in the night air.

A trap door within the recess flung open, and from what Ammin concluded could only be the marsh below, came a large group of women, looking shaken but resolute.

"The rest are coming," one of the women announced with a sideways glance at the trap door. "We hurried ahead to help out as soon as we got the signal."

"Thank you, Martha" said the doctor, not removing his focus from the man he was operating on. "Take a group with you to Jacob's hut. Heather, take another group over to Michael's." The two women led their groups hastily from the room. "The rest of you — dammit Adam, I need some pressure on the wound! He's losing too much blood!" The doctor shook his head angrily and gave the man who had opened the false panel in the wall an irritated look. "The rest of you just find someone in need and get to work…"

A kind-looking woman came over to where Ammin was kneeling next to Quincy. "I can tend to his wounds," she said in a gentle voice.

"I thank you," Ammin replied gratefully. As the women worked and Ammin's fear of losing Quincy subsided, his curiosity grew. He couldn't help but notice that the women's clothes were completely dry. "Ma'am, if you don't mind my asking, shouldn't that trapdoor lead straight into the marsh?"

The women chuckled indulgently "One would think so, yes. But it is not the case. There is a network of rooms built under the city to house the women and children in the event that we should be attacked."

"I see," said Ammin. "Very clever."

"*Come — on!*" a squat little woman yelled irritably as she emerged from the trap door. "Nicholas! Ryan! Stop horsing around and get up here! This isn't time for games you two! You're in the way of the others climbing up."

"Bet Lizzy likes the view though," one of the boys hollered back.

"Nicholas, I will smack that view so hard you won't be able to sit for a week if you don't get up here this instant!" bellowed the now extremely frustrated woman.

"Oh, alright," replied the voice from below; seconds later a boy wearing a mischievous grin climbed out of the trap door, followed closely by another boy who was undoubtedly his little brother.

Ammin watched as child after child and their mothers came up from the underground hiding place. Most of them looked extremely shaken. He turned back to the women tending Quincy's wound. "Is there anything you need from me?"

"No no, if there's something else you need to do, it's quite alright for you to leave. Your friend is going to be fine. He will just need plenty of bed-rest."

After bowing his thanks to the women, Ammin got to his feet and exited the hut. He headed back toward the main boardwalk to see if he could help with any of the others that might be injured.

"Ammin." A female voice near the marsh called his name. He had to scan the area for a moment before he found who had addressed him.

Lolani was perched atop one of the wooden posts that held up the boardwalk. "You and your crew have done well."

Ammin gave her a thankful nod.

"Not many could have entered a fight with that many Bazza and lived. Allow me to say thank you on all of Rohwen's behalf."

"We had the help of the Idenites," Ammin replied modestly.

"Indeed..."

Ammin stared wordlessly at Lolani for a second. A thought occurred to him. "Where did you come from anyway?"

"I was on my way here to ask the Idenites if they were ready to take up arms and join our forces against Vellix. However, before I arrived, I saw the owl, Katina — the one who nearly killed me, and in fact, thought she had. She was perched on a tree a short distance from here, no doubt ready to attack if necessary."

"When I saw her, I knew what must be happening — that Adrial and his men were here to do the very same thing in which I was intending to do. I attacked her. When she saw me, it was as if she had seen a ghost — like I said, she thought I was dead. I did not waste this advantage. I showed her no mercy, and in the end, I was victorious. Once I was sure she was dead, I flew as fast as I could to aid the Idenites against the Bazza. When I arrived, I saw that you and your men were already here... You clearly know the rest of the story."

Ammin nodded again.

"Well," Lolani said, glancing to the north, "I must go find Medwin and the others. But first, I need to ask... Where do you stand as an ally for the approaching war? Can we count on you?"

Ammin remained silent as he contemplated her words. He had been so consumed by his drive to avenge Bellamy that he hadn't taken the time to truly contemplate what was going on. The Bazza were recruiting, which could only mean one thing: war was definitely coming. "When you say 'we,' are you referring to Satria forces?"

"Yes. And any others we can get to join. Vellix's army is extensive. I don't know for sure the actual size, but it is safe to say they outnumber the Satria warriors by a great margin."

Ammin mulled over her words. It wasn't like him to get involved in such affairs, but he couldn't help feeling in the core of his gut that this case was different, as if the future of the world was at stake. "You can count on the aid of my crew and any other residents of Beach Bay that are willing," he said, his tone resolute.

Lolani gave him a thankful nod. "You are a good man, Ammin. My master is lucky to know you." Ammin made a gesture of thanks and Lolani continued. "You will let the Idenites know that we are in need of their allegiance?"

"Yes, of course."

"Very good. We will see one another again. Until then, keep your eyes open and keep your ears sharp. Vellix will learn that a legion of his most valued men have been defeated before long. He has many spies." Lolani took flight and disappeared into the night.

Ammin turned to find Marcella sprinting toward him.

"Come with me," she urged.

As Ammin followed her, he couldn't help but notice that she appeared to be unscathed — minus the bruising that consumed the right side of her face. His assumptions had been correct. She was definitely more than proficient with a sword. To emerge from a fight with the Bazza with nothing more than a bruised face was quite the feat.

She led him into the room where Lenny was still lying on the floor, in far worse shape than before. His skin was a pale shade of grey and sweat was dripping profusely down his face.

"Oi … Cap'n … di' we win?" Lenny asked, groaning with pain.

"Aye, lad," Ammin replied as he stared down upon Lenny with a look of pity. "We won."

"He needs medical attention!" Marcella exclaimed, gazing at Lenny with a similar look of pity in her eyes.

"Help me carry him," Ammin said, reaching down for Lenny's feet. "I know of a hut we can take him to."

They carried Lenny down the boardwalk as carefully as possible. All the while, he rambled incoherently.

It wasn't until Marcella told him to save his energy and keep quiet for the third time that he finally fell silent and allowed them to carry him the rest of the way without another mumble.

CHAPTER 22

The Traitor and the Legend

Slow, steady snores filled a small underground room. Conner tried to match Medwin's breathing pattern, hoping that it would help him fall back to sleep. He had no idea what time it was, but based on how tired he was, he assumed it was the very early hours of the morning, certainly early enough to be trying for at least a few more hours of sleep. But sleep felt like something distant that he would never attain. No matter how hard he pushed to reach it, it remained maddeningly far away.

Thoughts swirled around in his mind like a furious blizzard. If it wasn't bad enough that he was worried about the fate of Ammin and the crew, he now had Zelimir to worry about as well. The wolf still hadn't returned from his hunt. Anything could have happened to him.

True, he was a wolf and could clearly take care of himself, but what if something *had* happened? Conner scrunched up his face, angry with himself for his negative thoughts. He couldn't do anything for Zelimir if something had attacked or captured him, so why dwell on the thought? It was better to stay positive. Maybe the wolf had gone to extreme lengths to secure a good meal for his companions. Or maybe he had been so tired by the time he'd gotten his kill that he decided to rest a bit before bringing it back to camp. Either way Conner knew that he had no control over the situation.

Moxie stirred uncomfortably on his bed and started to mumble. "Must — find — way... ...Must — be — way — out..."

Conner glanced over at the dark figure of Moxie, the misery he felt for him contorting his face. Moxie was still having dreams about the years he'd spent searching to find some way of escape from Vellix's holding chamber. Even though he had escaped his prison in the physical sense, he still hadn't escaped it mentally. 'What if he never escapes it mentally?' Conner thought, a sudden surge of heartache for the hunchback causing his eyes to burn.

Why did innocent people like Moxie have to be subjected to such evil? Why did there even have to *be* evil? Why couldn't people just live their lives without seeking power and control at whatever the cost? Was power really worth ruining the lives of so many? Of course it wasn't. What would drive someone to lead such a life?

For the first time, Conner found himself wondering what had driven Vellix to become the evil man he was. A new web of thought began to spin itself meticulously.

'Well, for starters, Vellix's childhood must have been really tough,' he thought, recalling the conversation he and Medwin had had on Ewaun. 'Being raised by a race of people that are not your own because yours were wiped from existence would be awful...'

'Yeah, but he didn't know the truth,' a separate part of his mind retorted quickly. 'He thought he was from Edelan.'

'Yes, but later he found out the truth, and that was probably a huge part of what drove him. Imagine how betrayed he must've felt when he found out that the one he called mother had lied to him his whole life. She could have told him why he and his brother were different. She could have told him that he was the last of a proud race. The last of the Hylan.'

'But was that really enough to cause him to become truly evil? A lot of people grow up with hardships and turn out okay,' Conner thought conclusively. 'In fact,' he continued, hoping to vindicate himself even further, 'due to Vellix's oppression upon the people of Rohwen, many of them have grown up dealing with far worse childhoods than he did... Look at what he did to the Edelish. He scorched their homeland into nothing more than a desert wasteland.'

Suddenly, something occurred to him. 'What if he didn't just punish the Edelish for their allegiance to the Satria? What if he punished them for not giving their allegiance to *him?*' They would, after all, know exactly who he was, being that one of their own ancestors was the one who raised him. Vellix would have known they were keepers of lore, which would have given them no reason to ignore their own past: a past in which he had been a part, whether they liked it or not.

'What about Vivek, though?' Conner thought realistically. He was Vellix's twin brother. Evelina had raised him just as she had raised Vellix, and he had turned out to be a great man. So, was it even his upbringing that led Vellix down the path he chose? Or was it his profound abilities that caused him to thirst for the power he had stopped at nothing to secure?

'Do not let the knowledge held within the last scroll warp your mind as it has Vellix's…' The warning Salix and Lolani had given Conner floated across his mind. 'Was it the scroll, alone, that shaped Vellix's path?'

His thoughts continued to stir inconclusively for a few minutes. Then, as if the answer was a ripe apple waiting for the plucking, he knew the truth of it. It came to him in a calm voice of wisdom that reminded him of Vivek. 'Every moment of life shapes our path… It is up to us to remain on the right one…'

Conner's stomach growled angrily. He hadn't eaten since the food Azalea gave him. His hunger was so immense that he actually felt nauseous. He supposed that fighting off the Tantherians' toxin had used quite a bit of the food energy he normally would have been able to store. The temptation to leave the underground room and see if he could find something to eat started to creep into his mind.

Finally, after another half hour lying there, hopelessly trying to fall back to sleep, he grabbed his bow and arrows and left.

The air was brisk as he stepped out into the night. It purged him of all unwanted thoughts, leaving nothing but a clear focus of his goal. He heard the faintest noises around him: the leaves of the sparse trees rustling in the wind, the blades of grass sweeping gently across each other, the trickle of a stream in the distance.

Conner's heart gave a powerful jolt as the sound of footsteps met his ears. He fumbled to string an arrow and spun around to locate the source.

"Medwin … you scared me half to death!" Conner hissed, not wanting to make any noise that would scare off potential game. He took a deep breath.

"Sorry, Conner, I heard you leave and felt like it would be safer if the two of us went to find food."

Conner gave Medwin a questioning look that went unnoticed because he was busy rummaging around his pack. "How did you know I was going to find food?" Conner asked, a little taken aback.

Medwin eyed Conner for a moment.

Conner felt his face burn with embarrassment as Medwin's expression told him he was about to be made to look a fool.

"I assure you, I'm just as hungry as you are," Medwin replied calmly. "Plus, you brought your bow and arrows."

"Right," Conner said quietly.

They set out, side-by-side, their eyes scanning the landscape in opposite directions. Conner was grateful to have Medwin with him — he was nowhere near the hunter Medwin was. It was a good feeling knowing his chances of finding food had probably just tripled.

"Did you hear that?" Medwin whispered, breaking a long-lasting silence.

Conner stopped and listened intently. The faint sound of something creeping along through the grass was coming from somewhere just ahead of them.

"What are you waiting for?" Medwin hissed. "Get an arrow strung." His voice was quiet, but it still carried plenty of command.

Conner strung an arrow as quickly as possible. Whatever animal was lurking in the grass lunged out abruptly and ran off in the opposite direction. Conner took a shot and missed. The animal made a sharp left turn. The shadow of a bird flew out of the grass. With one great leap, the creature giving chase seized its prey and broke its neck with a mighty jerk. It then headed straight for Conner and Medwin, a bit of a flaunty trot to its step, its kill flopping lifelessly around in its mouth.

"Medwin, it's Zelimir," Conner said, excitement rising in his voice. "Help me gather some wood."

"Good thing you missed," Medwin uttered gravely.

Conner stopped scanning the ground for kindling and looked up at Medwin, his expression grim.

"But you did, though, so no point worrying about it," Medwin added, as it became clear he shouldn't have put the thought in Conner's mind.

By the time Zelimir arrived, Conner and Medwin had gathered enough wood to start a small fire. Medwin prepared the meat while Conner went to get enough wood to build a fire worthy of cooking over.

Less than an hour later, they were enjoying a quail dinner. Zelimir sat cleaning himself, giving each of the boys an occasional amused glance.

Medwin stashed some of the meat in his pack. "Let's save this for Moxie. I'm sure he'll be starving when he wakes up."

Conner nodded, got to his feet, and stretched. Now that he had something in his stomach, sleep was calling him, and he knew he would have to answer.

Medwin stamped out the coals of their fire and started to head back for camp, leaving Conner momentarily paralyzed by awe. The fact that Medwin was able to do such a thing without the protection of shoes was incredible. He made to follow Medwin, but Zelimir didn't move.

"What's up?" Conner asked curiously.

Medwin stopped walking to listen to Zelimir's reply.

"I smell something… Something familiar," Zelimir replied slowly. "I just can't place — wait! Follow me." He started to run.

Conner and Medwin exchanged confused looks and then did their best to catch up with the wolf.

"What do you figure?" Medwin yelled to Conner, projecting his voice over the sound of air rushing past their ears.

Conner, who was quickly growing short of breath, shrugged in reply because he didn't want to waste any precious oxygen.

After running nearly two miles, Zelimir came to a quick halt.

Conner and Medwin gratefully seized the chance to stop, both of them gasping for breath. Zelimir turned to them. "Keep quiet," he whispered severely.

Voices drifted from the other side of a thick wall of shrubbery. Conner inched forward until he had a decent view of where they were coming from.

Two men stood facing each other, both of them wearing dark robes. One was hooded, his face lost in shadow, while the other's hood hung loosely over his shoulders. His appearance was hard to make out, but with the sliver of moonlight trickling over Rohwen that night, Conner could tell the man was extremely old. Behind the two men, buried in darkness, was the outline of a vast tree.

"What you seek, you will never find," said the man with no hood, confidence striking every word.

The hooded man remained quiet for a moment — perhaps contemplating his response. Finally, he spoke. His voice was dim yet powerful. "What makes you so sure? I have done a great many things that most would have thought impossible."

"This may very well be true," the old man responded, "but you have not yet even located the entrance of the ruins, so I feel quite confident that you will not be finding the scroll anytime soon."

"I have the stone," the hooded man replied, trying to keep anger from inflecting his voice. "I could force you to show me. You may have been a legend in your time, Xellore, but I have your stone."

Conner and Medwin both clapped a hand over their mouths to stop themselves blurting out gasps of shock. How could this be? Xellore was supposed to be dead.

"I will not allow you to force me to show you anything," Xellore said calmly.

"I don't really know that you have a choice," the hooded man replied.

"Of course I have a choice, you fool… We always have a choice. I, having made the wrong choices on more than one occasion, know all too well the importance of making the *right* ones."

The hooded man didn't seem to know how to reply. He stood silently for another moment before saying, "I will torture you," his voice carrying a sharp edge.

Xellore was unmoved. "I will fight for as long as my body permits it. If I end up being tortured… Well, I really can't say it's not what I deserve." Sensing that his words had taken the hooded man to a realm where idle conversation meant very little, Xellore entered a fighting stance and awaited his opponent's first move.

The ground began to rumble.

Xellore remained motionless.

Thousands of roots burst from the soil and spiraled around Xellore like tiny snakes. As the roots tightened their grip, Xellore let out a slow breath. The roots became frail and dissipated, causing the plant life all around him to wither and die.

It was Xellore's turn to attack. The ground behind the hooded man launched itself skyward, forming a gaping cave entrance in a matter of seconds. It remained suspended in the air for a split second before falling heavily, swallowing the man.

Dirt, grass, and rock sprayed in all directions as the hooded man erupted from his newly formed prison.

As the debris settled, Conner noticed that the man's hood was no longer covering his face. He was just able to make out his appearance.

Skin hung loosely from his face and, like Xellore, he was extremely old.

Medwin, try as he might to cover his mouth, made an audible gasping noise. Fortunately, the two dueling men didn't notice. He turned to Conner and whispered in a voice so low that Conner had to strain to hear it, "That's Yorick!"

Conner tried to place the name. He felt like he'd heard it before, but he wasn't quite sure. He glanced over at Medwin, who had turned his attention back to Xellore and Yorick, and saw that his fists were clenched tightly. His expression was of the deepest loathing. 'Whoever Yorick is, he must be an enemy of the Satria.' Conner concluded, returning his attention to the dueling men.

A cluster of rocks rose up from the ground, mimicking Yorick's hands as he raised them above his head. The rocks quivered in mid-air for a moment. Yorick thrust his hands forward, and they shot toward Xellore like a swarm of pestering insects.

The rocks crumbled as they came within a foot of Xellore. Soon, a perfectly circular shield of dust hovered in front of him. Xellore stabbed his hands at the air in front of him. The dust shot back at Yorick, turning into one large shard of rock as it went.

Yorick sidestepped in time to evade. Emerald-green balls of flame materialized in his hands.

As countless green fireballs rained in on Xellore, he lit violet-purple ones in his hands and started to blast Yorick's out of the sky. Purple and green sparks showered the night and settled into the surrounding dirt and grass.

A solid minute of intense battle passed, and neither Xellore nor Yorick were able to land a single attack. They ceased fire, both men breathing heavily.

Yorick regained his composure well before Xellore. "How long can you keep this up, Xellore?" he goaded, careful to put as much sting into his words as possible. "If you would just tell me where —"

"*I won't tell you!*" Xellore shrieked. He made mirrored gestures with his hands. Two trees from off in the distance uprooted. He heaved them at Yorick, grunting from the immense effort the attack cost him.

Yorick pointed his hands at the two trees as they hurtled toward him. They whittled into small spears as the came within range. He caught and threw them back at Xellore in one swift motion.

Xellore batted away the two spears, but Yorick had already conjured another attack.

The ground under Xellore's feet ripped open, sending deep fissures in every direction. Xellore fell from view. A dull thudding sound echoed into the night, followed by the sound of hard wood splintering. The huge silhouetted tree behind Yorick came crashing down in two separate pieces.

Conner and Medwin swapped worried looks and quickly set their focus back on the fight. 'Please let him still be alive,' Conner pleaded silently.

Xellore rose up on a platform of stone. As the platform grew level with the ground, it latched firmly to its surroundings. Xellore had saved himself from falling to his death, but his body was now lying in a broken lump.

Yorick advanced on him. "You should have told me what I wanted to know. Now you will suffer." He pointed his hand at the two fallen pieces of tree; they exploded, scattering tiny slivers of wood across the night sky.

"No!" Xellore cried in horror.

Yorick pointed his other hand at Xellore. "You should have realized that when I said I would torture you, I meant mentally as well as physically. I want you to suffer wholly!"

Xellore started to jerk violently, his body contorting into positions that were far from natural. His screams filled the night, and for the first time Conner had seen in Rohwen, rain began to fall. It was almost as if the world could feel Xellore's pain and was weeping for him.

Conner couldn't take it. Xellore was going to be tortured to death if he didn't do something. He grabbed three arrows from his quiver and fired them in quick succession. Each found their mark, striking Yorick in his ribs.

Yorick shrieked and turned to look at what had hit him.

His mind focused intently, Conner pictured each deeply imbedded arrowhead breaking into hundreds of pieces and flinging themselves in different directions.

Yorick fell to the ground, writhing in agony.

Conner stepped out from the bushes that had concealed him, blue flames burning bright in his hands.

Medwin and Zelimir both made gestures of disapproval, but neither of them pursued him.

As Yorick got to his feet and realized what was facing him, fear shaped his features. He had just expended nearly all of his energy dueling with Xellore. There was no way he could enter a fight with a fresh opponent. "Who are you?" he asked, ripping the arrows out of his side as if they hadn't fazed him, but making the telltale expression of someone who was trying to conceal their pain.

Before Conner had a chance to reply, Yorick's eyes grew with understanding. He was facing the one who was destined to have power in cognition greater than all others. He turned on the spot and fled for his life.

Zelimir sprang out from the bushes and gave chase.

"Zelimir, wait!" Conner yelled out to him, but it was too late. He had already disappeared from view.

A distinct yelping sound echoed through the trees a few moments later.

"You go to Xellore," said Medwin as he leapt out from behind the bushes and took off after Zelimir.

Conner moved over to Xellore. The ancient man was still whimpering quietly in a heap on the ground. Conner bent down next to him. "Xellore, sir," he said sympathetically, "are you alright?" Even as the question left his mouth, he knew it was a dumb one. Of course he wasn't alright. He had just fallen a great distance and been tortured.

Xellore turned to look at who was speaking to him. As Conner met his eyes, he was surprised to see that Xellore was wearing a satisfied smile. "I knew I would meet you before I died," he said weakly. "There is much that I need to tell you — things that you must know."

Conner's mind burst into attentiveness. His thirst for the knowledge Xellore had to offer was beyond any that he had ever known. He returned Xellore's smile and then looked at him as though he wanted nothing more than to listen, to learn.

"Have you read the scrolls?" Xellore inquired.

"Yes," Conner replied with a nod. "All except —"

"The one Yorick just tried to get me to help him find…"

"Yeah," Conner said, wondering again who Yorick was, but feeling it was a subject more suited for him and Medwin to discuss. He didn't want to take his conversation with Xellore down any path but the one Xellore chose.

"So you know about the stone then?" Xellore went on.

Conner had to think for a second. "You mean the one that you infused with cognition?"

Xellore smiled, and for a brief moment there was a youthful gleam in his eyes "The very same."

"Is that what Yorick meant when he said he had the stone then?" Conner asked.

"Yes, that is what he meant. He thinks that because he holds the stone, he will be able to grow more powerful than his master. This, however, is not true. Yorick has no Hylanian blood, and therefore has no chance of exceeding Vellix's skill, stone or no. What's more, there is a vital piece of information Yorick does not know, and if I'm not mistaken, neither does Vellix."

Conner could feel himself edging closer to Xellore, his curiosity at its peak.

"The stone Yorick holds is not the only one." Xellore smiled as he watched his words sink in.

"There's more than one?" Conner asked hungrily.

"Indeed," Xellore replied.

Conner was already imagining what possessing a cognition infused stone would do for his skill. He would actually have a good chance against Vellix if he could double his power.

"In fact," Xellore continued, "there is more than two. I made three altogether. And one of them is in your —"

"*Pocket!*" Conner exclaimed, reaching into his right pocket and pulling out the little stone that he found just before Lolani had led him to the gate between his world and Rohwen. He examined the stone again. Its bluish-grey surface was just distinguishable in the moonlight. He rotated it in his hand to investigate the etching on the other side and realized that the lines made a crude, yet unmistakable version of the Hylanian symbol. "So it was you that Zelimir smelled in the forest behind my house. But then… that means…"

"Yes, I have been to your world. In fact, I have been there twice."

Conner couldn't find a response. He just stared at Xellore, unable to close his gaping mouth.

"The first time I entered your world," Xellore said, moving on, "was during the seven years in which I explored the expanses of Rohwen. As you might already suspect, due to your sharing a similar experience, I was unaware of the fact that I had entered another world at first. The transition between Rohwen and Earth is seamless."

Initially, Conner was shocked to hear that Xellore knew the name of his world, but after a moment's contemplation, he felt that it made a certain amount of sense.

Xellore could tell that Conner's mind was working furiously to make sense of everything. He paused for a second before continuing. "It wasn't until I met a woman by the name of Alice that I learned I was in a land by the name of Montana: one of many places on the world known as Earth.

"Alice was planting saplings in the forest behind her home when I first saw her. I knew right away that there was something odd about her. The clothes she wore were" — Xellore surveyed Conner's tennis shoes and jeans — "strange…"

Conner couldn't believe what he was hearing. Xellore had crossed the gate into his world two thousand years ago, but, due to the vast difference in the timelines between the two worlds, he had met Conner's grandmother, Alice. He wondered how she could've possibly kept a secret as huge as meeting someone from another world for so long.

"I stayed with Alice for just over a week," Xellore said, a note of shame entering his tone. "She was, in every way, a beautiful person. I found myself falling for her, contemplating the idea of remaining on Earth permanently. I set up a small camp — nothing elaborate, just a fire-pit and a makeshift bed — and on the ninth night, we lay with one another… It was then that I saw the error of my decision. I knew that I did not belong in that world. Why get involved with a woman who did? And so, as sad as it made me, I left her in the early hours of the morning…"

Conner felt himself burning with anger. Xellore had slept with his grandmother and then left her without any explanation. Now he knew how she had kept such a secret. He put his feelings aside and listened intently as Xellore started speaking again.

"For quite some time the idea that I may have left her expectant of child haunted my thoughts, but as the years passed, so did the thoughts." Xellore stared blankly at the sky for a moment, engulfed in thoughts from a past long forgotten.

"Now," he said weakly, snapping back to the present, "as you already know, after creating Salix I documented the information that she gave me into five scrolls. Every aspect of her knowledge astounded me, but none so much as her foresighted nature. It wasn't, however, until far too late that I realized everything she had predicted only came to pass at my own hand: The destruction of Hylan… The great evil that would plague Rohwen for centuries… The arrival of the one who would have the power of cognition more powerful than any other…"

Conner was staring at Xellore so intently now that his eyes were burning. Why hadn't he figured it out sooner? It was so obvious now. "So, what you're saying is that… that I'm…"

"My grandson …yes." Xellore gave Conner a warm smile. "Your mother is my daughter…"

This was almost too much to comprehend, yet it made perfect sense. 'I am part Hylanian,' Conner thought, touching his face instinctually, almost as if he had just become a new person and was curious what he felt like. 'That's why I have the power of cognition. That's why I'm the one destined to defeat Vellix. Everything Salix ever predicted happened because of Xellore… Including my existence.'

Xellore watched in silence as Conner worked everything out in his head.

For minutes, the two of them remained silent. Conner threw occasional glances at Xellore, each time finding that his grandfather was gazing upon him intently. The silence grew awkward and Conner searched for a means of breaking it.

"I know what happened to Areona," he said, speaking softly.

Xellore closed his eyes, a look of the deepest grief etched into the deep lines of his face.

"And how Hylan was destroyed," Conner added. He awaited Xellore's response, but got none. Finally, he decided to continue. "Xellore, sir, how did you survive when the tidal wave struck Hylan?"

Exhaling a grunt of pain, Xellore adjusted himself into a more comfortable position. "I am a cognition master," he said simply. When Conner didn't reply, he decided to elaborate. "I buried myself deep underground and waited for the danger to pass… I only wish that I could have saved others. I was on the outskirts of the city when it happened. I had no time to warn them. I was almost killed myself... Now, I must ask. How do you know these details about events that happened so very long ago?"

"I was told by a woman named Odriana — she is a keeper of ancient lore," Conner said matter-of-factly.

"She is, no doubt, Edelish, yes?" Xellore asked, even though he clearly knew the answer to his own question.

"Yeah..." Conner replied.

Xellore stared off into space, as if he was miles away from his body, submerged in memories. "For hundreds of years, I had no idea she had left... Areona," he started, almost speaking to himself more than Conner. "I thought she had died when the wave struck Hylan. I never forgave myself for my limitless pride and arrogance. If I had just listened to her... She was wiser, by far, than I..."

Xellore turned his focus to Conner, as if suddenly remembering that he was still in a conversation with someone other than himself. "It wasn't until I realized Vellix was extremely gifted in the art of cognition that I understood the truth: Areona had left the city when she concluded I would never be swayed from my foolishness and given birth to our child. She loved me very much, but nothing can stand in the way of a mother and the safety of her child." Xellore coughed and tried to grab more of himself than was possible with two hands, his face twisting with pain.

Conner knew that his time was running short. Xellore was dying. He had to tell him before it was too late. He couldn't let Xellore die thinking he only had the one son: a son who lived a life of evil. "Areona gave birth to twins," he said, placing a hand on his grandfather's arm.

Xellore gazed at Conner, his expression a battle between curiosity and confusion.

"She gave birth to two sons," Conner went on. "Your other son's name was Vivek…"

"Was?" Xellore asked quietly.

"Vellix… killed him, a short time ago… I — I'm sorry, Xellore, sir."

"And…" Xellore coughed again, cringing from the pain it caused him "…he, was, a good man?"

"He was a great man," Conner replied without hesitation, thinking about how unfair it was that he had been able to spend at least a short time with both Vivek and Xellore when they, as father and son, had not been able to meet. No sooner than he had had this thought, it spawned a new question. "Xellore, sir, what have you been doing all these years?"

"Waiting," he answered simply.

"Waiting?" Conner repeated.

"Yes, waiting…"

"For what? Sir?"

"For your arrival," Xellore replied, giving Conner a serious look.

"You've been waiting all this time for my arrival?" Conner asked incredulously. "But why?"

"Well, I would think based on the knowledge you already have that the answer would be quite obvious."

Conner stared at him blankly.

"It is because I am the reason that you will be able to defeat Vellix, Conner. Don't you see? It is I who am about to tell you where the entrance to the ruins of Hylan are; I who planted the stone for you to find. This gives you a power Vellix will never expect you to have."

Conner shifted slightly, listening avidly.

"It is I who is going to warn you that Vellix has used cognition to riddle the ruins of Hylan with traps that would make it impossible for one seeking the scroll to find it, if they aren't previously aware that these traps were merely illusions."

"So… I'm going to have to get past Vellix's traps?" Conner queried, unable to conceal how concerned this made him.

Xellore nodded grimly.

Conner rotated the stone in his pocket absentmindedly. He hoped it would be enough to get him past the obstacles ahead. "Sir, how did Vellix get the other stone?" he asked without even realizing he had formed the thought.

"He took it from me," Xellore said, giving Conner a solemn look as he answered.

"But… how — I mean, if you had the stone, how was he powerful enough to take it from you?"

"I didn't fight him… He had already read all five scrolls at that point. And he had mastered every aspect of cognition they could teach him. I could feel his power when he confronted me in the ruins, and what a power it was."

"So, what you're saying is that you were scared of him? Even though you had the stone?" Conner asked, half understanding; half shocked.

"No, that is not what I'm saying. I was merely letting you know how impressive his power was, even then. The reason I did not fight him is this: had I attempted to defeat Vellix at that time and succeeded, you wouldn't be able to fulfill your destiny. I had already caused enough damage, thinking that I could take matters into my own hands. I knew that I had to let Vellix continue on his path until the time that he would meet you." Xellore coughed again. He had grown extremely pale.

"But, what if I can't beat him," Conner said, feeling the full weight of the task ahead on his young shoulders. "What if he kills me…"

"I can't begin to pretend like I know what would happen at that point, but you are right to be worried about it. Just because you are destined to defeat him does not mean you can behave arrogantly, as I'm sure you are well aware." Xellore's voice was growing weaker.

The sounds of someone struggling to move through the grass drifted amongst the trees.

"So what are you saying?" Conner asked, desperate to finish his conversation. "What do I have to do?"

"You must become the person that you are destined to be…"

Xellore was speaking through a terrible grimace now. "…Become the one powerful enough to defeat him."

"Conner," Medwin yelled from somewhere out in the pitch-black night, his voice straining as if he were putting great effort into something.

"Medwin, where are you?" Conner called back. Xellore made a gurgling noise. "Don't die, sir! Sir, you can't die!"

Xellore gave him an extremely weak smile.

"Over here," Medwin said with a grunt. His voice sounded closer now. "I don't know what Yorick did to Zelimir, but he's hurt really bad."

"Did you give him a reviver?" Conner asked, not wanting to take his attention away from Xellore.

"Of course… Only — it doesn't seem to have done as much for him as it should have."

Conner tore his eyes from Xellore and threw a quick glance over at the barely visible outline of Medwin. He was dragging the limp body of Zelimir alongside him.

"He's going to be okay though, right?" Conner asked to confirm that Zelimir was fine before turning his attention back to Xellore.

"Yes, I believe so," Medwin said, breathing hard. "He just needs to rest. His heart rate is steady.

Conner gave Medwin a nod. "Xellore, sir…"

The motionless form of Xellore didn't respond.

At first, Conner was worried that he had died, but then he saw his grandfather's chest rise ever so slightly.

Xellore looked over at Zelimir, lying in the grass a few feet away. "The lone wolf," he whispered with an awed tone.

"Can't you heal him?" Medwin asked, eying Xellore piteously. "I mean, can't you use your cognition to heal him, and I'll give him the last reviver," he added, sounding urgent.

"Yeah, I can give it shot," Conner said, even though he was almost positive that Xellore's wounds were far beyond repair — at least at his level of cognition. A small voice in his head said, 'Use the stone…' His heart gave a leaping jolt. He was about to find out how much the stone would increase his skill.

Before Conner could do anything, Xellore whispered something inaudible.

"What was that, sir?"

Xellore whispered again, this time just loud enough for Conner to hear. "…No…"

"No," Conner repeated skeptically, as if he hadn't heard properly.

"No," Xellore said again, this time making sure there was no way Conner could misunderstand him.

"What do you mean, no? You don't want me to try and heal you?" Conner asked, completely stupefied.

"No, I want you to let me die. I am at peace for the first time in two thousand years. I have been waiting a very long time to die..."

Conner looked at Xellore, hardly able to understand how someone could *want* to die.

"You are young, Conner," Xellore uttered. "If you choose to use cognition to prolong your life for as long as I have, you will understand what it is like to accept death with open arms… My one request is that you bury me alongside Salix. In some ways it feels fitting that we should die on the same night…"

"What do you mean, 'die on the same night?'" Conner exclaimed, barely aware of the fact he was yelling.

Xellore gazed at Conner compassionately. "Don't you realize" — he glanced at the splintered remains of the tree a few hundred feet away — "what tree it was that Yorick destroyed?"

"No," Conner yelled, "it can't be!" He heard Medwin gasp somewhere behind him.

"I assure you that it is. Now, listen carefully," Xellore ordered, his tone becoming hard to ensure that Conner knew this was no time to mourn losses. That he needed to remain focused.

Conner pulled his eyes away from Salix's remains and looked at Xellore.

"There is a steep slope in the landscape to the east. If you use cognition on the largest boulder upon that slope, you will discover the entrance to the ruins of Hylan…" Xellore's voice trailed off with his last few words.

"So, the entrance is east of here?" Conner asked quickly, wanting to make absolutely sure that he had heard Xellore's scarcely decipherable words correctly. But no reply came.

A gust of wind whispered through the grass and trees, and as it carried on in its timeless journey, Xellore's being was carried away with it.

CHAPTER 23

Acceptance

Conner gazed quietly at Xellore for a moment. He wasn't really sure why he was sad about him dying. After all, the ancient man had told him he was ready to die just moments before he passed. Maybe it was the fact that he would never speak with Salix again that was truly weighing on his heart. Or maybe it was because death had always been taught as something that was supposed to be sad. He had never considered the idea that some people may actually welcome death. He contemplated the tasks ahead. 'Dying would be easier,' he thought, allowing himself a dismal smirk.

As Conner stood up and saw that Medwin was looking at Xellore with a grieved expression, he concluded that to understand the acceptance of death at their young age was truly a waste of time. He wasn't ready to die. He was only fourteen years old. He had just started living.

"Well," Medwin said, finally pulling his eyes away from Xellore's dead body, "we should get started burying him."

Conner nodded, his expression distant. The revelations that had come from his conversation with Xellore were stirring in his mind: questions he'd asked, answers Xellore had given him, things that he had known about Xellore's past that Xellore himself had not. They were playing back as if he'd put them on repeat.

He was vaguely aware that he had helped Medwin drag Xellore's body over to the remnants of Salix, and that Medwin had used cognition to dig a grave and was now placing Xellore's body within it. As Medwin lodged a rock at the head of the grave, Conner remembered what he had written on Vivek's gravestone. The memory of it felt like a lifetime ago now. 'Here lies Vivek: Last of the Hylan.' This statement was false, owing to the fact that he himself had Hylanian blood in his veins.

He almost felt like the first fourteen years of his life had been fake, pointless, or at the very least, useless. How skilled would he be right now if he'd spent all those years in Rohwen, learning cognition?

A sharp stab of guilt pierced his heart as his parents' smiling faces drifted across his mind. If he had grown up in Rohwen, he wouldn't have spent all those years — years in which he had many wonderful memories — with his parents. Before he could stop them, small tears were trickling down his cheek. What were his parents doing now? How worried had his mother become at this point? Did she think he had run away because his father and she had forced him to move to Montana? He remembered how short he had been with her the morning he left, eating as fast as he could and not even thanking her for the meal she had provided for him.

"Conner… …Conner…"

Medwin was calling his name from somewhere as distant as another planet. "Conner," Medwin said again, waving a hand in front of his face.

Conner snapped back to reality, feeling as though his head had just gone on a dismal and depressing vacation. "What's up?"

"Are you okay?" Medwin asked with a concerned glance in his direction.

"Yeah — fine," Conner replied unconvincingly.

"Are you sure?" Medwin probed, clearly not fooled by Conner's pitiful attempt at a lie. "Because it looks as though you've been crying."

"It's just sad, isn't it? Xellore and Salix dying…" Conner lied again, this time successfully fooling Medwin.

"Yeah, I suppose it is… But he did say he wanted to die, and that it was fitting for Salix to have died on the same night… I mean, I guess that makes it less sad, don't you think?" Medwin looked at Conner hopefully, not wanting him to think he was being cold-hearted about the whole thing.

"I guess so," said Conner, who couldn't have agreed more with Medwin's logic. He felt like Medwin probably thought him an oversensitive little baby at the moment. But he didn't care about that. He was determined not to bring up the subject of parents. If the subject was emotional for him, it was nothing in comparison to what it was for Medwin.

"What should we put on the headstone?" Medwin mused, tilting his head artistically, as if hoping it would give him a new, more revealing angle of the stone.

"Well," Conner said thoughtfully. "Probably just something simple… Like, 'Here lies Xellore: master of cognition,' or something like that." He didn't want to find himself inscribing false information upon another headstone as he had on Vivek's. It felt like an insult to Vivek's memory that he had called him 'The last of the Hylan,' now that he knew it wasn't true.

"Yeah, that's perfect," Medwin agreed, apparently quite taken with Conner's word choice. "You're going to have to do the inscription though" — he frowned, but quickly recovered himself — "because my cognition isn't advanced enough to do it…"

Conner was about to start the lettering when a thought occurred to him. Medwin was more than capable of this level of cognition. All he had to do was focus. Had he not created those stairs in the face of the Cliffs of Elders on their way to seek out Vivek? "Why don't you do it, Medwin?" Conner said, putting as much encouragement into his words as possible.

"Me?" Medwin pointed at himself, shocked that Conner had asked him to do it. "But, I figured you would do a good job of it."

"Maybe," Conner replied modestly, knowing that the task would truthfully be no problem for him and itching to use the stone in his pocket. However, he felt that Medwin needed this confidence booster. The more skill he had with his cognition, the better.

"So, okay, let's see," Medwin said to himself, now tilting his head so far that it was nearly touching his shoulder.

Conner watched, feeling the urge to laugh. He controlled his impulses, knowing it would deflate Medwin faster than a punctured balloon. He didn't have to fight the laughter for long though; Medwin had closed his eyes — surely summoning the picture of their chosen words engraved upon the headstone. His expression looked oddly strained with focus and detached from the world around him.

After a brief moment, in which Conner hoped beyond hope that he hadn't just set Medwin up to fail, words began to scribe themselves into the headstone.

Soon, Medwin was investigating his work with an air of someone who suffers from the disease of over-critiquing. "Well, it's not very good, is it?" he finally grumbled, looking unsatisfied.

Conner pretended to still be making a decision on what he thought of Medwin's work, which he had already concluded looked as though it had been written by a child in grade school. "I think it looks fine," he announced encouragingly. "It's perfectly legible, and that's what matters, right?" he added quickly.

"Yeah, I suppose so," Medwin replied, determined to accept Conner's compliment. "It was kind of crazy doing it," he said, his voice becoming suddenly confident, almost smug. "You know, picturing the words in my mind and then having the cognition work. It's not like I don't know what it feels like to do cognition" — he gave Conner a shrewd look and went back to appraising his work — "but this was different. There was a bit of art involved in it, you know?"

It seemed that once Medwin had forgiven himself for his less than tidy letters he was quite keen to give himself a hardy pat on the back. "Yeah, for sure," Conner replied, grinning from ear to ear as he continued to watch Medwin act overly pleased with himself.

"I should really be practicing more often, shouldn't I?" Medwin said seriously.

"Definitely!" Conner agreed. "I mean, look at that, Yorek, or whatever you said his name was. He wasn't of Hylan descent, and he is obviously a cognition master. I suppose all it really takes is the right mindset and a lot of…" Conner trailed off as he noticed Medwin was giving him a murderous look. "What?"

"It's not 'Yorek,'" Medwin flared up with a dismissive gesture. "It's *Yorick*, and I don't ever want you to compare me to him again! Understood?" Medwin's eyes were bulging, making him look completely out of his mind.

"*Sorry*," Conner retorted indignantly.

"It — it's okay…" Medwin mumbled. Hearing Conner respond so heatedly seemed to have pulled him back to his senses. "I suppose you would have no idea the severity of the fact that Yorick is Vellix's pupil, would you?"

"No, I wouldn't," Conner said, not only grateful for Medwin's ability to rationalize, but also for the fact that he was going to get an explanation.

When Medwin started to speak, it looked as if he were forcing back a large quantity of vomit. "Yorick…" he began; just saying the name seemed to bring him physical pain, "…was my father's primary advisor…"

Conner's jaw dropped.

"...Not only that," Medwin continued after soaking up Conner's expected reaction, "but he was also head of all thirty elders... I held council my first day back from Mt. Cirrus. Once the elders and warrior captains had gathered, the seat to my immediate right was empty. I was informed that Yorick had died in battle, and that his body had not been recovered. I grieved the loss of the man who knew my father better than anyone... *I grieved, Conner!*" Medwin looked deranged against the faint moonlight, his features contorting with rage.

"I — Medwin... I'm —"

"And he was Vellix's spy!" Medwin spat, flinging aside Conner's attempt to console him. "He was the one giving Vellix inside information! Do you know how many lives were lost at his hand? Just the Edelish alone!" Medwin stopped talking abruptly, looking as if he didn't close his mouth, the vomit he'd been fighting back would spew up uncontrollably.

Conner searched for something to say and quickly realized the right words weren't there. What was there to say? The man that Medwin's father had trusted above all others was Vellix's understudy and spy.

"He will pay," Medwin said through tightly clenched teeth. "I promise you, he *will* pay!"

Conner had only seen Medwin this furious on one other occasion, and that rage had been directed toward the Mirthless that killed his father — Conner had used cognition to give him wings and he proceeded to cut off the beast's head.

A long silence crept over them, eventually broken by a low growling moan. Zelimir had finally woken up. Slowly, he got to his feet, whimpering.

Concentrating intently, Conner focused on Zelimir's internal wounds healing. The wolf attempted to take a step and fell back to the ground. Conner was shocked to see that his cognition had done nothing to better Zelimir's condition. He couldn't understand why his effort had failed. Eventually, he attributed it to his having no idea what Yorick had done to Zelimir, no idea where the inflicted area, or areas were.

"I feel wonderful," Zelimir sighed sarcastically. "Really wonderful…"

"You've been spending too much time around Lenny," Conner laughed. Medwin started to chuckle lightly beside him; then stopped abruptly, as if he had suddenly remembered he was furious.

"Maybe so," Zelimir replied, sounding much more like his stern self.

"Where are you hurt?" Conner asked as he knelt next to the wolf.

Medwin looked on attentively.

"It's all over," Zelimir groaned. "My insides feel like someone grabbed them and squeezed as hard as they could..."

Conner shivered involuntarily as the vivid memory of Vellix torturing him invaded the front of his mind. He quickly suppressed the thoughts. "So it's your insides in general," he queried, wondering why, if Yorick's attack had afflicted all of Zelimir's insides, his cognition hadn't been effective.

"Yes," Zelimir said, grimacing.

Conner reached into his pocket and pulled out the stone.

Medwin saw that he was holding something in his hand. "Is that… Xellore's —"

"— Stone?" Conner turned to look at Medwin. "Yeah, it's one of them…"

"One…?"

Conner nodded. He gripped the stone tightly in his hand and summoned all his mental focus into Zelimir's wounds repairing themselves. Before Conner even felt strained, Zelimir had let out a long-winded sigh of relief.

"That was incredible," he said, standing up with his usual speed and agility. He ran a few laps around the general area to make sure he was back to fitness.

A sense of power came over Conner unlike any he'd ever felt. He couldn't believe how quickly and efficiently he'd been able to heal Zelimir. Looking down at the stone — a seemingly useless piece of rock in his palm — he thought to himself, '*Wow!*'

"I think we should get to bed," said Medwin, barely stifling a massive yawn. "As it is, we'll probably only get a few hours of sleep. And that's if we're lucky."

Conner nodded, realizing he could probably sleep standing up if he wanted. "Come on, Zelimir, we're going back to bed."

* * *

Conner awoke, feeling more refreshed than he had in weeks. He felt sure it was because his confidence had shot through the roof with the realization of how Xellore's stone affected his power. It had given him a magnificent feeling: hope.

"Mmm… Oh, this is nice!" Moxie pronounced with vulgar bliss as he ripped through the chunk of meat Medwin had saved for him.

Medwin watched him for a moment, his expression a mixture of amusement and disgust.

Conner crossed the room, opened the door in the ceiling, and stepped into the morning. Light, puffy clouds had replaced the rain clouds from the night before. They looked strangely cheery in the early morning sunlight. He drew a deep lungful of air and exhaled it with a content sigh.

Things had gone better than he could've imagined. He pretty much knew exactly how to find the entrance to the ruins now, he finally knew why he was the one to have the power of cognition, he had the stone that Vellix didn't know existed, and the task of being Rohwen's liberator now had cemented justification. All in all, he felt that things had finally shifted in his favor. He wasn't just some boy going on the luck that he felt could only last him so long. He was the grandson of

Xellore: master of cognition, creator of Salix — in his opinion, the most incredible thing ever produced by cognition.

Moxie clambered out of the underground room with a squeaky grunt and came to a halt next to Conner, who was still staring up at the bubbly puffs of cloud that were drifting peacefully across the sky. After taking in the view, Moxie asked, "Which way are we heading?"

"That way," Conner replied, pointing east.

Medwin and Zelimir exited the room. Medwin shut the door behind him, closed his eyes, and scrunched his face in concentration. The thin line encompassing the square door regressed, starting at one corner and continuing until the ground where it had existed was seamless once more.

Conner noticed that Medwin had a different air about his use of cognition now. It was completely evident that he wanted to be better. His discovery of Yorick being a traitor had infuriated him beyond description, and he had vowed to make the traitor pay. But in order to face a master, he would first need to become one himself. Determined to do all he could to prepare Medwin for the task ahead, Conner set off, flanked by his companions.

It was a short trip back to Xellore's grave. Conner paid a last respect to his grandfather, and as he stood there, the reality of Salix's destruction hit him like a swift blow. He would never speak with her again. Where would he be without her? 'I would be dead,' he told himself, glancing at Moxie. 'If it hadn't been for Salix's words of wisdom, I would have killed Moxie without question. I would have killed the sole reason I survived my duel with Vellix.'

"Conner, look." Medwin was holding something tiny and brown between his fingers. "You know what this is?" he asked, grinning boyishly. "It's a seed!" he went on before Conner could reply.

Hope bloomed inside Conner like a spring flower. 'What if,' he thought.

Medwin bent down and planted the seed some ten feet from Xellore's gravestone. He turned to face Conner and gave him a serious nod.

Conner pulled the stone from his pocket and closed his eyes. He allowed the few images of Salix he had to form in his mind: her age-weathered trunk and weeping branches, her towering height and shimmering leaves.

A small stem pushed diligently through the soil and continued to grow upward. Leaves began to mature around it as branches sprouted in all directions. Soon, bark covered the stem as it grew thick and strong, still pushing upward as if it could grasp the sun. But as the branches reached their peaking height, and realized the sun was unattainable, discouragement overcame them. They wept back to the soil from which they came, brushing lightly across the grass and wild flowers.

Conner stood facing his creation. The tree looked exactly as Salix had. Feeling confident, he stepped under the umbrella of branches. 'Salix?' he whispered, speaking within his own head.

"… …"

"Salix," he said again, this time speaking aloud. "Can you hear me?" Again, he got no reply. His heart knew the truth before he was ready to accept it. "*Salix!*" he yelled desperately as someone placed a hand on his arm. He turned and found Medwin giving him a consoling look.

Moxie and Zelimir stepped through the tree's curtain of branches.

"You tried, Conner," Medwin said, his voice warm and full of solace.

"Salix's consciousness was of Xellore's design," Zelimir started, bringing his unceasing logic to the conversation. "It was a great thought" — he locked eyes with Conner — "but the chances of recreating her were incredibly slim, if there even was a chance."

Zelimir's words were hard to swallow, but Conner knew the truth of them was absolute. He put a hand on the willow tree's trunk and admired the endless patterns in the bark.

"You should cherish the fact that you had a chance to speak with her," Zelimir went on after a moment's silence. "How many can say the same?"

Conner looked away from the tree. He gave Zelimir a thankful nod, stepped out from under its branches, and left Willow Grove without a backwards glance.

CHAPTER 24

Deception

Hours later, the countryside began to slope — just as Xellore had said it would. Large boulders integrated into the landscape near the bottom of the hillside, their dingy grey surfaces covered in moss and poking out at all angles.

"I think this is it," Conner said, stepping up onto the nearest boulder and turning to face the steep incline.

Medwin and the others turned toward the slope as well.

"What is 'it?'" Zelimir asked incredulously.

"That, right there," Conner replied, pointing at the largest boulder, imbedded deeply in soil.

Zelimir didn't reply. He merely gazed at the spot where Conner had pointed with the look of mild curiosity.

Conner started toward the boulder, envisioning an opening in its place. The huge rock didn't shift an inch. Feeling baffled, Conner tried again — still nothing. He reached out and touched the rock. It felt completely normal. 'This has to be it,' he told himself. 'What am I missing?'

Medwin arrived next to Conner and began investigating the rock as well. "Are you sure this is the right spot?"

"Xellore said if I used cognition on the largest boulder I would discover the entrance." Conner made a thorough visual sweep of the hillside. "This is definitely the largest boulder." Medwin nodded, and Conner went back to examining the rock.

"Did you try it with the stone?" Medwin asked curiously as Zelimir and Moxie arrived next to him.

"No, I didn't think it would be necessary to use it for this," Conner replied with a shrug. He pulled the stone from his pocket. Holding it tight in his hand, he pictured the boulder removing itself.

...Nothing...

"There must be something we're missing," Medwin said, running his hands along the rock's largest surface. "Just keep trying."

Fighting back his frustrations, Conner made another attempt to remove the boulder.

"Whoa!" Medwin yelled as Zelimir and Moxie inhaled startled gasps.

Conner quickly opened his eyes to see what had caused such an alarmed reaction. Half of Medwin's body had disappeared into the face of the boulder, leaving only his waist and legs visible. "What the? Are you okay?" Conner asked, not entirely sure how to react. "What happened?"

"I'm fine," Medwin replied, his voice distant and muffled. He tried to stand up, but didn't budge. The rock had become solid again, lodging him within. "I can't move!"

"Hold on," Conner said. He grasped Xellore's stone and reformed a picture of the boulder disappearing. "Okay, try again."

Medwin stood up, and his upper half emerged from within the boulder, as if the large chunk of rock was nothing but a hologram.

Conner held the picture of the ruin's entrance in his mind and walked into the boulder. After a few short steps, he felt the temperature drop considerably. He opened his eyes and found himself swathed in total darkness. "Walk through guys," he called out to the others, while maintaining his focus on the entrance.

Medwin, Zelimir, and Moxie arrived a few seconds later.

"I can't see anything," said Moxie.

Bright blue flames lit up a tunnel that descended into darkness. Conner led the way as the path took them deep under Rohwen's upper crust.

The tunnel ended abruptly, leaving the four of them standing on the edge of a sheer drop. Conner lifted his hands high, and the pale blue light of his flames revealed a remarkable view of the valley below.

The remains of a city stood, sprawling into the veil of darkness. Even in its crumbling state, it was a beautiful sight to behold.

From atop the cliff it was hard to see much detail, but Conner could tell that a great amount of time and care had gone into the planning of Hylan's development. Its architectural design was as logical as it was artistic. A maze of cobblestone streets meandered through the city, forming patterns while never coming to dead ends. Lining the streets were thousands of buildings, which reminded Conner of the neighborhoods in his world. A moment of nostalgia brushed his senses.

"Well" — Zelimir looked up at Conner. Then back at the deteriorated city below — "shall we then?"

Conner nodded, and stairs began to carve their way into the sheer wall, echoing dissonantly through the silent air. "Come on guys." Conner gestured for the others to follow him.

When they reached the valley floor, Medwin separated from the group, scanning the ground carefully.

"What are you doing?" Conner asked, completely puzzled by Medwin's behavior.

"Looking for a couple decent sticks," Medwin said as he bent down to pick something up. "We can use them as torches."

"Well, why didn't you ask for help?" Conner strode over to Medwin, holding his flames in a position that would cast the least shadow over the area Medwin was searching.

"Didn't really think about it," Medwin replied. He bent down and grabbed a second stick. After a moment's examination, he deemed it worthy of use. "Here, Moxie, take this."

"I should probably use a torch as well," Conner said. "It would be nice if I didn't have to concentrate on keeping my flames burning the whole time we're down here."

"Here," Medwin said a second later, handing Conner a long stretch of branch.

The ruins came into better view as Conner lit all three torches.

"It might be wise if we split up," Zelimir advised, taking in the more revealing view of the city. "There is a lot of ground to cover. We will have a much better chance of finding the scroll in a timely manner if we're searching in four separate locations at once."

"That's a good point," Medwin agreed as he took in the city's extensive size.

Moxie didn't seem to like the idea of being alone in this place. His eyes shifted around the ruins as though he was sure something would jump from the shadows and snatch him up at any moment.

"I don't know," Conner said reflectively, contemplating Zelimir's suggestion. "Xellore told me that Vellix set traps down here to make it hard for the one seeking the scroll to find it…"

The four of them stood in silence for a minute, during which Moxie's eyes never stopped shifting from side to side.

"I think it would be best if we just stick together for the time being," Conner concluded. "At least until we get a feel for what we're dealing with." Medwin and Zelimir conceded to his rationality with polite nods.

They decided to start by methodically entering what was left of the houses to search for any possible hiding spots within. Conner was nearly positive that this was a complete waste of their time, however. He felt that if he were the one hiding the scroll, he would have wanted it to be somewhere significant.

But, just in case Vellix had assumed a seeker would think exactly that, he entered the first of countless houses and grasped his stone, focusing on the scroll showing itself. When an hour passed, and each house he'd entered proved to be as pointless as the last, he gave up on the idea.

As they moved deeper into the city — without so much as a fragment of an idea where to look next — Conner found that he was unable to stop himself from becoming increasingly irritated. It didn't help that Medwin and Zelimir had started making rather unhelpful comments about how their attempt to find the scroll was obviously useless; that to find something as small as a scroll in a place so large was a fool's errand. Moxie wasn't much better with his constant on-edge movements, making the place seem more threatening than it had to be.

Conner wanted to tell all three of them that he didn't need their help. He would find the scroll alone and they could just head back up to the surface and wait. What good were they doing him anyway? It was he who had the power of cognition — he who was capable of learning what the scroll had to offer.

"Seriously, Conner," Medwin sneered, his tone of voice sounding uncharacteristically rude. "What is the point of this? We've been down here for hours now. We're not going to find the stupid scroll."

"Go then!" Conner flared up, pointing a finger back in direction they had come. "It's not like I need you! I can find the scroll on my own."

"Oh, yeah, I bet you'd love that!" Medwin spat back. "Conner — the one with special power. Conner — the one to defeat Vellix. Why not add another? Conner — the one to find the scroll singlehandedly."

Conner looked like he was about to punch Medwin when Zelimir interjected.

"The two of you are just idiot children," he began coldly. "Neither of you have a clue! I don't even know why I'm still sticking with you fools!"

Moxie grabbed his patchy hair and started tugging at it, yelling as if he were having a nervous breakdown. "No! No — no — no!"

As they bickered, the light of Conner's torch found its way onto the front wall of a vast building. Although crumbling, the structure had clearly been built for something, or someone, very important. Stone columns lined the first story, supporting the five that rested above it. Multiple stages of trim framed every window, making the design appear busy, while achieving the effect of depth and dimension.

'This is it,' Conner thought, excitement rising. He didn't know why, but he was absolutely convinced that the scroll was hidden somewhere within this building — almost as if it had called out to him. He started running toward the building's front entrance, Medwin and the others right behind him, as if trying to be the first to reach a finish line.

As Conner entered the vast structure, he tried to decide which way to go first, but his attention fell instead to the others. He found himself wanting nothing more than to rid himself of the fools. What were they doing, looking around the room like that? They were going to try and get the scroll first. They wanted it for themselves, but he wouldn't let them get it. He would kill them before they could get it.

'What are you thinking?' implored a small voice at the very center of his conscious thoughts. 'These are your best friends! They're not trying to —'

'I said kill!'

'No!'

'Kill!'

"*No!*" Conner cried as Medwin lunged at him with his hatched drawn.

Conner ducked before Medwin's strike made contact. Zelimir sprang at Medwin from out of the shadows. Medwin was quick enough to evade the attack. He turned his attention from Conner to the wolf. "If you think you're going to get the scroll, you're dead wrong!"

Zelimir replied with a viscous growl.

Moxie slipped away, giving the other three a defiant glance. He ran up a nearby flight of stairs and out of sight.

Conner dropped his torch to the floor, grabbed his bow, and quickly strung an arrow. "Neither of you move!" he yelled in a demented voice that wasn't his own. "I swear, I *will* fire!" he promised, switching his aim back and forth between Medwin and Zelimir in quick succession, the underside of his facial features lit by the torch burning below him, exposing a twisted expression of rage.

Zelimir leapt at him with ferocity. Conner fired. Multiple howls of pain rang around the room like a duet of agony. Conner was on the ground, his left pant leg ripped and soaked with glistening blood. Zelimir lay next to him, an arrow protruding from his side.

Medwin gazed down at the two of them. A flicker of comprehension crossed his dark brown eyes. He took off at a run. "Just hang on guys!" he told Conner and Zelimir as he leapt up the same flight of stairs Moxie had taken.

Conner struggled to his feet, clutching the horrific wound on his leg. The immense pain had cleared his mind. He felt like himself again. 'This is deception at its best," he thought darkly, looking over at Zelimir, whose cries of pain drove through him like a knife. 'What have I done? I attacked one of my closest friends.'

Shame threatened to consume him, but he fought it, knowing that allowing his mind back into a place of weakness would grant Vellix's cognition enchantment on the building the ability to overtake him once more.

"Conner…" Zelimir murmured weakly.

"Zelimir, I am *so* sorry," Conner whispered sincerely, kneeling down next to the wolf.

"As am I… I am ashamed that Vellix's enchantment was able to overtake my mind in such a way. It wasn't until I felt the overpowering pain of your arrow that I was able to regain control."

Conner looked into Zelimir's face. The wolf looked as though he was about to die. His eyes had started to close slowly. Conner ripped out the arrow, pulled the stone from his pocket, and stared intently at the bleeding wound on Zelimir's side.

'Why would you save him?' hissed a cruel voice in his head.

'Shut up!' Conner retorted, trying with all his might to maintain the mentality necessary to heal Zelimir. He took a steadying breath and focused with every ounce of his being. The flesh around the wound started to weave itself back together, but with none of the precision he'd seen on the occasions he healed his own wounds.

'You're not doing it right,' the evil voice jeered. 'It's not going to work.'

Blood continued to poor freely from Zelimir's gash. Conner put a hand over it to slow the bleeding his heart beating so fast it might burst through his chest. He was out of time. Zelimir's breathing was so weak it was practically non-existent.

'Please!' he begged himself. 'Please let me be able to heal him.'

'What's the point in trying? You're not —'

"*I said shut up!*" he screamed at the top of his lungs. "I *can*, and I *will!*" Conner turned the stone over in his sweating palm to remind himself of the power he held and refocused on Zelimir. Once again, the flesh began to weave itself together. This time, however, it was working far better.

Moments later, he was able to remove his hand from Zelimir's side. "You're going to be okay," he said reassuringly. Zelimir didn't reply, but he was still breathing slowly.

Conner looked down at the wound on his leg; the familiar sensation of his own flesh healing itself began immediately.

"Arrrghh! Get off me, Moxie! You're not in your right mind!" The muffled sound of Medwin's yells found their way down from somewhere in the building's upper stories.

Feeling that Zelimir would be okay where he was, Conner grabbed his torch and took off up the stairs.

He reached the first landing, straining his ears. Medwin and Moxie's yells echoed through the ceiling. They were still somewhere above him. He ran up the next flight, still listening intently.

"Moxie, I'm warning you!" Medwin's voice reverberated down the long corridor to Conner's right.

"I won't let you get it first!" Moxie shrieked, his small voice sounding completely deranged.

Conner moved quickly down the corridor and entered the room from which he had heard the commotion.

"Sorry about that, Moxie," Medwin said, bending over the hunchback's knocked out body and picking him up.

As Conner watched Medwin throw Moxie over his shoulder, he knew that Medwin had overcome the enchantment. He was looking at the real Medwin.

Medwin stopped moving abruptly. He turned his head ever so slightly and said, "I know you're there, Conner. I don't want to have to hurt you…"

It was obvious that Medwin wasn't foolish enough to assume Conner was in his right mind. Last he saw, Conner had shot Zelimir with an arrow.

"It's okay, Medwin, I'm —"

'No it's not! Kill hi —'

'Shut up!'

"— I'm dealing with it now. I won't let the thoughts overcome me again."

Medwin tuned to face Conner. The tense expression on his face eased up. "Good… You know what this place reminds me of?"

Conner thought for a second. "The lake behind Mt. Cirrus?"

"Exactly," Medwin replied.

"I hate this place," Conner muttered, staring up at the ceiling.

Medwin replied with an adamant nod of his head. "Do you think the scroll is even in this building?"

"No, I don't think so," Conner admitted thoughtfully.

"Why is that?"

"Because as soon as we came in here all I could think was that the scroll *was* in here."

Medwin tilted of his head curiously.

"Think about it. Why would Vellix make the pursuer of the scroll feel positive that what they were searching for was hidden in the place he actually hid it? I expect this building is a trap to make you search endlessly for the scroll that isn't even here."

Medwin nodded again, grunting as he hoisted Moxie into a comfortable position on his shoulder.

Conner saw Medwin's face twitch, changing his expressions as if he was in battle with himself. He knew that it could only mean Medwin's mind was being attacked again. "Come on. Let's get out of here."

"Yeah, definitely!" Medwin said enthusiastically.

* * *

The building had been a serious letdown for Conner. For one shimmering moment, he had truly felt that they would find the scroll there. He had to keep reminding himself that the only reason he had thought that at all was because the building itself had told him to feel that way.

The thought that he would never find the last scroll was like venom corroding his mind, telling him to give up, telling him he was wasting his time. The worst part about it was that he wasn't sure if these were his own thoughts, or ones planted in his mind by Vellix's enchantment upon the ruined city.

Their search was agonizingly slow-going. With Zelimir still feeling weak, they were only covering half the ground Conner knew they should have been. It was all he could do not to let this infuriate him. Deep down, he knew there was nothing he could do about it, but it didn't make it any easier to deal with — if anything, it made it that much harder.

Uncontrollable anger had welled up inside him. He wanted to scream. He wanted to give up. 'Do you really need the scroll?' he asked himself, his voice sounding sly and deceptive. 'I'm sure you'll be fine without it.'

'I won't give up,' he replied to the deceitful voice. 'I *will* find the scroll.'

They came upon a circular plaza encompassed by towering, axe-wielding stone statues. The incredible force of the tidal wave that struck Hylan, combined with the erosive power of time, had greatly damaged the appearance of most of them: some were headless, while others were nothing more than legs. A few, however, had withstood the wave's damage and defied the test of time.

The feeling of excitement rose up in Conner again. This was the most significant thing they had seen in hours. "Hey, let's light a few new torches. I want to make sure we have plenty of light to search by."

"Yeah, let's make sure we have plenty of light, so we can see really well when we find nothing," Medwin scoffed.

"Fight it, Medwin," Conner implored.

Medwin shook his head violently, gave Conner a shameful glance, and started scanning the ground around him.

"Found one," Moxie pronounced a minute later, waving a long branch above his head and sounding pleased with himself. Conner lit the end and continued his search. Soon, he and Medwin had torches lit as well.

Conner started toward the plaza.

"Careful now," Zelimir said warningly when he noticed Conner was moving with quickening pace. "We don't know what to expect."

Conner gave the wolf an understanding nod. He moved cautiously into the plaza, examining every detail. His desperation to find the scroll was overwhelming. He didn't know how much longer he would be able to stand the way this place made him feel. It was all he could do to stop himself from lashing out at the others for no reason. To make matters worse, he was painfully aware of the fact that the others' minds were being attacked in the same way.

Medwin and Moxie entered the plaza and began searching in separate locations.

Conner watched as the light of Moxie's torch reached the center of the plaza. It almost looked as though there was something carved into the ground. He moved eagerly toward it. His stomach did a somersault as he got close enough to realize it was an engraving of the Hylanian symbol. "I think this is…" his voice tapered off as the ominous sound of massive slabs of stone grinding upon one another met his ears.

He threw his torch, grabbed his bow, and turned just in time to watch as one of the statues came to life, its eyes glowing red. It thrust its axe straight for Conner's head.

Conner rolled out from under its attack and quickly stowed away his bow — it wasn't going to do him any good against something made of stone. "Moxie, get away from the plaza!" he yelled. Moxie fled without hesitation.

Medwin was about to enter the fight, hatchet drawn, but Conner told him to stay back. There was nothing a hatchet was going to do to harm a stone monster.

The colossal statue hewed the spot where Conner had been only moments ago. A large plume of dust rose into the air, fogging the stone giant from view and causing its red eyes to look as though they were floating in mid-air.

Conner seized his chance to hide, hoping that Vellix's sentinel hadn't seen where he'd gone. He grabbed the stone from his pocket. Knowing he was likely to need the free use of both hands during the fight, he shoved it under the vambrace on his left arm, making sure it was flat against his skin.

The huge sentinel demolished the statue Conner was hiding behind; fragments of rock pelted his arms and torso, causing painful welts to rise almost instantly.

Conner pictured the sentinel crumbling into bits. It fell to the floor in a heap of rubble, but it reformed immediately, in one flawless motion.

Gaping in horror, Conner tried again, and again, the stone giant reformed seamlessly. Conner was at a loss. He had the cognition infused stone. His skill was more proficient than ever. But if his cognition attacks weren't going to affect the sentinel, how was he supposed to win.

The monster's axe smacked the ground with thunderous force again.

'At least it's slow,' Conner thought, feeling relieved that he had one thing going in his favor. It still wasn't enough to ease the realization of how desperate his situation was though. Without cognition, he was virtually helpless.

He thought hard, racking his brain for some answer to his dilemma — all the while dodging the sentinel's slow yet disturbingly powerful attacks.

'You need an object that's harder than *it* is,' he kept repeating diligently, begging himself to conjure a solution.

'Diamond!' The answer came to him, just as precious as the item itself. 'What I need is *diamond!*'

Conner's eighth grade teacher's voice entered his head. 'Carbon can be found in all things organic. When intense levels of heat and pressure are applied upon the carbon, we get diamond.'

Feeling like he had never been so grateful for school in all his life, Conner reached for his bow. He strung an arrow while dodging another of the sentinel's attacks. Then, focusing as hard as he could on subjecting the head of his arrow to the heat and pressure needed to form diamond, he released it, aiming at the space between the sentinel's eyes.

Conner watched his arrow approach the monster as if it were happening in slow motion. The bright, red light of the sentinel's eyes shone through the arrowhead a split second before it struck and refracted, glimmering with a rainbow sparkle.

The sentinel fell to its knees, its blazing eyes flickering on and off. Its upper half plummeted face-first into the ground as the red of its eyes died out permanently, turning back to the cold and lifeless shade of grey they had been.

Conner let out a long sigh of relief and sank to the floor from exhaustion. Medwin, Zelimir, and Moxie came to congratulate and applaud his victory, all three of them moving buoyantly.

"What I don't get," Medwin said disbelievingly as he arrived next to Conner, "is how an arrow was strong enough to penetrate it." He gave the huge sentinel a sideways glance.

"Indeed," Zelimir agreed. "I was wondering the very same thing."

"I used cognition to turn the arrowhead into diamond," Conner said, feeling like the idea was possibly one of the best he'd ever had.

Medwin seemed to share his sentiments. "I don't know how you thought of that, but I'm impressed."

"I wouldn't have thought of it if it wasn't for Mr. Weaver," Conner laughed, knowing he had just thoroughly confused Medwin and the others. None of them had a clue who Mr. Weaver was, but he felt that his teacher deserved the credit on this one.

"Who?" Medwin asked, wearing a funny look of curiosity. "Who's Mr. Weaver…?"

"He's a school teacher in my world," Conner replied, laughing again. "…You know? Someone who educates people about things?"

"Oh, so you mean like an elder," Medwin concluded, tapping his chin knowingly.

"Um, yeah… sure." Conner giggled silently.

Moxie headed over to the center of the plaza, and started investigating the etching there.

Conner jumped to his feet, feeling exhilarated. "This has to be it guys!" he exclaimed, pointing down at the Hylanian symbol. The etched area opened at his mental command. There, lying a few feet below the rest of the plaza floor, was the scroll, waiting to be taken.

Conner reached down and picked up his prize, finally the holder of the last scroll.

The feeling he got as he held the scroll in his hand was indescribable. He finally had it. The search was over. "Come on guys," he said, gesturing for the others to stand around him.

Once they'd gathered, the circular plaza broke free from the ground around it, emitting a loud cracking noise.

As they began to rise, the ceiling ripped open above them, allowing dazzling sunlight to flood the vast underground chamber. Conner's eyes adjusted to the light as they rose higher. He gazed down on the ruined city below them. Now bathed in light, the buildings and streets had come into much better view. A murky greenish brown color stained their once beautiful stonework. Conner wondered briefly how many years the city must have remained completely submerged in water, but as he continued toward the surface, his thoughts shifted. He suddenly became inescapably aware that his finding the scroll had just set a new level of finality for his future. The days in which he could allow his focus to linger on the task of finding the ancient document were past.

A new Chapter of his journey had begun.

Made in the USA
Charleston, SC
05 May 2016